To Hannah —

Good luck with your
graduate studies
and best of luck
in all future endeavors!

11/6/21

Also by John Adam Wasowicz
Daingerfield Island
Jones Point
Slaters Lane

ROACHES RUN

John Adam Wasowicz

ROACHES RUN

Publisher: Clarinda Harriss
Editor: Charles Rammelkamp
Graphic design: Ace Kieffer
Cover art: Alex Herron Wasowicz

BrickHouse Books, Inc. 2021
306 Suffolk Road
Baltimore, MD 21218

Distributor: Itasca Books, Inc.

ISBN: 978-1-938144-83-7

Printed in the United States of America

To my nephews
Michael, Matthew, and Douglas

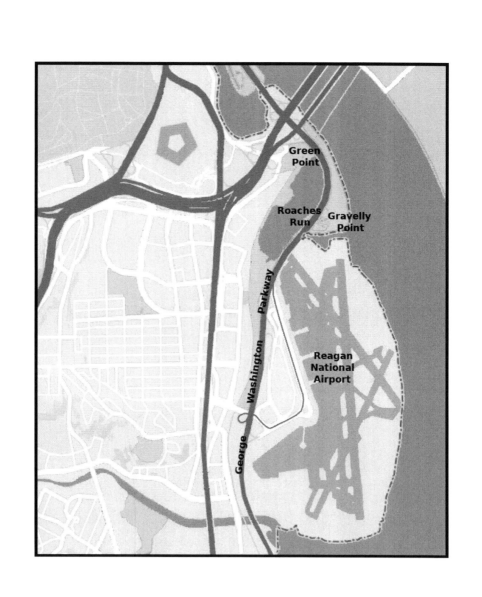

"To live outside the law you must be honest."

– Absolutely Sweet Marie by Bob Dylan

TABLE OF CONTENTS

PART I
Saturday, May 29

Chapter One: The Rhythmic Cycle of Life

The Rhythmic Cycle of Life

by

Henry David McLuhan

to R.H.

"The past resembles the future more than one drop of water resembles another."

—Ibn Khaldun

AUTHOR'S NOTE

I'm delighted you have purchased a copy of *The Rhythmic Cycle of Life*. I hope this book provides a new prism through which you can look at yourself and study the rhythm of your life. I am optimistic that it will change your life and enable you to avoid dangerous shoals, find safe harbor, and catch the winds that will propel you to new horizons.

I'll check back with you in twelve years, at the end of the next cycle. Either you'll be cursing me as a fraud or you'll be acclaiming me as a New Age guru. I certainly hope it's not the former!

Begin today by making a chart for yourself, like the one displayed in the early chapters of this book. It's a great time to learn from your mistakes and start effecting change.

By the time we meet again, another cycle of our lives will have passed. If you're making the same mistakes you made when you were first introduced to this book, then either you didn't follow the instructions or I failed you. But if you're in a better place — if you actually solved a recurring nightmare that afflicted you personally or professionally — then we both succeeded.

I will be taking my own medicine. I'm committed to redirecting myself as I approach benchmarks in my current cycle. I'm not entirely sure of what lies ahead, but I am confident that I possess the tools to identify calamities before they occur, effect change, and get to a better place.

Ready? Set? Go! Let's take a spin and see where we end up! With hope and promise for a better and improved tomorrow, I am, affectionately yours,

Henry David McLuhan, Ile Saint-Louis, Paris

June 1, 2009

The Rhythm and The Circle

Your life has a rhythm. It is unmistakable and unavoidable. Uniquely your own. No one else on the planet has it. It is the rhythmic cycle of your life.

Sometimes that rhythm is ascendant. Other times it spirals downward. When your life is moving in an upward progression, you cannot fail at succeeding. But when your life is heading in the opposite direction, you are helpless to reverse course. Seemingly.

You actually can change the rhythm of your life by choosing to understand it. To take the time to write it down. Examine it. Study and analyze and evaluate it. As a result, you will be able to navigate your way through life. Not a perfect navigation. But a smarter one. One that enables you to guide yourself further than you ever imagined possible.

Your life runs in twelve-year cycles. To take advantage of the lessons in this book, you have to have lived long enough to complete close to two cycles. The older you are, the better.

After you chart your twelve-year cycle, you will be able to affect your life as never before. You will be able to intervene on your own behalf. In advance. You will be able to avoid disaster. Enhance your riches. Avoid disasters. Expand your horizons. In sum, you will be able to control the cycle. By controlling the cycle, you will control your life.

The circle is the universal symbol of totality. Astrology, astronomy, mysticism, and mathematics all use the circle. There is a reason for that. The circle is all-encompassing. It is continuity. We see it everywhere. The clock. The compass. We can put things inside of it. We draw pies to explain our accumulation of investments or the distribution of assets. Tires. Plates. Buttons. Coins. The sun.

Assume you were born in the year 1976. The rhythmic cycle of your life would look like this:

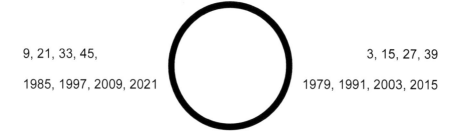

1, 12, 24, 36, 48

1976, 1988, 2000, 2012, 2024

9, 21, 33, 45,

1985, 1997, 2009, 2021

3, 15, 27, 39

1979, 1991, 2003, 2015

6, 18, 30, 42

1982, 1994, 2006, 2018

Using this circle, write in the year of *your* birth and three-year cyclical dates. Now, let's color it in!

The First Cycle

Begin with your birth year. You have no memory of that year, so you have to rely upon records and the recollections of others.

How did the birth go? Maybe a planned vaginal delivery turned into a C-section because the fetal monitor detected distress. Maybe an exceptionally easy delivery. Did your mother's water break in a taxi on Broadway? Were you the first baby born after midnight on New Year's Day? Was your father present? What about brothers and sisters and family members? Were you born at home or in a hospital?

What happened that night? That year? Who else was born? Who died?

Now complete the entire twelve-year cycle. Pay particular attention to the beginning of each new quarter: the third, sixth, and ninth years. Of those three, focus most on six, the year opposite your birth year in the twelve-year cycle. This is a balancing year. The middle of the cycle. The year that best compliments the first/last year of each cycle.

In "Ode: Intimations of Immortality from Recollections of Early Childhood," William Wordsworth coined the oft-quoted expression: "The child is father of the man." The first cycle establishes the foundation of your entire existence, including the ground rules that will govern the remainder of your life. Set them down scrupulously and honestly.

Be brutally frank about yourself with yourself. This could be a painful exercise. But also fun. Take your time.

Did you get seriously sick? Were you hospitalized? Where did you go to elementary school? Or were you home schooled? Who were your best friends? What colors do you remember? Smells? Did you have a pet? Were you involved in school-related activities? Outside activities? Where did you go on vacation? What were your favorite songs and clothes? What were you most proud about? What embarrassed you?

What happened to your family during this twelve-year period? Were brothers and sisters born during this cycle? Did anyone die? What about your grandparents? Did your family move? Where were you most comfortable? What was your family's socioeconomic position? Did your family become more prosperous? Did the family's fortunes ebb?

But don't start looking at ways to improve things yet. We need a little more information about the rhythm of your life. So let's get started on the second cycle.

Chapter Two: Morning

ELMO KATZ slid the e-book reader onto the patio table. Closing his eyes, he leaned back in a chair in the postage stamp-sized backyard of his townhome on Harvard Street and listened to the sounds of Old Town awakening.

A delivery truck rumbled by tiny retail stores sandwiched together along the city's main thoroughfare. A Metro train sped into the nearby King Street station. Around the corner, a city bus labored down Diagonal Drive toward Gardens Park.

As the COVID-19 pandemic receded, the sounds of the city had returned. Restaurants and retail businesses were springing back to life. People were still cautious and wary, but more pedestrians, joggers, and cyclists now filled the streets and sidewalks.

Memories of 2020 were fixed in Katz's mind. George Floyd's death; the political protests; the holidays spent in isolation to slow the spread of COVID-19. The breach of the U.S. Capitol in January seemed like a continuation of that tumultuous year.

Katz opened his eyes and looked up. A slice of moon hung in a sky sprinkled with vanishing stars. With each passing second, the night's illumination was erased by dawn's light as the milky gray of morning emerged.

Katz wasn't sure what to make of *The Rhythmic Cycle of Life*. He didn't trust self-help books. He believed people naturally and intuitively knew the answers to most of their problems. He certainly didn't need gurus or shamans to find them.

Ironically, however, that was the very premise of *Rhythmic Cycle*, which left him conflicted and wondering whether he might actually agree with it.

His eyes swept down and focused on the phone resting beside the tablet.

When it first rang two hours ago, Curtis Santana, his chief investigator in the U.S. Attorney's office, was on the line. A man's body had been found beneath Richmond Highway along Four Mile Run, Santana said. The victim had been shot at point-blank range. Half his brains were splattered against the bridge abutment; the other half were spilled on the bike path that connected Four Mile Run to the Mount Vernon trail.

Katz and Santana suspected the vic's identity, but they needed confirmation. While Santana gathered more information, Katz pulled himself out of bed, went downstairs, and brewed a pot of strong coffee: eight ounces of water and five scoops of Misha's Arabian Mocha Java beans, coarsely ground. He drank his first cup, refilled it, and, clutching the cup in one hand and his phone and e-book in the other, went outside to the patio.

A few minutes later, the phone rang again.

"It's Morley," Santana confirmed.

Katz rubbed his bare toes over the moist moss that grew between the bricks on the patio. The kitchen lights suddenly turned on. Through the glass door, Katz saw Abby Snowe, his girlfriend, standing at the counter beside the coffeemaker.

"I think Spates figured out Morley was an informant," Santana said. "If he has any sense, he's probably hightailed it to points unknown."

Katz doubted the shooting was deliberate. The fact that the gun had been fired at point-blank range suggested a scuffle. Rodney Brown, the chief medical examiner, would confirm it for them.

"That's the key point," Katz said.

"What is?" asked Santana.

The patio door slid open. Snowe, lithe and blonde, appeared in jeans, a long-sleeve cotton shirt, and rubber boots.

"Hold on a minute," he said into the phone as he stood and stretched.

"Hey," Katz said, addressing Snowe. "Sorry if I woke you."

"You didn't," she said matter-of-factly, holding a cup of coffee in her hand.

"Where are you going?"

"I told you last night about Maggie Moriarty's relapse," she said. "If that woman doesn't straighten up, she's going to lose her little girl, which would be tragic for both of them." She stared at the steaming hot coffee. "Maybe Katie should be placed with Child Protective Services. I don't know." She looked up. "Anyway, I have to go. Maggie's living in a tent village somewhere down in the Eisenhower Valley."

Katz pictured shrubs and bushes along the shallow riverbed hiding a camp of homeless people. "It's no place to raise a little girl," he said.

"You think?" Snowe asked sarcastically. "She should be in preschool, even if it's only online. Maggie just carts Katie around from one hellhole to another, exposing her to things that no child should see, especially a four-year-old, to say nothing of COVID-19 and other shit that's out there."

Katz felt bad. He had obtained a financial settlement for Moriarty following the tragic death of Katie's father, Tony Fortune, along the Georgetown towpath in 2017. Regrettably, Moriarty used the proceeds to finance a downward spiral fueled by drugs and alcohol.

Snowe caught Katz's guilty look.

"You're not responsible," Snowe said. "That decision is on her. You tried to give her and Katie a better life. She's the one who messed it up." She pointed toward the phone, eager to change the subject. "What's going on?"

"They found a body at Four Mile Run."

"One of your cases?"

"It belongs to the antiterrorism task force," he replied. "Stone's in charge." He referred to Alexandria Detective Sherry Stone, with whom he'd collaborated last year on the Slaters Lane case. She was chair of a metropolitan area interagency task force that pulled together law enforcement resources in case of a terrorist threat or attack.

Given his job as U.S. Attorney and hers as a senior probation officer in Alexandria, their conversations routinely touched on murder and mayhem. Their communications were stunted and superficial to avoid sharing confidential information, particularly if it involved a criminal case.

Katz was one of the few U.S. Attorneys who had been asked to remain in the new administration. No one was surprised. The decision to nominate him had been the brainchild of Senator Abraham Lowenstein based on his adept handling of the Daingerfield Island espionage caper. His confirmation in 2018 was based on ability, not politics.

"All right," Snowe said. "I'll see you later."

Like Katz, Snowe had gotten her COVID-19 vaccinations in March. She felt more confident about returning to her routine work. At the rate things were going, life would be back to normal by the summer.

As the sliding glass door closed, Katz caught his reflection on the glass panel: tall, lanky, kinky steel-wool hair graying at the temples, olive skin, an inscrutable face, and dark, piercing eyes. He ran an open palm over the stubble on his cheek. He raised the phone in his other hand and said, "Hey."

"I was about to hang up." Santana replied. "I call with details about a murder and you put me on hold. What the fuck, Mo?"

"Sorry."

The door slid open. "And don't forget Constitution Hall tonight," Snowe said. "They're only allowing a limited number of people into the event."

Katz pointed triumphantly to the e-reader lying on the table.

"Yeah, right," she said. "I know what you think about self-help books." The door closed again.

Katz smiled to himself. Even if he was uncertain how he felt about the book's premise, any writer who used a *nom de plume* as pretentious as Henry David McLuhan had to be a fraud. Just another hipster running a hustle, he thought.

"Don't forget your mask!" he hollered toward the house. "You may have gotten your shot, but you're not invincible."

From behind the glass Snowe waved a blue mask at him before she disappeared.

He spoke into the phone. "If Spates has any sense."

"What?" Santana asked.

"That's the point, Curtis. You said Spates is probably already hightailing it to points unknown if he has any sense. The *point* is Spates doesn't have any sense. From what I've been told, he's a fool. He's going to stay right where he is."

Santana pondered the response and said, "So you *were* listening."

"Of course," he said. "I always listen."

**

PHIL LANDRY was in his national security office a short distance from the U.S. Capitol. He dropped his Personal Identity Verification card into the card reader on his desktop computer. Once the computer program opened, he checked the time and location of this morning's briefing and the list of attendees.

The lead briefer was Alexandria Detective Sherry Stone. All of the usual suspects would be attending, including Mo Katz, the cocky U.S. Attorney for the Eastern District of Virginia; Curtis Santana, his lead investigator; and Mai Lin, a research assistant who, since helping solve the Slaters Lane murders, acted as though she was the managing partner of a law firm.

Landry had expected the U.S. Attorney's office to fall apart last spring following the loss of the lead attorneys for both the civil and criminal divisions. Much to his surprise, the opposite occurred. The unprecedented events of April 2020 created a stronger *esprit de corps* than had previously existed. Landry was bitter that Katz's star ascended while his fortunes plunged. Two years ago, he was close to being selected for the top position at the Department of Homeland Security. Then the long knives came out. Articles about his past imbroglios appeared in The Washington Chronicle. Despite much of it being nothing more than conjecture and innuendo, there was a scintilla of truth that roiled his supporters. When Abe Lowenstein, chairman of the Senate Select Committee for Intelligence, withdrew his endorsement, Landry's supporters tripped over one another to find the exit. Although he maintained the title of director of security operations, he was relegated to a crummy office and wielded little influence.

He tried unsuccessfully to rehabilitate his public reputation. In 2020, he sought a role in the national response to COVID-19 but lacked the credentials to make a meaningful contribution. Next he tried to rebuild his reputation as a tough law-and-order guy by criticizing groups like Black Lives Matter, only to see mounting public support for police reform following the deaths of George Floyd, Breonna Taylor, and others. Then, at the first of the year, he stated publicly there was no need to fortify the Capitol during the congressional session to certify the Electoral College vote. He adopted the wrong position at every turn, he reluctantly admitted to himself.

Though he was repulsed by rioting in the inner cities, he made an exception for the January 6 breach. He chided those who labeled January 6 as an "insurrection" while referring to protests in Portland and elsewhere as "peaceful."

Beneath Landry's exasperation was an unquenchable hatred toward three individuals whom he held primarily responsible for derailing his career in law enforcement and national security. That was why, last summer, he conceived of a plan to *destroy* those three individuals. With all of the insanity going on in Washington, he believed this was the perfect time to carry out his plan.

He hoisted his squat body from his desk chair. Smoothing his slightly greasy, graying hair, he approached the cubicle outside his nondescript office. "I'm headed to Ashburn for the briefing," he told Vanessa Wilson, his administrative assistant.

"Duly noted," replied Wilson. She did not look up. Wilson was reed-thin, with raven hair and a sardonic smile. A devout Bible reader, she was reminded of a line from 2 Corinthians 1:19 whenever she interacted with her boss: "For ye suffer fools gladly, seeing ye yourselves are wise."

Landry detested Wilson. She was a busybody and a troublemaker. As soon as that harassment complaint she'd filed against him was dismissed, he was going to fire her ass.

"I'll check from time to time to see if there are any messages," he said. He knew she wanted to avoid returning to the office because of COVID-19. She had only been in the office a handful of times since March 2020. Furthermore, the pandemic had taken a toll on her; she had lost her mother — also a federal employee — to the coronavirus last year. Landry had no sympathy. The way he looked at it, it just meant there was one more unproductive fed six feet under. He was also secretly gleeful that he had an excuse to call her into the office on a Saturday of a holiday weekend when he knew she would rather be home.

Landry took the elevator to the underground garage. His chunky form lumbered across the empty parking area toward his vehicle. He thought of Ruth Hammond. Thick saliva formed in his throat. He hawked up a glob of phlegm. It landed with a splat on the concrete. He swept his hand across his mouth to catch the remaining spittle and wiped it on his trousers.

He pulled out of the parking garage onto Maine Avenue and then onto the freeway. He crossed the 14th Street Bridge, maneuvered the car into the far right lane, and swooped down the ramp onto the southbound lanes of the George Washington Parkway.

Gravelly Point and Reagan National Airport were to his left, bordering the Potomac River. To his right was a patch of marshland and a National Park Service sign announcing the Roaches Run

Waterfowl Sanctuary.

Roaches Run wasn't really a bird sanctuary, in his mind. Rather, it was a staging ground for taxicabs and limousines that trolled the airport. No one even noticed the crescent-shaped asphalt parking area at Roaches Run. It resembled a pit stop at a race track.

Landry believed that, if a survey was conducted of 100,000 commuters who drove by the "waterfowl sanctuary" on any given day, 99.9 percent would not remember it and the 0.1 percent who did never visited the place. That was why he parked a panel van at Roaches Run earlier in the week. He was hiding in plain sight.

Landry made a sharp turn into the parking area and pulled up next to the van. A smattering of taxis and limos filled the lot. No one walked nearby. He turned off the ignition, exited the car, clicked the fob, and walked casually to the windowless back door of the van on the passenger's side. He climbed inside and locked the door behind him.

**

BREAKING NEWS
Holiday Gatherings Expected at Washington Landmarks
by Tom Mann, City Editor @The Chronicle Newspaper

An enthusiastic crowd is expected to descend on Washington this weekend to celebrate the Memorial Day holiday. Many restaurants and hotels will be open for business, a respite from the coronavirus pandemic that decimated the tourist season last year in the nation's capital.

The National Park Service is expecting the National Mall and historic landmarks — including the Lincoln Memorial, Washington Monument, and Jefferson Memorial — to welcome a limited number of visitors.

Since the Inauguration in January, the city of Washington is seeing increased attendance at public events. Regrettably, the most heavily attended event in the past six months was a rally on the Ellipse that was the jumping-off point for the ransacking of the U.S. Capitol.

A U.S. park ranger preparing to greet the crowds at the Washington Monument said, "I think a lot of people want to be here to make up for the emptiness we all felt last year, but they know it's not yet totally safe to do so."

To those who do come to the city, Lafayette Square has joined this year's list of places to visit. Last spring, the park was the focus of peaceful protests that followed the killing of George Floyd.

"I think we can use this holiday to reaffirm our commitment to systemic change for racial equity and to pay homage to those who died at the hands of the police," said one visitor from Minneapolis.

The president will lay a wreath at the Tomb of the Unknown Soldier at Arlington National Cemetery. The cemetery will be open to the public, although face masks and social distancing will be required.

Last year, the cemetery was only open for gravesite visitation to family pass holders. Members of the Army's 3rd U.S. Infantry Regiment, The Old Guard, wore face masks as they placed flags in front of headstones for "Flags-In" at the cemetery.

"At least Washington will recognize the solemn nature of this holiday, even if we have to wait for the crowds to return," said one local vendor.

Flags are flying at half-staff for a three-day period under a presidential order in remembrance of those who died to safeguard the nation.

"This weekend we also pay tribute to the men and women who died of the coronavirus, those who survived the pandemic, those who continue to persevere through tough economic and social conditions, and those who remind us that Black Lives Matter," said Sen. Abe Lowenstein, chairman of the Senate Intelligence Committee.

Unlike most members of Congress, Lowenstein will remain in Washington for the holiday. That is one of the few things that hasn't changed from last year. And there will be no ceremony, virtual or otherwise, honoring the Washington Nationals for winning another World Series championship, since the banner will fly in Los Angeles, home of the L.A. Dodgers.

**

KATZ SHAVED and showered. He grabbed another cup of coffee, unplugged the coffee maker, and went to his car. The morning air was crisp and the sky was clear. He made two calls as he started the engine. The first was to learn from Santana whether there were any new developments concerning Morley. There weren't. The second was to Sherry Stone, who headed the investigation into Hugh Spates, the man suspected of killing Morley. She had directed Santana to call Katz in the middle of the night about the body's discovery.

"I don't know about you, but I expect Spates to continue his plan," Katz said.

"No doubt," she agreed. "Spates is a delusional a-hole. I expect him to move forward as though nothing happened."

"Exactly. That's what I told Curtis."

"I know," she replied. "I was with him when he called you. You sounded pretty sure of yourself."

Katz tipped the rearview mirror to check for oncoming traffic before pulling from the curb. "I am," Katz explained. "Spates has the same DNA as every other member of the criminal class, whether a small-time hood or a white-collar criminal. Once they put something into motion, they act as though they're bulletproof. It's what makes them dangerous, but it's also the root of their undoing."

Stone grunted her concurrence. "Where are you?" she asked.

"I just left the house. Why? Do you need a ride?" Stone shared a townhouse with Santana five minutes away on Prince Street.

"No," she replied. "I'm at the station. I'll take a car from the motor pool in a little while. Say, guess who else is going to be at the briefing?"

"Abe Lowenstein?" he asked.

"No," she laughed. "He's welcome to join, but I suspect he's only in town to monopolize on media inquiries rather than actually do any work." She paused and then said, "Phil Landry."

"Talk about delusional assholes," he said.

They both disliked Landry, whom they held responsible for manufacturing a terrorist plot to bring surface-to-air missiles into the nation's capital two years ago. They were only too happy to see his nomination sabotaged by others, resulting in his demotion to a meaningless job.

Stone had another reason for detesting Landry, but that was personal and Katz didn't need to know about it.

"Landry keeps turning up, like a bad penny," Katz said.

"I'm actually afraid he's up to something," Stone said.

"What makes you say that?"

"He never accepted his rejection for the homeland security post. He wants back in. People like that never quit. Landry's up to something. And it's no good. Mark my words."

**

AS LANDRY locked the door, he manually switched on lights inside the van. A bank of television monitors glowed. In front of the screens, three computers and a keyboard rested on a console beside a comfortable leather swivel chair. Landry sat down, entered a code, and waited for the program to open. As he waited, he rehearsed the scene he had choreographed for tomorrow.

Landry had arranged for three individuals to go to the GreyStone Hotel. They would each retrieve orange H-Pack backpacks and head to a different corner of Lafayette Square. The backpacks would be filled with explosives timed to detonate at 11 a.m.

Landry had selected security personnel to be stationed at the corners of the park. He had specifically chosen three trigger-happy goons. Like him, they felt threatened by the reforms taking place in local, state, and federal law enforcement.

The computer program opened.

Landry entered three names: Ahmed Suleiman. Maria Pena. Ari Hammond.

As he adjusted himself in his chair, he went through a ritual he repeated several times each day. He checked his cell phone. He felt his wallet in the back pocket of his trousers. Then he glanced at the lanyard around his neck. "Shit," he uttered. He had left his PIV card in his office computer.

**

WILSON ASSESSED the situation. By forgetting to remove his PIV card from the computer, that fool had granted her unimpeded access to a treasure trove of information. But unless she kept wiggling the mouse every few minutes, the computer would lock and she would lose access to the Outlook program for his government email account.

She wasn't sure what she was searching for, other than incriminating evidence of *something*. That evil man was up to no good. She felt it. For months, she had fantasized about searching his files. But she always hesitated.

If he ever found her snooping around his business, he would fire her. As a result, she avoided doing anything that would give him a reason to get rid of her. As it was, she knew he would seek her removal as soon as her harassment complaint was resolved. But she didn't want to give him the satisfaction of getting rid of her for cause beforehand.

The phone rang.

She ignored it. Her eyes surveyed the folders cascading down the computer screen. She recognized the names of most of the files as projects that Landry handled on a day-to-day basis.

Then her eyes fell on a folder titled "Personal." She clicked on it. Inside were three subfolders titled "Target A," "Target B," and "Target C." She opened the first subfolder. The subject was Ahmed Suleiman. She opened the second: Maria Pena. And then the third: Ari Hammond.

The phone rang again.

30

**

"PICK UP!" Landry shouted into the phone. The ringing stopped. A recording came on. "Hi. This is Vanessa. Leave a message. And have a blessed day."

Landry ended the call. He tried to remember whether he closed the door to his office when he departed. If he had, there was nothing to worry about. She didn't know the combination to the cipher lock on the door. But what if he hadn't?

Unfortunately, there was no time to go back to the office and retrieve the PIV card. Assuming the worst, that Wilson might go snooping through his computer files, there was a strong likelihood she wouldn't assign any significance to the folder. Landry didn't think Wilson was smart enough to identify a dead body in the road if she stumbled upon it. There was probably nothing to worry about, he concluded.

Landry called Ahmed Suleiman.

**

SNOWE PARKED her car on the gravel shoulder of Eisenhower Avenue, climbed over the guardrail, and headed down to Cameron Run. In her rubber boots, she waded across shallow water that trickled down the channelized stream to the Potomac River. Ahead of her, buried in the bushes and newly budding trees, a brown and green camouflage tent came into view.

She donned her mask. As she approached the tent, smoke wafted up into the sky and she smelled burning wood and leaves. Maggie Moriarty sat by a campfire, dressed in soiled jeans, a tattered flannel shirt, and unlaced hiking books. In front of her, a pot of coffee balanced between two logs. Moriarty stared vacantly at the low-burning fire and poked the embers with a stick that she held in her shaky hand.

"How are you doing?" Snowe asked.

Moriarty looked up zombie-like and shrugged. She wasn't

wearing any facial protection.

"Where's Katie?"

"What's it to you?" Then, recognizing the visitor, she snarled at her probation officer. "Don't you have better things to do than badger parents about their kids? You should be home taking care of your own. Oh, sorry, I forgot, you don't have any kids." She smirked. "Maybe that's why you take such interest in mine. Maybe you've got some guidance about how to be a good parent."

Snowe ignored the hostile tone. "Mind if I sit?"

Moriarty removed the stick from the fire. The tip was burning. She twirled it around like a wand. "There's plenty of room," she said.

Snowe sat on a rock. "You're right," she said. "I don't know a lot about the day-to-day challenges of raising a child. But I know a little about what's expected of a parent, and it looks to me as though you're failing miserably. Look around. You're living out in the open. There are no bathroom facilities. There are no other children. This camp lacks the physical infrastructure and emotional support systems that a child needs. No sidewalk to ride a tricycle or place to color with crayons, no…."

Moriarty poked the air with the stick. "Shut your trap. Don't talk to me about *infrastructure* and *support systems*." She pointed the stick menacingly at Snowe. "I don't need any of your social welfare bullshit. Go back to where you came from and take all your textbook crap with you."

Snowe realized she was taking the wrong approach. She was speaking *at* Moriarty rather than talking *to* her. She knew she was wrapped up in her own emotion and could not retreat. "And then there's drugs, Maggie," she said. "You're using again. The test results came back. Social Services is going to lodge a formal action against you next week to have Katie placed in foster care."

"No!" Moriarty staggered to her feet. She waved the smoldering stick as though it was transformed from a wand to a sword. "You're not going to take Katie!"

Snowe looked around. "By the way, where is she?" Moriarty just glared at her defiantly. Snowe got up and walked to the tent. Peeking inside, she saw Katie lying fully dressed on top of a grubby sleeping bag. Her long blonde hair was stringy and her clothes were wrinkled and dirty.

The sleeping bag wiggled and a man's head emerged, his eyes straining as he squinted at her.

"You go away!" Moriarty hollered from her post at the campfire. "You're no good. You're just going to cause trouble. Get the hell out of here!"

Snowe shook Katie awake and said softly, "Come on, Katie, let's go." The sleepy girl let Snowe lead her out of the tent. Snowe stepped on a syringe as they made their way outside. The man in the sleeping bag emerged from the tent wearing boxer shorts and a T-shirt. "What do you think you're doing?" he hollered. "Let go of my little rag doll."

Jesus Christ, Snowe said to herself. *Little rag doll!*

**

"AHMED?"

Ahmed Suleiman said nothing. He held the phone to his ear and looked across the table toward his uncle Trey. The old man was wearing a mask. A chessboard was positioned between them.

Suleiman knew the voice on the phone belonged to the man who stood outside the mosque about a year ago, soon after he and his family had celebrated Eid al-Fitr at the end of Ramadan. The man had spoken about a terrorist attack that had just occurred at Naval Air Station Corpus Christi, Texas. The man also talked about the October 2019 assassination of Abu Bakr al-Baghdadi and the need to avenge his death.

"Your move, Sully," said his uncle.

Suleiman glanced at the chessboard. His queen was dead and his king was cornered by a bishop, a castle, and two knights. Uncle

Trey was two moves from checkmate.

"You win," Suleiman said, nudging his king to topple it and quickly rising from the table. As he turned, his hand inadvertently swiped the standing pieces. A pawn tumbled to the ground.

Trey Carr looked at Sully with sad eyes as the young man retreated to the far end of the park. Carr picked up the pawn and put it with the other pieces. Inside, he felt despair. Despite his best efforts, Sully had not received the upbringing he deserved. He blamed himself. After all, what kind of a role model had he been?

When he looks at me, he sees a failed soul. I don't instill any desire in him to succeed. All I do is remind him of a rigged, oppressive system that needs to be attacked and destroyed.

Suleiman was well out of earshot from his uncle but still spoke into the phone in a whisper through his mask. "What do you want?"

"It's time," Landry said, staring at the computer screen inside the van parked at Roaches Run. Of his three recruits, Landry considered Suleiman the easiest prey. He came from a shitty past and he faced a bleak future. Landry prided himself in taking advantage of such shortcomings. Still, he knew Suleiman needed to be coaxed into the gate.

"Tomorrow at 10:45 a.m., go to room 909 at the GreyStone Hotel in D.C. It's near Farragut Square," Landry instructed. "Use the keycard I mailed you last week. Inside the room, you'll find three orange H-Pack backpacks. Strap one of them on your back and walk toward Lafayette Square per the instructions I mailed with the keycard."

Suleiman glanced toward Uncle Trey. The chess pieces were already stored in a burlap sack. The old man was bent over and talking on his flip phone. Suleiman wondered who he was talking to. *Does the old goat actually have any friends?*

Suleiman spoke into the receiver, "What about the other backpacks?"

"That's not your concern," Landry said. "Your job is to pick up one backpack at precisely 10:45 a.m. and go to your designated place. Understand?"

"I understand," Suleiman answered. He believed the plan called for multiple explosions around Lafayette Square. He just wanted to know who else was involved. Did they harbor the same uncertainty that he felt today? Why was it necessary to set off bombs to maim and kill? He knew something big had been unleashed last year. He remembered a report that on June 6 of last year over 500,000 people participated in protests at 550 places throughout the U.S. There was a movement going on and it was going to bring about change. He wanted to be part of the positive energy and didn't want to emulate the insanity he'd witnessed in Washington back in January. *Was bombing really the best way to seek systemic change?* He knew the answer to his own question. *No.*

"And don't wait for the next person to arrive," Landry instructed. "The mission is synchronized. If you delay, you'll throw off the timing for everything."

"I understand," Ahmed repeated.

"Now get some rest so you'll be ready for this important mission." Landry sensed hesitation. "What is it?" he asked.

"I don't know about this anymore," said Suleiman. "All of the insanity that occurred back in January. Violence begets violence. It's not the way."

"You don't know what you're talking about," replied Landry. "Just do as you're told. Any more questions?"

Suleiman hung up. He did not have any more questions, but doubt still lingered in his mind. He turned back toward the table. Uncle Trey was gone.

Landry hoped Suleiman would not renege on his promise. He put the odds at 50/50. Then he made his next call to Target B, Maria Pena.

**

Twelve Years Earlier

The room was shaped like a shoebox, with a narrow metal table in the center. A chain was bolted to the middle of the table with a handcuff at the end of the chain. As Trey Carr remembered it, the room's side walls were covered with white tiles of soundproof material. The rear wall had a small window, high up. He could not remember if there were bars on the window.

Carr sat beside his attorney, Sean Matthews. The guy wasn't known for his courtroom prowess, but his retainer was cheap. Carr felt it was better than going with the public defender, though he now had doubts. Facing Carr and Matthews was a squat, wide-shouldered Alexandria cop.

Carr, 36 years old, had a rap sheet for petty offenses, including petit larceny and urinating in public.

"This time it's serious," said the cop.

Carr wasn't good at remembering names. But this one was easy. The officer's last name was the same as the legendary coach of the Dallas Cowboys, the nemesis of his beloved Washington team. "What are you talking about?" Carr asked angrily. "I got stopped for a busted headlight." He knew there was a pipe in the glove compartment that he used for free-basing, but that could only result in a drug paraphernalia charge. Since he didn't have drug-related convictions, he assumed Matthews would get him a suspended imposition of sentence, which meant no jail time provided he didn't get caught again.

"I'm talking about a recent spate of robberies off Seminary Road," Landry said.

Carr looked at Matthews. "I don't know anything about that," he said. Matthews motioned for him to address Landry. He turned to the cop. "I didn't rob any houses."

"Well, if it wasn't you, it was someone with your DNA," Landry laughed.

Carr stared at the cop in shock. *Did Landry just say what I thought he said?*

"What DNA evidence are you referring to?" Matthews asked.

"Don't worry about it," Landry replied. "Your client understands what I'm talking about."

Carr rubbed his chin. Landry had sprung something unexpected on him. Well, maybe it was not totally unexpected. After all, he suspected his "nephew" Ahmed might be involved in some B&Es. The fancy clothes and high-end electronics that appeared out of nowhere were disconcerting. If Carr's surmise was correct, Landry was attacking his one vulnerability. That wasn't right. Family should be off limits.

"Robbery is a felony," Landry said. "Someone gets convicted of a robbery, their life is effectively over. No chance of getting a job to do anything meaningful. No right to vote. No right to possess a firearm. That person is basically in the same hole as your ancestors, Trey, except there's no hope for emancipation."

Carr waited for Matthews to say something, anything, but the attorney just sat there, giving Landry *carte blanche* to say and do whatever he wanted. Two against one. Those weren't the odds Carr was counting on when the interview began.

"That's racist," he said.

"That so?" Landry laughed.

Matthews snickered. Carr looked at his attorney in disgust.

Landry said, "You come from shit and your future is shit. That applies not only to you but to everyone associated with you." He glanced at Matthews. "Even your attorney knows it's true." Then he added, "If you had any money, you wouldn't have walked in here represented by Mr. Matthews. You got your poor, sorry ass in a heap of trouble, Trey, and anyone close to you will be in trouble too."

Carr closed his eyes. His fingertips rubbed his eyelids. Then he lowered his hand, opened his eyes, and turned to Matthews. "Can we talk alone for a minute?"

Landry pushed back his chair. "I'll step outside and let you two confer," he said.

"Mighty considerate of you," said Matthews. "Thanks, Phil."

As the door closed, Carr, furious, asked Matthews, "What the fuck is going on? I expect advance warning if a cop is going to spring something like this on me. And you just sit here. He's making a fool of me and he's making a chump out of you. And you thank him for being considerate."

Matthews remained silent for a long moment. "I know exactly what's going on," he said finally. "Landry wants you to take a plea. In exchange for doing that, he's willing to drop an ongoing investigation against a member of your family. I'd say that's pretty generous."

"I can't believe this," Carr said, incredulous. "You knew all the time that this was going to happen? And you didn't tell me? You didn't warn me? I mean, you set me up. And now he's fucking me over."

Matthews suppressed a laugh. Carr reminded him of former D.C. mayor Marion Barry. *The bitch set me up.* He wondered what people saw in Barry anyway. The man was a low-life, just like Carr.

Matthews wanted to be done with the case. All he wanted to do was collect his retainer and move on to the next case. "It's SOP with this cop," he said. "I didn't find out about your nephew until I got here this morning. If I'd known earlier, I'd-a told you."

"Shit," Carr said, disgusted and angry. "It's 2009, for God's sake. This isn't supposed to be happening, not here, not now. This is old school. I say we alert the higher-ups to what's happening. This cop's trying to get me to take the fall for my nephew's crimes, but we both know he's also going to add a bunch of other unsolved cases to improve his stats at my expense."

Matthews had actually known for days that Landry was going to pull this stunt. He hadn't told Carr because Landry knew Matthews occasionally slid a Benjamin under the table to finagle a favorable disposition from the police in his cases. If Landry leaked word of those arrangements, certain members of the local police force would be disciplined, and Matthews would be disbarred.

Matthews opened his notepad and removed several 8x10 inch photos of Ahmed Suleiman accepting cash for small vials containing rock-like substances. He slid the photos across the table like he was putting down a royal flush.

"This is bullshit," Carr said.

"It may be an unfair way to pressure you," Matthews admitted, "but it's not bullshit. The contents of those vials tested positive for crack cocaine. Landry's got an ironclad case against your nephew. Maybe these are nickel-and-dime sales, but you know what they do to crack dealers. If Landry goes forward with this stuff, the kid's gone for life."

Carr stopped breathing. The neighborhood was being hollowed out. Young ambitious Black men were being put behind bars in droves. The Crime Prevention Act looked a lot like another urban renewal project to clean up the ghetto.

He grabbed the back of Matthews' chair and inhaled deeply, filling his lungs with the stale air of the interview room. He was trapped, like an animal. "I need to talk to my nephew," he said.

"There's no time for that," Landry said from behind them.

Carr and Matthews spun around, startled. Neither of them had heard Landry reenter the room. "Either we work out a deal now or I present this evidence to the grand jury," Landry said. "And once I do that, all bets are off."

"Get the fuck out of here!" Carr screamed. "I need to think."

"Fine," Landry said. "Go ahead and think. Just don't think too long. Grand jury convenes tomorrow. I need to get this case on the docket if we can't reach an accommodation."

After Landry departed for the second time, Carr put his head down as tears of frustration overcame him. Months later, when he reflected on what happened next, he concluded Landry was simply playing him. He wanted Carr to overreact and get caught up in his own emotions. Landry was betting that once Carr broke down, he would backtrack. And once he backtracked, he would plead guilty to whatever shit Landry put in front of him.

After all this played out according to Landry's plan, Carr was bitter about taking the rap for crimes he did not commit. He was aggravated about being manipulated by Landry into accepting the devil's offer. And he prayed for the day when this vicious cycle would end and crooked cops would no longer be able to act with impunity against people like him.

**

"MARIA?" Landry asked when she answered the phone.

Maria Pena froze. She felt she had done something wrong. She wanted to reverse course. Yet she felt she couldn't untangle herself from the web spun around her. She knew she bore some responsibility for the predicament in which she now found herself.

This man was uncanny. From the moment they met, it was as though he understood her better than she understood herself. *How was it possible? How could he identify my vulnerabilities and take advantage of them so effortlessly?*

"Yes," she said hesitantly.

Landry smiled to himself. "It's time," he said. His words were soft and soothing. "It's time to put our plan into action."

"I don't know." The words came out as though each was a stand-alone sentence. "I." "Don't." "Know."

"Okay," Landry replied soothingly. His voice evidenced no anger. "I understand. Not everyone is motivated when it's time to act. It takes passion and commitment. Maybe you just don't have what it takes."

She knew he was manipulating her. Yet, for some reason, she was attracted to him. Maybe it was a self-destructive impulse, she thought. "Tell me again what you want me to do."

"I want you to take a stand, Maria. I want you to find expression in your life. To live."

It started with a random email advocating environmental protection. That wasn't her thing — she was still searching for her purpose — but something in the email drew her to the author's message. Then, out of curiosity, she went to the website. And there, to her surprise, she found praise heaped upon her hero: her father.

The website stated:

We need to follow the example of Fernando Pena, who railed for social justice. He staked everything on an unwavering devotion to truth. It cost him his career and caused untold suffering from the death of the woman he loved, but he never faltered in his quest. We must emulate him in our effort to reverse past environmental injustices.

She read and reread the words. A tribute to her father! Finally, someone recognized his brilliance and paid tribute to his work. She wondered whether it was a first step toward rehabilitating his reputation. When she got the next email, she contributed $20 to the cause.

Then the third email arrived. It thanked her for her support. She was surprised, since her contribution was only $20. Yet the email reminded her that, while money was good, personal involvement was better. And it implored her to enlist in a demonstration planned for Washington, D.C.

In late July, she answered a call from an unfamiliar number.

"Maria, I'm calling you from the Environment First Fund. Thank you for supporting the EFF. I wonder if you've had a chance to read my blog about our planned demonstration in Washington, D.C.?"

"No."

Actually, she had, and Phil Landry knew it because he had monitored her activity. But it was easy playing dumb with Maria Pena. Landry knew that despite an impressive academic background and a more impressive pedigree, she had mental health issues. Like father, like daughter, Landry thought. From what he had learned, she would be psychotic if she didn't take medication on a regular basis. In fact, she might be psycho even with her meds. *Like father, like daughter.*

"Do you have a minute for me to tell you about it?"

"I'm busy right now."

He knew she wasn't. She had nothing to do. She was unemployed. All she'd been doing for the past two months was going down to Lafayette Square and joining in the protests.

"I know you're busy, but I'd appreciate it if you could just give me a couple of minutes," he implored.

Her silence served as his opening. Landry spent the next 20 minutes extolling her father's virtues and explaining how the EFF wanted to apply her father's principles in criminal justice to environmental fairness.

"He was a trailblazer who ignited a movement," Landry said. "When he saw injustice, he immediately took action to address it. His work at the Justice Department was unequaled. His dedication to find a just and verdant outcome harkened back to the days of Attorney General Robert F. Kennedy. I want to employ that same set of principles at the EFF. Verdant means green and lush, you know, and that's the image I want to create for this organization. I can't think of a better way of expressing environmental beauty than by using 'verdant' and I can't think of a better person who symbolizes the pursuit of justice than Fernando Pena."

Landry had studied Pena's Facebook page and had seen a photo of Robert Kennedy on it. He didn't think much of RFK; Landry considered RFK a belligerent rich kid who built a favorable image from a malleable media. But it didn't matter what he thought. What was important was that it was a selling point.

The same for "verdant." It was a word that had been used in an ad by the Catherine T. MacArthur Foundation — "committed to building a more just, verdant, and peaceful world" — and Pena quoted the phrase in some of her tweets. It was meaningless drivel to him, but he echoed the words back to her as a means of effective seduction.

"Meet me," he cajoled her. "I have something planned. I would like you to participate in it. And I'd like to tell you about it in person."

She agreed to meet at the coffee shop at the Key Bridge Marriott in Rosslyn since it was close to his "office." Pena had limited her contact with other people since the middle of March, when she began staying indoors to fight the spread of the coronavirus. She had spent over four months isolated from the world, afraid for her elderly father's health as well as her own. And, when she did come out, it was as though she lacked the social skills to navigate her way through the day.

She never intended to spend the afternoon in bed with Landry at a hotel. It broke all the rules. So much for six feet of separation! But that's what happened. First it was just talk about the environment and her father, of course. As she gazed intently into his eyes she sensed a strong magnetism drawing her to him. The fact that she hardly knew him added to the attraction. When he suggested that they move upstairs to a room in the hotel, she could not resist the temptation.

Afterwards, she spent several days trying to make sense of it. She had been social distancing for months, and now she'd become intimate with a man she'd known for barely two hours. As she tried to process the relationship, she grew anxious in anticipation of his next call.

"MARIA?"

She started as she heard her father's booming voice.

"Who's that?" Landry asked on the other end of the phone.

She lowered her phone. "Just a minute," she called out.

"Who's that?" Landry repeated.

"My father," she whispered.

Fernando Pena appeared in front of her. Shrunken by age and cruel fate, he was a deflated caricature of the commanding presence who roamed the halls of the Justice Department a decade ago.

His daughter ignored him and walked out of the house and onto the porch. If, by following her, her father was somehow trying to affect or influence her actions, he was having the opposite effect. "Tell me what you want me to do," she said. "I'm ready. I'm so ready."

"That's my girl," Landry replied.

**

WHEN SHERRY STONE arrived at Cameron Run, the campfire was still smoldering but the makeshift campsite was deserted. Two marked cruisers pulled to the curb a minute later, their emergency equipment blaring. Uniforms exited and surveyed the area. A senior family counselor emerged from the passenger side of one of the vehicles.

"Where is everyone?" Stone asked.

"They grabbed the little girl and headed into Old Town about ten minutes ago," replied Snowe. "You should be able to find them without any problem."

"Don't bet on it," Stone said. "Druggies are a wily group, and Maggie and her boyfriend are a particularly difficult pair to corral. We've had several run-ins with them during the past few months. They think they're fooling people by living at this campsite, but we keep it under surveillance."

"You're familiar with them?" asked Snowe. "Why didn't you notify me? I'm Maggie's probation officer. Plus, you know Mo and I are invested in her case."

Maybe you are invested in the little girl, but I've never heard Mo mention her to me one time, Stone thought. "We'll find them," she said. "If Maggie needs more treatment, we'll haul her skinny ass into court and ask a judge to order it. The last thing we want is for Katie to be a motherless child." She remembered that Tony Fortune, Katie's father, died the night Katie was born. She hoped the child wasn't cursed.

"Mind if I ride along if you go out looking for her?" Snowe

asked the uniforms, who nodded their consent.

Stone wished them well. She looked at the time on her phone. She was late for the briefing. Of course she knew there was no need to rush. She was giving the brief.

**

LANDRY RELAYED his instructions to Pena. She was to go to the GreyStone Hotel. She was to arrive no earlier than 10:30. There would be two H-Pack backpacks by the credenza. She was to strap one on her back and go to the designated corner of Lafayette Square. "Got it?"

She did. But there was one more thing. "I need to see you," she whispered. "Can we get together tonight?"

No way, he thought. There was too much for him to do. Yet he could not afford to alienate her. "There are so many logistics to work out," he said gently. "Maybe tomorrow night." Of course, if things went according to plan, there would be no tomorrow for her.

"Okay," she acquiesced.

Landry hung up. He stepped out of the van. He lit a cigarette and looked across the water at Roaches Run. Smoke curled out of his mouth. He finished the cigarette and snuffed the butt in the dirt with his heel. He still had to call Ari Hammond, number three, the one that gave him the most trouble.

Standing at the far end of the sanctuary, he dialed the number. No answer. He took a deep breath, turned, and looked east across the G.W. Parkway toward Gravelly Point. The sun hung over the Potomac River. Further to the left, the Washington Monument was visible, with one side of the obelisk glistening while the adjoining side was hidden in shadow.

As Landry surveyed the area, a man stood at the edge of the soccer field at Gravelly Point with a pair of binoculars focused on the van parked at Roaches Run. The phone inside his jacket pocket rang. He lowered the binoculars, which hung around his neck by a nylon cord, and pulled out the phone.

"Hello."

"Took you long enough," Landry replied as he moved from the van to his car. "Where are you? What are you doing?"

"I am in D.C., preparing to die."

Landry brushed the statement aside. "Tomorrow morning, I want you go to room 909 at the GreyStone Hotel at exactly 11 a.m., retrieve an H-Pack backpack, and take it to the southeast corner of Lafayette Square."

"And blow up like a firecracker."

"You aren't going to die."

"Yeah, sure, if you say so." Hammond laughed. "You recruited me to strap explosives to my body and stand at a congested corner during the height of the Memorial Day weekend. And you have the audacity to say that I'm not going to die. Your plan is modeled after the December 2009 attack inside Camp Chapman in Afghanistan."

Landry was taken aback.

"We both know the score," Hammond said. "No one's walking away unscathed from this thing."

Landry considered the lengths to which he had been forced to go. To win over Suleiman, he presented himself as a radical extremist. With Pena, he adopted the persona of an environmentalist nihilist. And lover. For Hammond, he acted like a lunatic. All three of them had mental health issues, but Hammond was a certified nutcase. He had actually been locked up in an asylum at one point.

"It's cool," Hammond said. "I'm ready to go out in a blaze of glory."

"You exaggerate."

"Do I? Just look at what those fools did in January, breaching the Capitol. People died. It doesn't take much to ignite things in this town. But I don't give a damn. Like I say, I'm ready to go out in a blaze of glory."

Landry suddenly felt a pain behind his left ear, like a hairpin driving into his temple. It was the feeling he got when he was being watched. *Did someone have him under surveillance?*

On the other side of the parkway, Hammond raised the binoculars and trained them on Landry. A plane appeared in the sky moving left to right, its engines announcing the plane's descent. Hammond pressed the mute button with the thumb of his left hand.

"Where exactly are you in D.C.?"

Hammond waited until the sound of the roaring engines diminished. He unmuted the phone. "Lafayette Square," he said. "I'm casing out the area."

"Hang on a second," Landry said while walking swiftly to his car. He jumped in, threw the vehicle into reverse, backed up, downshifted into drive, and darted out of the parking lot. He merged with southbound traffic, navigated a straightaway between taxis and Uber drivers, turned 180 degrees, drove by the arrival gates, and took the ramp to the northbound lanes of the G.W. Parkway.

He signaled right and swept into the entrance to Gravelly Point. It had taken less than three minutes. His eyes surveyed the parking lot, the soccer field, and the open field leading to the river. He stopped the car and jumped out.

Another plane descended overhead, its engines echoing across the field and drowning out all other sound.

"Sorry about that," Landry said into the phone when the noise had died down. "Something came up. I couldn't talk."

"Not a problem," Hammond said.

When he had seen Landry's car tear out of Roaches Run, Hammond surmised Landry smelled something fishy. So he dashed to his car, drove up the parkway at breakneck speed, and stopped at the monument north of the 14th Street Bridge. *Your instincts are good, but mine are better. Give it a little more time and you'll get the full measure of how much better.*

"Listen," Hammond said. "If there's nothing else, I'll be going. But to be clear, I have no illusions about your plan, and be assured that you can count on me. This is the sort of moment I've fantasized about for a very long time."

He hung up.

Landry stood in the Gravelly Point parking lot and looked across the parkway to Roaches Run. The van was visible from where he was standing. He sensed something. Yet it was inconceivable for him that he was the prey. After all, he was the alpha.

**

"DAMN," Wilson cursed. She was logged out. She had been distracted by the files she had printed and lost track of time. When she finally punched the keyboard, the system requested a password. She tried to recall how many times she could guess at a password before the system locked her out. *Was it ten? Fewer than that?* She hesitated. Did she want to risk it? If so, what six to eight numbers had he used?

Hoping that Landry kept the password hidden somewhere, she frantically opened the drawers to his desk, then the credenza, and finally the overhead cabinet. Nothing. Then she discovered a locked cabinet. She went to the credenza and fished for keys. They were stored in the back. She tried each key on the keychain until she found one that opened the cabinet. And there, taped on the inside of the door, was a code: 1793159.

Not particularly original, but par for the course, she concluded. He'd drawn a square with a diagonal strike through it. She typed the numbers in the box for the password.

It worked.

This was a game changer. Not only did she now have unlimited access to his computer files, but she could review the printed items at a leisurely pace. Once she gathered sufficient information, she planned to contact the media. And she knew exactly who to call.

**

KATZ ARRIVED at the operations center in Ashburn with ten minutes to spare. The building was on a nondescript cul-de-sac in a nondescript industrial park. It looked like the other large, three-story, flat-roofed buildings in the area, with one exception: the 10-foot fence topped with rolls of razor wire that surrounded it. There was also a guardhouse at the fence entrance manned by two tall sentries armed with long guns.

Katz stopped at the entrance and flashed his PIV card at the guard who stepped forward. The guard nodded and signaled to his colleague to open the gate and lower a metal barrier at the base of the entrance. Katz drove over the metal spikes that would pierce the rubber tires of his car if headed in the opposite direction. He parked in the half-empty lot. Since March of 2020, most people had been teleworking. Traffic and parking – once the banes of his existence – were no longer a problem.

Once inside, he used the card again to go through the turnstile and enter the lobby. He removed his personal and work phones from his pockets and placed them in a small metal locker, and dropped the key into his pants pocket. Then he entered the sensitive compartmented information facility, or SCIF.

Santana was already there, along with Mai Lin, his special assistant. They were both seated against the wall; there was an empty seat between them. The room was filled with some twenty people, half of them seated in chairs along the walls and the remainder seated at least six feet apart from one another around a long, oval-shaped oak table covered with phones, computers, and speakers.

On the wall was a huge screen with the faces of the remaining members of the group. There were more members participating remotely than in the room. The call was on a secure line.

Katz slid into a chair about six feet from Lin.

"You should be up there," Lin chided him, glancing at the empty seats at the table.

"*You* should sit up there," Katz said. "You're the superstar in our operation, not me. Plus, you've attended all the briefings. I only know what you and Santana tell me."

Over the past three and one-half years, Lin had repeatedly proven herself as a skilled analyst and prodigious worker in his office. Two years ago, while pregnant with her son, she had been wounded in a terrorist ambush. Last year, she played an instrumental role in identifying the person who murdered Jane Hutton, the head of the office's civil branch.

"Okay, I'll slide up there when Sherry finishes her presentation," Lin joked.

"I'm serious," Katz replied.

Lin made a motion for him to shush and turn his attention to the head of the table, where Sherry Stone was standing at a tabletop podium.

"Ladies and gentlemen, let's get started," Stone said. She adjusted her mask. "For those in the room, check your pockets. If anyone inadvertently brought any electronics into the room, put them in the lockers outside." Around the room there was a rustle as people reached into their pockets to be sure they had not brought a device into the SCIF. A few sheepishly stood and stepped outside.

Once everyone had returned and taken their seats, the lights dimmed and the room fell silent. A bright lens flashed an image on the screen, with part of the image falling across Stone's face. She shifted the podium slightly to the left to escape the glare.

The door to the conference room opened again, emitting light. A stocky figure entered and took a position along the wall. Landry would have been on time if he had only brought his PIV card. It was hell getting through the gate and into the building without it.

"After 9/11, a lobbyist named Hugh Spates helped pass legislation to reimburse businesses affected by a terrorist act near a federal site if that site was a potential target of the attack," Stone began.

A face flashed on the screen. The man was fit, with blond hair, a rugged chin, and blue eyes. His smile was contemptuous.

"It was a noble act," she continued. "But as sometimes happens, the angels of his better nature abandoned him. Now he's trying to use that law to stage a phony terrorist act and collect a handsome return from the federal government. Specifically, he's planning to detonate explosives to destroy buildings he owns near the U.S. Capitol."

The next slide was an overhead photo of warehouses along a railroad line. In the upper right corner was the U.S. Capitol building. "Spates owns several properties along this railroad track in Southeast D.C.," Stone said. The next slide showed a target with the bull's-eye directly over one of the warehouses. "The warehouse he owns and intends to destroy is around a quarter mile from some of the most important real estate in the city." The target's circumference covered several buildings below Independence Avenue, including the O'Neill and Rayburn House Office Buildings.

"He'll never get enough explosives onto Capitol Hill," someone said. "It's too heavily guarded." The point was well taken, Katz thought. Even though the National Guard troops brought to Washington to reinforce the Capitol grounds following the January 6 attack and to safeguard the city during the swearing-in of the new president had departed, there was still a robust presence of officers and heightened security.

"Nothing stops a fool," Stone said. "Spates thinks he's invulnerable. If anything, he believes recent events provide legitimacy to his plot."

Next Stone displayed a photo of a railroad line running through Crystal City parallel to the G.W. Parkway south of the 14th Street Bridge. "He's going to do it by train," she said. "The explosives are going to be loaded onto a train in Virginia and carried over into D.C."

The lights came back up. People shifted in their seats. Many members of the group already knew about the attack because they were involved in surveilling the operation. Due to their diligence, the attack was never going to be allowed to take place.

Stone reached down and picked up an orange canvas backpack. She placed it on the table in front of her. "In the late '60s," she said, "JanSport and Gerry Outdoors designed a lightweight nylon backpack for campers and hikers. In no time, students of all ages were using them, from kindergarten to professional school. More recently, they've moved to the workplace, where everyone from summer interns to CEOs uses them. They are, in a word, ubiquitous. Maybe some of you have one.

"This particular orange-colored backpack, called the H-Pack, has become the backpack of choice for terrorists. Maybe it's because of its large interior cavity, absence of zippers and side pockets, sturdy leather bottom, or canvas exterior. For whatever reason, most of the bombings in the past six years, domestically and around the world, have involved H-Pack backpacks. In fact, if security officers see someone with an H-Pack backpack at an airport or special event, you can be sure they're going to give that person additional scrutiny. So be aware of that if you own one."

Landry smiled smugly to himself.

"Yesterday," Stone continued, "our surveillance detected two H-Pack backpacks placed against a fence running along a strip of land south of Crystal City. An hour later, the backpacks were snatched by Spates' accomplices, Levin Wallace and Peter Morley. On this occasion, the backpacks were not filled with explosives. Instead, they contained a large amount of cash, namely $25,000 in $100 bills."

"Wasn't one of them whacked last night?" asked one of the better-informed members of the group.

Stone nodded. "Late last night or early this morning, Morley was found dead at Four Mile Run. He was also our confidential informant. Based on his information, we learned that Spates is planning to stage the event this weekend. We believe Spates retrieved the backpack from Morley's car after he killed him."

"Has Morley's murder jeopardized the operation?" someone asked.

"No," Stone answered. "Our information shows that Spates is driven by an intense ego and a sense of desperation. He thinks he's bulletproof. Plus he's in financial straits. We believe that he's not going to stop now and that he's confident no one is going to link the murder to the explosion. In fact, in the hours ahead, I expect him to place explosives along the same fence line where he previously put the money. He's not backing down now."

"That's not what I mean," said the person who had posed the question. "Do you think the operation might be jeopardized because someone on our side leaked information to Spates? I mean, why else would he kill Morley?"

Stone seemed surprised by the question. "I doubt that's the case," she said. "In fact, it never occurred to me until you just suggested it." She looked around the room. "I can't believe someone in this room, or anyone connected with this investigation, would leak the identity of our CI to the target of our investigation." She paused. "If I find out otherwise, there will be hell to pay."

Katz leaned over to Lin. "There's no leak. The shooting was accidental. Spates had no intention of killing a member of his crew. And Stone's right when she says Spates is going to proceed with this insane plan."

Lin looked at Katz. She knew him well enough to know he was probably right.

**

IN THE CARNAGE following the terrorist attacks of 9/11, few people focused on real estate insurance policies. Hugh Spates was the exception. As a young lobbyist for the real estate insurance industry, he paid close attention to the Terrorism Risk Insurance Act and the more than $30 billion that was paid in claims related to the attacks. While the media and the public focused on compensation for first responders and the families of victims, Spates saw real estate claims: developers, landlords and tenants, and others who suffered huge losses and received enormous compensation. In the horror of crushed bodies, mangled steel, and shattered glass, Spates saw opportunity.

"You know what would be funny?" another congressional staffer said to him while working on the bill. "What if someone bought property near a potential terrorist target in the hope the place actually got bombed? You could buy a piece of real estate and receive triple payback if the place got destroyed by terrorists." Everyone laughed, including Spates.

Over the next decade, he bought parcels of real estate along the railroad line near Capitol Hill. He didn't buy them with any sinister intent. He just thought the properties were underpriced and that he'd make a killing in the market in the long run.

He took a hit during the 2009 financial crisis. Real estate plummeted. Then it rebounded. And just when he was preparing to sell and cash in, COVID-19 hit. The commercial real estate market stalled in the big cities, including D.C. Although it bounced back, the future was uncertain.

He needed a way out.

And then he remembered the joke that one of the staffers made about the 9/11 bill. That night, Spate drew a series of concentric circles around Capitol Hill, using the U.S. Capitol as the center.

Now, as he prepared to execute the plan, Spates believed fate had dealt him a winning hand. The mayhem that unfolded at the U.S. Capitol on January 6 leant legitimacy to the belief that the nation's capital was a target for extremists. In the ensuing rubble, Spates saw dollar signs flashing in front of him.

**

"THOMAS MANN?"

"Yes," Mann replied. "Who is this?"

"I called you last year about Philip Landry."

"Oh, yes," Mann replied, acting surprised.

The screen on his phone told him it was Vanessa Wilson. Her name and number had remained in his phone since her last call. He had actually Googled her when she previously contacted him, and he had never forgotten that she was a beautiful woman. At that time, she discussed her complaint against Landry for sexual harassment. Slowly but surely the case was winding its way through the system. Landry was a predator and she wanted to take him down.

Mann leaned back in his chair in the editorial office of *The Washington Chronicle*. The newsroom was deserted. Congress was out of town for the holiday. Some of his friends remained isolated in their apartments while others had embarked for the Vineyard or the Outer Banks. Anyone who remained in town was teleworking and filing their stories electronically. "I'm glad to hear from you," he said. "What's up?"

"He's up to no good."

He knew she was referring to Landry. "What sort of *no good*?" he asked.

"If I tell you, will you write about it? Or will it be like the last time? I poured out my soul to you and you didn't print a single word."

"I wanted to, believe me, but I didn't have enough independent information to corroborate your story. I understand you're upset with me. But I can't print something based on one person's word. These are serious allegations and I have to be on solid footing."

Wilson sighed. "That's the problem," she said. "I've been looking at these documents for the past few hours and I can't make any sense out of them. All I know is he's up to something bad."

"Are you in a safe place?" Mann asked. "Physically, I mean. Are you in a safe location?"

"I'm okay," she said, a little surprised. "Thanks for asking."

"Can I see the documents you're talking about?"

"Yes," she said. "I can bring them home with me. You're welcome to come to my house and look at them."

"When's a good time to meet with you?"

**

Nine Years Earlier

MANN KNEW the *Chronicle* had submitted his series on the Pena Inquiry for a Pulitzer Prize but he never expected it to be seriously considered for the award. He was floored when he learned he'd won for writing the best investigative series. Champagne flowed in the newsroom and coworkers crowded around to offer their heartfelt congratulations. The prize boosted morale and created new hope that the upstart newspaper might defy the odds and stay in business. Mann had the scoop of the year, akin to vaunted D.C. journalism coups like the Pentagon Papers and Watergate.

His series focused on Fernando Pena, a Justice Department official who led an inquiry into alleged improprieties committed by Phil Landry, who at the time worked for the Alexandria Police Department. The investigation — dubbed The Pena Inquiry — concluded that Landry manipulated the system to coax pleas out of defendants to close cold cases. Mann's series raised questions about Pena's motives and techniques. It suggested he doctored documents, misappropriated funds, and withheld vital information in conducting his inquiry.

As *The Chronicle* published its stories, Pena lost credibility and came under suspicion himself. Within days, his investigation unraveled. In the end, Landry received a letter of apology for questioning his integrity.

Mann never revealed his "Deep Throat." If he had, there would have been an understandable skepticism about the legitimacy of the allegations against Pena. While Mann claimed the anonymity of his source had to be protected, the truth was he wanted to hide the identity of his source: Phil Landry.

⁑

MANN CALLED STONE. They knew one another from the days when he was a beat reporter covering the courthouse scene in Alexandria and Arlington. She was a rookie. Mann knew about her problems with drugs. At the time, she was a rebel and an outcast, a far cry from the role model and rising star that she appeared to be today. He recalled how her drug problems almost got her thrown out of the department. Only deft lawyering by Mo Katz — her defense attorney at the time — salvaged her career. Mann believed that, if ever there was a fallen angel who had earned her redemption, it was Stoner, a nickname that close friends used affectionately to the present day. One thing that escaped the reporter's watchful eye, however, was the fact that Landry had blackmailed Stone, using her weakness to get her to back off pursuing leads during the Pena Inquiry.

"On good authority, I understand something's brewing in D.C. this weekend," Mann said. "If you provide me with details, I'll keep my story under wraps until it breaks. Deep background."

Stone sensed Mann was fishing. "I haven't the foggiest," she said.

"Come on, Stoner. I just want to be on top of things when they break. You know how it is."

She did not entirely trust him, but she was curious as to what he knew about the Spates operation. And she was willing to trade information for whatever intel he possessed. *Maybe there's more to it.* "Where are you?" she asked.

"Downtown. I can drive to Virginia and meet with you, if you like." No response. "Come on, Stoner." He put down another card. "According to my source, it has something to do with that body at Four Mile Run." It was a gamble, but his instincts told him to take it. "I'm going to keep digging," he pressed. "If I inadvertently blow the lid off this thing, don't say I didn't give you fair warning."

Stone was hooked. Coming on top of that comment this

morning about someone possibly leaking information, this call seemed too timely to be just fishing. Plus, she acknowledged, Mann could do more damage with a little information than with a lot. "Okay. I'll meet you in Tysons in a half hour," she said. She gave him the name of a restaurant on Route 7 and they agreed to meet outside of the place.

"Damn," Mann said to himself after he hung up. "I'm good."

Chapter Three: Afternoon

THEY SAT outside at a small square table on chairs that scraped the sidewalk. The inside of the restaurant was nearly empty, a continuing sign of the impact of COVID-19. Mann didn't record Stone or take notes. Their conversation was short and to the point.

"We've been keeping tabs on Hugh Spates," Stone began.

Mann knew Spates by reputation: slick lobbyist, in and out of trouble with congressional oversight committees and federal investigators, sued twice for failing to adhere to regulatory requirements. Acquitted both times. Spates was either a sleazy operator or an effective advocate, depending on whether you were investigating his services or paying for them.

"He's planning to take advantage of a provision in a bill he helped write to provide compensation to property owners whose buildings get damaged from terrorist attacks on nearby federal facilities," she said.

From his surprised look, she immediately sensed that she'd said too much and shared no further details with him. She also knew he would have an easy enough time piecing this information together and checking public real estate records to know where the "attack" would be staged. "I've got to go," she said, rising abruptly. "If you release anything about this, I'll kill you, metaphorically speaking, of course."

Realizing the conversation had gone sideways, Mann said, "Listen, before you go, there's something I have to tell you. Full disclosure, Stoner. You shared something with me that I didn't know about. Now it's my turn to share something with you."

Stone sat back down and pushed her chair closer to the table. "Go on," she said.

"Phil Landry is up to something. I don't know the details. I got a call from his assistant, who's got an outstanding complaint against him for harassment. I'm going out to look at some documents she pulled off his computer. I'll share them with you, if you want."

"Okay, what exactly did she tell you?" Stone asked.

"He's got some crazy scheme. It involves three people. That's about all I know. If you're interested, why don't you join me?"

Landry again. "I'd like to," Stone said without hesitation. She looked at her phone to check the time. "Hang on a minute." She texted the team that her brief would resume at 3 p.m., later than scheduled.

She wondered if there was a connection between the operations planned by Spates and Landry. If so, Landry was gathering inside information by attending her briefing. She would have to tailor the afternoon session accordingly.

**

"IT LOOKS like we've got a reprieve," Santana said, looking at the text message on his phone. "Stone just postponed the briefing." He was having lunch with Lin and her husband, David Reese, in a half-filled diner. Since Santana and Lin worked closely together, they had formed a work "pod" so they felt safe dining together. Now with time to spare, they summoned the waitress back and ordered dessert.

The conversation turned to Reese's first jury trial as a newly minted assistant commonwealth attorney.

Jury trials had been shut down until late in 2020, when the Virginia Supreme Court approved a plan to resume them in compliance with CDC guidelines.

"It's been a logistical nightmare, but it's something that couldn't be delayed any longer," Reese said. "People are wearing masks, temperatures are being taken, riders are restricted in elevators, and jurors are sitting apart from one another in the jury box."

"It's remarkable," Lin commented.

"People have a constitutional right to a trial by jury," Reese said. "Smart defense attorneys began demanding juries for cases that normally would plead out. The docket got all snarled up. As a result, we cut some incredibly attractive deals to get people to plead. In this case, there wasn't room to negotiate so we took it to trial."

"So tell me about it," Santana said.

"It was an aggravated assault case against a woman who rammed her vehicle into her ex-boyfriend's car," Reese explained. "She was waiting for him, pulled her car from the curb, gunned her vehicle into his, and struck the driver's side. They needed the Jaws of Life to get him out."

"How much time did she pull?" Santana asked.

"They found her not guilty."

Santana chuckled. "What was her defense?"

"Sexual assault."

"No, I mean, what was her defense for driving her car into his?"

"Sexual assault."

Santana waited for a further explanation.

"She claimed he assaulted her earlier in the day and was driving to her apartment to do more harm," Reese explained. "She cut him off at the pass, so to speak." Santana chuckled, but Reese didn't appear amused. "Here's the thing," he continued. "There was no evidence he ever physically assaulted her. No prior police report, no bruises, nothing. I think she acted out of a jealous rage and then made up that story to win over the jury."

"Well, it worked," Santana observed.

Reese winced. "Yeah, but she took advantage of the jurors' sympathy to escape punishment."

"You shouldn't feel bad about it," Lin interjected. "It happens all the time, doesn't it, Curtis? I mean, maybe it was a credible defense. And you can't blame her attorney for being creative in trying to get her off."

"She's right, David," Santana said.

Reese shook his head and said, "It shouldn't be that way."

"You're too altruistic," Lin said.

"You have to expect results like this," Santana added. "A defendant will use every trick in the book to win an acquittal. And you can't blame them. After all, they're fighting for their lives."

"Even so," Reese said, "a jury is supposed to view a case dispassionately and return a verdict of guilt if the elements of the offense have been proven beyond a reasonable doubt. In this case, there was no evidence supporting her claim. All of the evidence pointed in the opposite direction, namely that she planned to assault him.

"It's not like she was acting in self-defense. The jury was seduced by her story." He sunk his head. "It was my first case and I did it the right way. The jury disregarded everything I presented and set her free. It was a sham."

Dessert arrived and everyone was momentarily distracted by the sweet treats before them.

"Here's my take," Santana said after swallowing a spoonful of an ice cream sundae. "The truth — the real truth — is always somewhere in the middle. The ex-boyfriend probably did abuse the defendant, just not that day. And she probably was seeking retribution for a lot of things. Juries pick up on that stuff. I think the jurors saw something that led them to acquit her. Don't be too hard on yourself, David. People take justice into their own hands all the time. It's a fact of life."

**

STONE RANG KATZ. "I just met with Thomas Mann from the *Chronicle*," she said. "He had a lead on the Spates operation."

"I figured something was up when you postponed the afternoon briefing," Katz replied. "Tom's alright. He's never burned me. But you have to be careful not to fall into a trap and tell him more than he needs to know."

"Too late for that, great wise one."

Katz, seated on a cushioned bench outside the conference room, looked up as Lin and Santana appeared around the corner. Santana handed Katz a cup of coffee and plunked a paper bag down on the bench next to him. "Your lunch," he said. "A cold burger and fries, and a cup of cold black coffee. You owe me twenty bucks. We can square up later."

Lin and Santana headed to the lockers to secure their phones before reentering the SCIF. With his free hand, Katz opened the bag and popped a fry into his mouth. "What happened?" he asked Stone.

"I provided Tom with the outline of the Spates case. After I finished, he reciprocated and told me that our friend Phil Landry has something up his sleeve."

A smile spread over Katz's face. "Smartly played," he said.

"I can't claim that I forced the issue," she said. "Tom and I spoke at cross purposes. He called about a rumor of something happening in D.C. over the Memorial Day holiday. I assumed he was referring to Spates. He's just a stand-up guy and shared the information about Landry."

Katz glanced around the hallway and lowered his voice. "So what exactly is this tip about Landry?"

"Hard to tell," she said. "Landry's assistant has it in her possession. Tom and I are going to meet her and review some documents."

Katz took a bite out of the burger and nibbled some more fries. "This could be serious," he managed to say with his mouth full. He swallowed. "The last time he pulled one of these stunts, shipping those dummy surface-to-air missiles into D.C., a real live SAM ended up in the mix." Two years ago, Landry conned a bunch of criminal miscreants into helping him import surface-to-air missiles into D.C. It was a case of entrapment, but Landry came away smelling like a rose and was nearly nominated as DHS secretary because of it.

"Don't remind me," Stone said. "I was there. Where the hell were you?"

"Why does he do this shit?" Katz asked.

"Hell if I know. The man's a narcissist. He should be in prison instead of at DHS."

"What's your next step?"

"Not entirely sure," she answered. "After this afternoon's briefing, I'm going back into the District. I'll review the documents with Mann and figure out if we need to take any action."

"Keep me apprised."

"I always do," she replied.

**

KATIE FORTUNE raced down King Street like a spring breeze, stopping to stare in store windows, weaving in and out of the crowds, and dancing merrily along the brick sidewalk. Looking at her, no one would have thought she was lost, alone, vulnerable, and frightened. She looked like an average precocious four-year-old whose family was trailing behind her.

A patron stepped out of the Principle Gallery and watched as Katie skipped by, heading toward the river. A moment later, the girl ran up the opposite side of the road. The woman noticed that Katie's golden hair was unwashed and matted, her complexion was waxen, and her clothes didn't quite fit. The woman quickly pulled out her phone and dialed 911. "Perhaps it's none of my business, but there's a little girl running unattended in the 200 block of King Street," she said.

The dispatcher asked for a description. It matched Katie's. He asked for the woman's location and the direction in which the little girl was headed. Then a message went out to the police that the little girl they were searching for had been found.

The closest officers were on the upper end of King Street near the Masonic Temple. They drove down to the river and began searching on foot. Streets, stoops, alleys, and stores were inspected to no avail.

Abby Snowe accompanied the police. At times, she seemed to lead the effort. She created an air of anticipation among the search team; it was only a matter of minutes before Katie would be found.

Then a report came about a blonde-haired waif at the intersection of Cameron and Washington Streets. And another Katie sighting three blocks further up Henry Street. A third report placed the little girl on Prince Street. Katie had become a whirling dervish. "I don't think we're going to find that girl until she's ready to be found," said one officer, hitching his britches and catching his breath as he trotted behind Snowe.

**

LATE IN THE AFTERNOON, Stone resumed the briefing. She kept a watchful eye on Landry, who again arrived late and stood against the wall.

"We have four teams assembled to monitor the situation along the rail line," she said. "The first team will be in a high-rise along the railroad track." She pointed to a building at the edge of Crystal City overlooking the railroad tracks north of Four Mile Run. "I'll be there if we learn the operation has been activated. And the second team is going to be based at Roaches Run."

Landry rocked back on his heels. He clasped his hands behind his back, his palms pressed against the wall. *Roaches Run!* She had to be kidding. It was the one place he concluded that was hidden in plain view. It was the reason he had selected it as his mobile operation base.

"Why there?" he piped up.

"The rail line runs directly along the perimeter of the sanctuary," Stone explained. "It's a perfect location from which to observe the train at ground level."

"Don't you leave the team exposed at that location?"

Katz, seated at the table, lowered his head. *Why the interest in Roaches Run?* Such keen interest was odd and might mean Landry was involved, he concluded.

"There's a line of trees and bushes along the shoreline," Stone said. "They'll be able to conceal themselves from onlookers. Plus, by that time, it'll be immaterial whether they've been detected. The explosives will already be on the train. And it'll only be a few minutes before the train is stopped."

Katz looked closely at Stone to see whether she was surprised by Landry's line of questioning. Something clearly was bothering Landry. She was expressionless. To Katz, that meant she shared his suspicion.

"The third and fourth teams will be on either side of the Potomac," she concluded. "One team will be on the Mount Vernon Trail directly beneath the 14th Street Bridge, and the other at Hains Point. From these locations, we'll have eyes on the train at all times."

**

TREY CARR watched Suleiman from the corner of his eye. Normally, Sully would be texting with friends and scrolling through his Twitter and Instagram feeds. But this afternoon he was nervous and distracted.

"Are you okay?" Carr asked. Suleiman fidgeted and walked around aimlessly. "Don't worry," Carr said. "Everything is going to be okay."

Suleiman looked at his uncle with disdain.

Look at you! You have been betrayed by this country and you don't even know it. You are a convicted felon. They stripped you of your past, present, and future. I did bad things, but I was smart. I escaped unscathed. Yet, while I have no scars, I feel aggrieved. Perhaps my anger is for you.

Carr knew his nephew thought he was a weak and broken man. After all, since being released from the penitentiary, he found that his job applications repeatedly ended up in someone's wastepaper basket. What Suleiman didn't know was that had escaped prosecution at Carr's expense. Carr was not looking for gratitude; he just wished the young man would smarten up and quit acting like a martyr.

**

66

Twelve Years Earlier

"WHAT DO you think my nephew's chances are?" Carr asked Matthews. He wished he had a more competent counsel, but he had already shelled out $5,000 and had no more to spare on another attorney. "If I don't go along with Landry's offer, that is."

Matthews shook his head and replied, "It's always a roll of the dice. You can never predict what a jury is going to do."

Carr wanted to laugh out loud. He knew Matthews never took a case to a jury, regardless of whether the client was guilty or innocent. Mathews pushed his clients to plead guilty and take their chances before the judge at sentencing.

"What if he's innocent?" Carr asked. "Or that the police offered to forget his case if I cleared out their backlog on unsolved cases?"

Matthews shrugged impatiently. "You're not seeing reality," he said. "In a way, I understand. He's your nephew. He's ashamed to confide in you about his involvement in some nefarious dealings.

"As to your allegations against Landry, let's be serious. He'll just deny it. No one is going to believe you. And your threats are not going to stop Landry from prosecuting Suleiman for every crime he can throw at him."

"They aren't allegations," Carr protested. "They're facts. Hell, you were there. Landry is trying to squeeze me to admit to crimes I never committed. He's a lazy, dishonest cop. That's enough to stop any prosecution against Sully in its tracks. You were a witness!"

Matthews said nothing.

Realizing that his own attorney would not stand beside him if he bucked the system, that his options were limited because of a lack of money, and that his nephew's future was in peril, Carr surrendered to the inevitable.

**

CARR ENTERED a plea in Alexandria Circuit Court to four residential robberies. Both the prosecutor and the judge were skeptical about Landry's methods in closing the cases, but neither said anything. The rookie cop assigned to the case initially raised concerns about the investigation, but then that cop went radio silent.

In preparing for the sentencing, Landry told the prosecutor a light sentence was appropriate. He acknowledged it might be hard to get a jury to convict Carr of the robberies. Despite feeling there was something wrong with Landry's presentation and knowing there were rumors about both Landry's tawdry tactics and Matthews' inferior defense skills, the prosecutor did as Landry suggested.

"How do you plead, sir?" asked the judge.

"I plead guilty, your honor," Carr replied, standing contritely in the courtroom, his attorney at his side. Landry sat in the back of the courtroom, his legs crossed and his arms draped around the adjoining empty chairs, looking like a spider that was waiting to capture its prey.

"And you plead guilty because you are in fact guilty and not because anyone has coerced you?"

"That's correct, your honor."

"I realize the prosecution is arguing for a light sentence, about two or three years, but I cannot agree with such leniency. You have to pay for your crimes. You are hereby sentenced to twenty years in the Virginia penal system on each of the four counts, with ten years suspended on each count, and the four counts are to run concurrently. Is there anything else you would like to say to the court?"

"No, your honor. Thank you, your honor."

**

EVERYONE ASSUMED it would end there, Carr thought to himself. *The rookie cop Sherry Stone was the only person who expressed reservations along the way. But Landry got to Stone, and I can only guess how he got her to shut up. Then, a year later, there was that research student, Ruth Hammond. She looked at my cases. She discovered discrepancies.*

I hadn't fully accepted my fate. I was willing to speak the truth when she visited me in prison. And then that wonk from DOJ, Freddy Pena. He initiated an inquiry into the whole thing. He was making headway. But Landry stopped Pena's inquiry in its tracks too. Not sure how he did it, but it might have had something to do with the bad press that Freddy got.

Everyone assumed it would end there, but it didn't. Not by a long shot. It was just the beginning.

**

THE BRIEFING ended at 5 p.m. Katz ran into Landry in the parking lot as he was leaving. Without any provocation or advance warning, a casual encounter turned into a nasty confrontation as Landry began a half-crazed rant.

"I saw you seated at the table," Landry said to Katz. "As a former criminal defense attorney, you must feel pretty good about yourself. Like you've arrived, you know. High-powered position, steady salary, lots of prestige, and even some future potential if you play your cards right."

"I play my role," Katz said nonchalantly. "At the end of the day, the title doesn't really mean anything. You are who you are."

Katz hoped that would defuse the situation. He considered Landry unstable and unpredictable and, based on Stone's recent disclosure, potentially dangerous.

"You certainly are who you are, Katz, and that's no one!" Landry burst out venomously. Some members of the team who were walking through the parking lot stopped and eyed Landry cautiously. A couple of them moved forward, prepared to jump in if a fight broke out. "There's nothing to you, man," Landry continued in a loud voice. "No substance, no center. Just a lot of parts that don't add up to anything, like in a junkyard. Part Black, part Jew, part prosecutor, part defense attorney. In reality, you're no one. No one and nothing."

Landry's words stung because there was some truth to them. At his core, Katz felt disconnected and incomplete. Katz knew he was a jigsaw puzzle but he also knew he didn't need an evaluation from the likes of Landry. It was complicated, but he was working on it. "Dr. Freud, is it?" he asked, keeping his tone even.

"You're an asshole," Landry hissed. He turned away abruptly and stalked to his car. The others in the parking looked at one another with expressions that asked: WTF? Landry wrenched open the car door, got in, and slammed it closed.

He tried to regain his composure. He was angry with himself. He should have kept his cool. But he blamed Katz for setting him off. His phone vibrated. He pulled it out of his pocket. Maria Pena was texting him.

Need you tonight. Room 901. Down the hall. Have a special treat. Not what you're expecting. Will not disappoint.

Chapter Four: Evening

AROUND 6 P.M., Stone and Mann were sitting spaced apart on Vanessa Wilson's patio, sifting through emails that Wilson had printed from Landry's computer. "Can you make sense of it?" Wilson asked. Stone and Mann didn't answer. They kept studying the messages.

Slowly, a picture emerged like a hologram. Landry was planning a fake terrorist attack. He had persuaded three people to carry backpacks filled with explosives to Lafayette Square. The parties were identified as A, B, and C in the subfolders. Landry had used different techniques to entice each of them to participate in his scheme. For one, he encouraged revenge for misguided U.S. policies in the Middle East; for another, retribution for years of environmental neglect; and, for the third, anarchy for the sake of anarchy.

Landry planned to have the three individuals arrested as they approached Lafayette Square and Black Lives Matter Plaza under the pretext that they were suicide bombers engaged in a terrorist plot.

"What a self-aggrandizing asshole," Mann said. "He should have been fired years ago."

"What are you going to do?" asked Wilson.

"I'm going to inform the people overseeing security that we've identified a potential terrorist attack," Stone said. "Even though it appears Landry intends to have these people arrested before they can carry out any bombings, it's impossible to know how this is going to turn out. People could get injured.

"I'm also going to recommend that Landry be picked up on suspicion." She looked at the documents again. "I want to try and figure out the identity of his three accomplices. They may be the ones in the most danger. If Landry carries out this plan, he might have them shot on sight to cover up his insane plan."

"Are you going to recommend that Memorial Day activities be

cancelled in D.C.?" asked Wilson.

"Not my call," Stone replied. "Someone else is going to have to make a decision whether this threat can be contained or whether we need to cancel events. At the very least, I think they'll take precautions to shut down this insane operation before it has a chance to be effectuated."

"That sounds reasonable," Wilson said.

In the back of her mind, Stone wondered if this might not be a terrorist plot at all, but something else, namely some form of payback, Landry-style.

"Listen, Tommy," she said, "I don't want you printing anything about this now. I want to have Landry taken into custody without being tipped off in advance."

"I won't write word, I promise," he said.

Stone continued to study the documents. Thirty minutes later, she discovered she was alone on the patio. Mann was in the kitchen sweet-talking Wilson.

**

LANDRY MADE one final trip to Roaches Run before heading to the GreyStone Hotel.

He opened the back door to the van, climbed inside, turned on the computers, and checked messages from his three targets. Then he closed his eyes. By this time tomorrow, he would have created the illusion of having foiled a terrorist plot. The purpose of his ploy, others would conclude, was to reverse the downward trajectory of his career and return to his glory days.

People were familiar with the way he operated in the past — always stirring the pot, advancing his career, stepping on or over others, and devising Machiavellian plots — and they would conclude this was business as usual.

Nobody would suspect he had created a play within a play. No one would see that it was not about advancing himself this time. No one would realize this was just a cover to reap revenge against some of the people who sought to undermine his ambitions in the past.

It wasn't about Ahmed Suleiman, Maria Pena, or Ari Hammond at all. They were simply a means to an end.

Landry jumped out of the van and secured the back door. He regretted he did not have a more secure lock, but replacing the standard lock with a more industrial one was not high on the list of things he had time to do now. The number one priority was to move the van before Stone's agents arrived tomorrow. He would do that later tonight, after he returned from the GreyStone Hotel.

Landry returned to his car. He drove south on the parkway, repeating the route he had already taken several times in the past days — turning into the airport, swooping around like a boomerang, passing the terminal, and exiting onto the northbound lanes.

Now, driving by Gravelly Point, from the corner of his eye he thought he saw a man standing near the van. He turned and looked again. There was no one there. A shiver ran down his spine. *What were the chances?*

His car crossed the 14th Street Bridge, drove by the U.S. Holocaust Museum, and headed toward the National Mall. Traffic remained heavy; people were flooding into the city for the weekend. The Washington Monument was to the left, the U.S. Capitol in the distance to the right. The traffic lights were green all the way to Farragut Square.

**

THE METRO CLUB was at the intersection of H and 17th Streets. It was open, subject to coronavirus protocols that included sanitizing high-touch areas, social distancing, and strict compliance with health and safety rules for preparing and serving food. Katz found a parking space a half block away. Within a few minutes, he and Snowe walked beneath the stone columned portico and entered the building. Dark paneled wood, sumptuous rugs, mirrors, gilded framing, and heavy furniture greeted them, as did a man in a uniform who ushered them to a table in a small private dining area.

"I feel like we're onboard the Titanic," Snowe whispered. Katz agreed. The club's interior certainly harkened back to the Gilded Age.

"Abby Snowe?" The man approaching the table had long silver hair that cascaded over his shoulders. He had gold stud earrings and was attired in a white suit and white mask.

"It's so nice to meet you, Mr. McLuhan," she gushed.

"The pleasure is mine," said the author.

They bumped elbows.

She introduced Katz. They eyed one another suspiciously, neither making an effort to touch one another.

Six other people were already seated around the room at small tables spaced apart. They began to buzz excitedly at the sight of McLuhan. Dinners like this one were standard fare on McLuhan's book tour. Before each lecture, he met with readers selected by book clubs to discuss *Rhythmic Cycle* and how the book had changed the readers' lives. During the pandemic, McLuhan continued the practice, albeit as a slimmed-down affair. When Snowe told Katz about it, he concluded it was a smart way to drive sales and spur attendance.

As excited as Snowe was to attend the dinner, her mind was elsewhere. The early morning interaction with Moriarty had unsettled her, as well as the hunt through Old Town for the little girl. Snowe prayed Katie would be found and cared for, particularly if Moriarty spiraled out of control.

**

"YOU'RE SKEPTICAL about the methodology of the twelve-year cycle in *The Rhythmic Cycle of Life*," McLuhan said pointedly to Katz. There was no anger or disappointment in his voice. Katz sensed it was part of a setup. "Pick an event and let's see if we can

74

trace its origin by studying a twelve-year cycle," McLuhan continued. "Let's see if we can deduce a way that would have prevented it from occurring or at least allow it to play out in some other way."

Without thinking, Katz blurted out, "9/11." The attacks on the World Trade Center and Pentagon by Al-Qaeda on September 11, 2001, were something he would never forget, even though he was a teenager at the time. It had inspired him to public service as a prosecutor.

McLuhan nodded. "You've chosen a historical event rather than a personal one." Turning to the guests around the room, he said, "One of the values of my twelve-year cycle is that it can be applied not only to your personal life experiences but also to the progression of historical events, whether you're looking at a sports team or a nation's march through history. You can define trends and figure out ways to effect change in subsequent cycles."

He watched as the dinner guests ran calculations through their minds, focusing on events that were meaningful to them. "The crux of 9/11 was less about Middle Eastern terrorism taking place on our shores than about America's resolve to identify and defeat an adversary bent upon destroying our way of life," he said. "So let's look at it that way."

The guests nodded their heads in agreement.

"It was exactly 60 years to the day, on September 11, 1941, that Charles Lindbergh delivered a speech in Des Moines, Iowa," McLuhan began. "It's hard to describe the division within our country between Lindbergh and the isolationists, on the one hand, and Franklin Delano Roosevelt and those who recognized that our entry into the war was imperative, on the other.

"People were repulsed by Lindbergh's isolationist rhetoric," McLuhan continued. "They denounced him and rejected his ideology. People saw through the falsehood of his speech and they formed a collective mindset against the real enemy. At that time, it was Nazi fascism. On 9/11, it was radical Middle Eastern terrorism.

Today, it's domestic extremism."

Katz surveyed the intent faces around the room. They were seduced by McLuhan's apparent insight. Katz saw something else, namely a showman pulling off a magician's stunt.

McLuhan probably had a list of 50 events that people would select, Katz figured. For each event, there was an answer. If necessary, McLuhan would redefine the question, weave other events and trends into the response, and provide an answer that appeared spontaneous. In fact, it was fabricated and rehearsed *ad nauseam*. Katz understood it only too well; it was his own modus operandi in preparing his opening statements in jury trials.

"There was a book by Lynne Olson titled *Those Angry Days* written ten years ago," McLuhan added. "She explained the nation's mood far better than I'm able to do and she singled out September 11, 1941, as the turning point between pro- and anti-interventionist sentiments in the months leading up to World War II." McLuhan spent the next ten minutes reciting events in 1953, 1965, 1977, and 1989 that reinforced his theory about a twelve-year repetitive cycle. To Katz, it was farce compounded by deceit.

**

"He was amazing," Snowe said an hour later as they walked six blocks toward a large white tent erected on the side street beside DAR Constitution Hall.

"He's a charlatan," Katz replied.

"You're just jealous he was the center of attention. It's a position you prefer reserved for yourself." Snowe sounded irritated and exhausted. The search for Katie Fortune was weighing on her, Katz thought, but so was the difficulty they were having as a couple in navigating the next step of their relationship.

"I'm not jealous," Katz said. "That 9/11 thing was a total scam. McLuhan simply researched important dates and gathered facts to support his theory. It sounds great, but it's a rip-off."

Snowe looked unconvinced.

"Trust me," he said. "I'm not proud to say it, but I've done the same thing hundreds of times in front of juries. Everything about his delivery — the understated showmanship, drawing comparisons that elude other people, making everything fit together so perfectly. It's all a show."

"You're such a — the word escapes me," Snowe said.

"Realist?"

"No," she replied briskly. "Cynic. That's the word. You're a cynic."

"Abby," Katz said. "Everyone runs a hustle. It's the way the world works. We spend our lives hustling others or being hustled by them. The sooner you figure that out, the sooner you realize not to take anything at face value."

"Maybe in your world," she reproached him, "but not in mine."

"It's true in everyone's world," he replied, "whether you admit it or not."

She resented his insinuation, which was that she was naïve and idealistic. "I hoped you would be impressed," she said. "That's why I invited you. Now I wish I had brought someone else who would have appreciated his insights."

When they arrived at the tent set up alongside DAR Constitution Hall, their conversation ceased. They took their seats, separated six feet from one another, appropriate for their present mood.

Despite the small crowd, McLuhan appeared to thunderous applause. He sat on a four-legged bar stool in the center of a wooden stage about six feet high. A microphone was clipped to his lapel. The event was streaming online, with thousands of adoring fans watching in rapt attention. An empty glass and a pitcher filled with ice water stood on a thin-legged table off to the side. Next to the glass were blue, yellow, and red markers. Behind the table was a whiteboard.

"Good evening," he began. People seated throughout the tent applauded loudly. "*The Rhythmic Cycle of Life* is a self-help book," he said when the applause finally died down. "It's based on a simple premise, which is that your life, like history, repeats itself. Life is not linear; it occurs in cycles. And, since your life is cyclical, the key to a successful life is to repeat your past successes and avoid your previous blunders. There is no easier way to accomplish that objective than to understand the cycles of your own existence. It's all about you, literally. You've already been around the block a couple of times."

Everyone laughed.

He filled the glass with water, took a sip, and placed it back on the table. "Provided you haven't burned out — and, from the looks of this audience, you are bursting with energy and facing the future with enthusiasm and optimism — you can take your life to a higher level simply by charting the past events of your life."

**

LANDRY PARKED in the alley behind the GreyStone Hotel. Earlier, he had paid the hotel's technician to disable the security cameras for three hours. He wondered why the hotel bothered to monitor its lobby with cameras, given the fact that bookings had plummeted due to the coronavirus. But, since the policy was still in practice, he paid whenever he had a rendezvous with Maria Pena. In fact, it had become routine, an easy way for the tech guy to pocket a few extra bucks about once a month, pandemic or no pandemic.

After looking around the alley to make sure no one was watching, Landry cautiously removed one of the three H-Pack backpacks from the trunk of his car and placed it in a large duffel bag. He entered the back entrance, took the service elevator to the ninth floor, unlocked the door to room 909, and gingerly placed the backpack against the credenza. Then he went back downstairs and repeated the process two more times.

**

"LET'S RECAP," McLuhan said. He held a blue marker. The whiteboard now showed a large circle he had drawn, along with years, events, and notes printed around it. "Once you've been through at least two cycles, you begin to see the rhythm of your life. You should be able to spot when good things happen in your cycle. By the same token, you should be able to identify when bad things happen. You need to study those progressions in order to figure out how to avoid bad things from repeating themselves and how to encourage good things to occur over and over again."

He took another sip of water from the glass on the table. "These are all ways to shake things up. Redirect your energy and take yourself off the road that previously led to bad destinations. Use today — right now, tonight, in real time — to change the past. You can do it." Then he paused. *You may have good instincts, but mine are a little bit better.* "You can definitely do it."

From the corner of her eye, Snowe saw Katz suddenly fidget in his chair. She turned her head and raised her eyebrows at him questioningly. He shook his head in response. But she knew something had happened, like he'd been hit with something from behind.

**

LANDRY SAT on the edge of the bed. Three backpacks were lined against the credenza. His phone vibrated. He saw the name Maria appear on the screen. He answered the call, but it must have been too late. A second later, a text appeared. 'I'm here. Same routine!' He replied: 'OK. Give me 15 minutes. Same routine as always.'

She was right down the hall. How convenient, he thought. She would be in the bathroom when he arrived. He'd get undressed, except for his socks, lie on the bed, and turn off the lights. She'd open the bathroom door dressed in a lace nightie, straddle him, and ask, "What's your pleasure?"

And, just as they used a routine to get started, things always ended the same way. Landry would turn a sensual evening into something disgusting and demeaning. He would slap and punch her, twist her hair, degrade her with lewd words and force her to submit to his perverted whims. Why she tolerated this treatment she was helpless to understand.

Landry reached in his pocket and pulled out a bottle of pills. He popped one into his mouth and waddled to the bathroom, where he scooped water from the faucet to wash it down. He knew Maria Pena was mentally challenged. She had had very few lovers, he believed, and probably didn't know the difference between being loved and being manipulated. *Good for me*, he thought. He reveled in the way he treated her, inflicting pain and humiliation. It got him off. That was all that mattered.

Landry looked at the bedside clock. He'd wait another five minutes before heading to the room. He planned to make it a night to remember.

**

A LONG LINE snaked along the sidewalk adjacent to DAR Constitution Hall as admirers queued up at the desk inside the tent where Henry David McLuhan autographed their copy of *The Rhythmic Cycle of Life*. Now wearing latex gloves and a mask, the author occasionally rose and fist- or elbow-bumped an admirer.

Snowe and Katz were near the front of the line. For Katz, the evening had been mildly entertaining. He still had no doubt that McLuhan was a fraud. The smoke-and-mirrors that the author used at dinner earlier in the evening were in full display inside the hall.

Looking at the stately building next to them, Katz said, "You know, we've been here before. I don't know if you remember, but I got us tickets to see Robin Williams' *Weapons of Self Destruction*."

"I remember," Snowe said. "It was filmed as an HBO special. It was back in 2009."

**

AN EMPLOYEE at a restaurant on Fayette Street was carrying

out the trash when he spotted a bundle of clothes in the alley. Upon closer examination, there were legs and hands curled under the clothes. It was a little girl, probably around four years old. Beside her were scraps of food fished out of the dumpster. The employee alerted the owner, who rushed outside, picked up the little girl, and brought her inside the restaurant. The child placed a tiny arm over the woman's shoulder, embraced the warm body, and uttered an exhausted breath.

"Call the Alexandria police," the woman said. "This must be the girl they're looking for."

A policeman arrived in ten minutes. It was the same officer who'd been huffing and puffing in his pursuit of Katie earlier in the day. He was a father of four and he'd never stopped looking, even when others had called it a night. Once he got Katie safely to the station, he would be able to go home.

**

KATZ AND SNOWE returned to their townhouse a little after 10. Snowe went to the kitchen to get something to drink while Katz went upstairs to change. When he came back down, he found her hunched over her phone typing a response to an email.

"What's going on?"

"They found Katie outside Meggrolls on Fayette Street. She's in family care overnight." She put down the phone. "Maggie's nowhere to be found. The police went back to the camp, but it's deserted. I've got a bad feeling, Mo. I'm afraid she might do something stupid."

"There's nothing to be done tonight." Katz poured himself a glass of wine. He turned on the television in the kitchen.

Snowe walked to the back of the townhome and opened the French doors to the slate patio. "Mo," she called. Piled against the wooden fence was a fleece jacket, a wool blanket, and a crumpled piece of paper. The jacket and blanket smelled of outdoor fires and body odors. The crumpled note was written in longhand, in large, oval letters composing short sentences. Snowe picked it up and took it inside. It read:

> *No one but me to blame.*
> *I miss Tony. I kid myself that I can get along without him.*
> *If something happens, you and Mo raise our little girl.*
> *You'll know what to do. I don't have a clue.*

Snowe found herself shivering. Katz put down his glass of wine and held her. "We should notify the police and see if they can redouble their efforts tomorrow."

Katz called the commonwealth attorney and the sheriff. Snowe contacted Child Protective Services, the city attorney, and a local nonprofit that provided 24-hour service to the homeless. Then Snowe sat and reread the letter. Her eyes welled with tears.

"Let's go to bed," Katz said. He turned off the television as the 11 o'clock news came on.

"We have to go look for her tonight," Snowe said. "I've got a bad feeling."

"Okay," Katz said. "Let me grab a couple of flashlights first."

They drove to the edge of Old Town near the location of the makeshift camp and parked on Duke Street below the Masonic Temple. They got out of the car and took opposite sides of the street checking bushes, front stoops, parking lots, dark corners, and deserted alleys. At Daingerfield Street, Katz crossed over to Snowe's side and together they walked down the narrow brick sidewalk along Hooff's Run to Jamieson Avenue and the cemetery.

A thick mist floated through the beams of their flashlights. A myriad of tiny winged creatures danced in the light as though auditioning for a fairy's play. In the distance, the rectangles of house windows glowed yellow and white in the night. To their left was the Wilkes Street Cemetery complex and ahead of them the Grave of the Female Stranger.

"This way," Snowe said, pointing her beam straight. They walked past gravestones dating back to colonial days. The moon cast shadows across the stones, some of which stood upright while others tilted to the side, finding their natural place in the soil, like trees. They spied the silhouette of a person slumped beside a gravestone. A hood covered the face and a blanket was wrapped around the body's legs.

Snowe focused her light on the lump. The light was intense in the dark, as though it was coming from a spacecraft landing in the cemetery. A head appeared. Snowe recognized the face. "That's the guy who was with her this morning," she said. *What a scumbag*, she thought. The man remained in a stupefied state as they drew alongside. He stumbled to get up, as though bound by tree roots to the plot of ground.

"Maybe death's pulling him down," Katz whispered.

Kneeling beside him, Snowe asked, "Where's Maggie?"

"No idea," he said with difficulty. The words were accompanied by a strong odor of alcohol. "I haven't seen her." Then he squinted his eyes at Snowe. "You busted up our place this morning." Katz gripped the man by his collar. Snowe touched Katz's sleeve and he slackened his hold.

"Where do you think she went?" Snowe asked. "Is she out here somewhere?"

The man shivered and pulled the blanket up to his chin. His breath formed clouds. "She might have gone to a shooting gallery," he said, slurring his words. "In the city," he added.

Then the man dozed off.

Snowe turned to Katz. "He's useless," she said.

Katz let go of the man's collar. "Do you want to drive downtown?"

"Where would we even look?"

"No clue."

She lowered the flashlight to her side. "I'll check to see if there are any leads first thing in the morning." They wended their way through the cemetery. Then they walked up Jamieson Avenue to Holland Lane and back to the car. It was 1 a.m. by the time they returned home.

**

LEVIN WALLACE stayed indoors all day. From the moment he returned from the railroad line with the H-Pack backpack, he had barricaded himself in the Anacostia apartment. He had received an advance of $25,000. And another $25k was coming as soon as he finished the job.

He had given clear instructions to his wife, Bonita, to hide the money. With $50k, they could do things. Move, put a down payment on a small condo out in the x-burbs. Start a family. Wallace hugged the backpack like it was his best friend.

PART II
Sunday, May 30

Chapter Five: The Rhythmic Cycle of Life

Review

Did you complete your work on the cycle, as instructed in the past chapter? If not, please do it now. This isn't intended as something for you to read. It's intended as something for you to do.

Done? Okay. Let's continue.

What you have written down is actually a summary of your entire life. Not just the first twelve years. Everything. All that has been. All that will be. You have just sketched it all out.

That's not possible, you're thinking. You're always opening new doors, exploring new chapters. Evolving. It cannot possibly be that who you are, where you've been, and where you're headed is all encapsulated in one puny twelve-year cycle. I mean, you're just getting started. Everything's ahead of you, right?

Well, you're right. There are a myriad of experiences that lie ahead. But the footprint of your life – the genius strokes, mistakes, successes, failures, highs, and lows – are already charted on that piece of paper of the first cycle of your life.

Consider a major interstate highway. If you look at old road maps going back hundreds of years, you will discover, almost without exception, that the road existed first as a footpath (perhaps for Native Americans and certainly for early settlers), then as a dirt road (for horse-drawn carts and stagecoaches), and then as a two-lane and eventually a four-lane, six-lane or even a twelve-lane highway.

But the route itself has hardly changed.

Your life is the same.

You travel the same worn path. Over and over. Life, you see, is not an upward trajectory. Nor is it a downward spiral. It is a line bent into a circle. A cycle. Understand the cycle and you can anticipate, prepare and plan for what lies ahead. You cannot avoid your fate, of course, those unique occurrences that compose your "life," but you can figure out what life is.

And you can make the most of it.

Let's consider the highway analogy we used a moment ago. That major twelve-lane interstate highway still follows the dirt path used by carts and horses a couple hundred years ago. But, along the way, the bedrock has been fortified, some rough corners have been smoothed, some straightaways have been marked with caution signs and speed limits, bridges have been built to protect against streams, and rock formations have been blasted to shorten the route and make it more direct. The same path is still being used, but getting from Point A to Point B has gotten a lot more convenient and assured.

The Second Cycle

The second cycle is where your life takes flight. And crashes. By the time the second cycle has ended, you have finished most of your schooling. Or maybe you're in graduate or professional school. You have had your first job. Maybe even your second or third job. And you have loved and been loved.

During this twelve-year period, you attain adulthood. In the process, the experiences that were critical in your first cycle find expression. They become deeper and more personal.

This is the second cycle, but it is the first time things are repeating themselves. Your life cycle is playing itself out. Again. Like tire tracks over the same spot of snow. Let's examine the tracks. How close is the second rotation to the first one?

Amazing things happen in the second cycle.

Let's fill in the second cycle of your life. Each year. 13, 14, 15. The end of the first quarter. Comparisons to the first time around? 16, 17 and 18. One and one-half times around the circle. Around the sun. Around earth. Around your whole life. Next 19, 20 and 21. And then on to the completion. Racing around the final turn, so to speak. Passing quickly: 22, 23 and 24.

Ending up where you started. It's all making sense, isn't it? It's all understandable. It's all a little familiar. Hmm, yes. It's all repeating itself.

Before we go into the third cycle – ages 24 to 36 – let's get one thing straight. These trends, similarities and repetitions are all going to happen again. And again and again. Are you content with that? If so, then maybe all you have to do is focus on how to make good times better. But, if not, then let's consider in short order how to make the bad times go away.

The Third Cycle

The third cycle is likely to be the one where you find a partner and maybe start a family. Or you discover that you're destined (at least for the time being) to blaze your trail alone. Either way, you are going to begin to create your own life now.

You will put your education to work. You will use your life experiences to figure out new challenges. There are a lot of ways things may be turning out for you right now.

By the time I reached 36, my life was off the rails. Not because of anything I did, but because of something that was done by an outsider to a member of my family. And I had to go back over my own life experiences to try to find my moral compass. Ironically, it was during that phase of my life that I discovered — that I created — the rhythmic cycle of life.

By exploring my past, I was able to foresee my future. And I was able to deal with the present. I was able to grasp what had gone wrong in the previous cycle and how I could avoid it in the next cycle.

And I also discovered how my actions in the here-and-now could actually change the past. Debts could be settled. Hurt could be healed. Losses could be avenged.

Chapter Six: Night

SNOWE SAT on the patio, her head craned upward and her eyes fixed on the stars in the night sky. The Moon was full last Wednesday. Now it was waning gibbous.

The moon was that exact shape the night she returned from the counselor's office. She'd gone for a stroll in the apple orchard near her family's home in Massachusetts. She'd never felt as alone as she did that night. She remembered a translucent moon in a starless night and thinking that she would see that exact moon again someday and, when she did, something wonderful would happen in her life. She rubbed her fingers across her forehead. In the distance, a neighbor's dog barked to be let back inside.

Eighteen Years Earlier

"ARE YOU SURE?"

Snowe had shocked her parents, forsaken an athletic scholarship, and lost a year of college. But nothing compared to this decision.

"Yes," she replied.

The affirmation — if that's what one could call it — was met with silence. The woman who asked the question was not going to be easy on Snowe. She knew what it meant to forever sever a relationship with an infant and that Snowe might regret the decision sometime in the future.

The woman, in her 60s, understood better than Snowe how long time was and what regret was like. She knew Snowe would never know the names of her daughter's parents. In fact, she would never know the name of her own child. At the age of 16, Snowe was operating on blind faith. She had to trust that giving away the greatest love she ever felt was the right thing to do.

"I'm good with it," Snowe said to the woman. "I'm sure."

**

TWO HOURS after the planned rendezvous with Maria Pena, Landry's car pulled from the curb behind the GreyStone Hotel. A piece of moon hung in the sky. Street lights, encased in gray smog, emitted faint light. The headlamps of Landry's car cut through the dark as it passed Farragut Square and headed in the direction of K Street.

The car stopped. The interior lights went on. Then the car continued on its way. Traffic was light as the car headed across the Key Bridge to Rosslyn, Virginia. In a few hours, all of the months of planning, secret meetings, clandestine emails and phone calls would bear fruit.

Landry's car navigated through Rosslyn and slid onto the G.W. Parkway, eventually turning into Roaches Run. Two taxi drivers were standing beside their vehicles in the parking lot, smoking and swapping stories. Landry's car pulled up beside the white van.

Best to wait until those two leave before going to the van and making final preparations for tomorrow.

Across the parkway, the lights from Reagan National shone in the dark sky. Further in the distance, on the opposite side of the Potomac, the dome of the U.S. Capitol appeared like a brightly lit lightbulb in the velvety night. One of the taxi drivers extinguished his cigarette and sauntered to his car. The other made a phone call before climbing into his vehicle. A few minutes later, both departed. The coast was clear to move to the van.

**

STONE RETURNED to the police station after reviewing the documents Wilson provided to her and Mann. She issued an APB for Phil Landry. She also sent out emails to several law enforcement agencies with jurisdiction in D.C. alerting them of Landry's plan.

**

HUGH SPATES was still mad. All Morley had to do was

listen. But no. Morley had to be large and in charge. He had to give orders instead of take them. Just shut up! Spates said. Just shut up and do what I tell you to do. Or else. *Or else what?* Or else you're going to regret it. Spates wondered why Morley had to say that. *Or else what?* He should have just let it go. Done as he was told.

Spates couldn't sleep this night. He kept reliving the minutes leading up to yesterday morning's shooting. He wished he could pull that bullet out of Morley's skull, stuff it back in the barrel, and place it back inside the cylinder. He wished he could turn back time.

It was the single most stupid, impulsive, and regrettable act of his life. Up until that moment, everything was going as planned. Then Morley had to go and spoil it. *Or else what?* The question left Spates no choice. He had to show Morley there were consequences for disobedience.

When Spates pulled out the gun, Morley started to laugh. *Go ahead, big man. Shoot me.* Morley was calling his bluff. *Shoot me and who's left to help you?* Then Morley lunged for the gun. He tripped. Spates tried to pull back. Their legs twisted around one another and they fell to the ground. The gun discharged. Spates expected to feel blood rushing from an artery. But there was only the ringing sound in his ears from the loud blast that exploded an inch away and reverberated under the bridge.

What happened? Had the bullet missed them? Had it ricocheted off the steel and cement undergirding the bridge?

He felt Morley's weight on top of him. Dead weight. He screamed. He squirmed to the side and tried to slide out from under the body. Blood from Morley's mouth trickled down onto his neck. The dead man's arm draped over his shoulder. With a horrified gasp, Spates finally wrenched himself out of the dead man's embrace, rolled on the ground, crouched on all fours, and stared in disbelief at the hulk.

"Morley?"

The stiff just lay there.

"Morley!"

Now Spates sat in his living room with an empty bottle on the coffee table in front of him. He was breathing heavily. His heartbeat pulsated in his ears so intensely he half expected his eardrums to burst.

He heard traffic. Trucks were racing down the interstate a few miles away, moving freight in the middle of the night along a deserted highway in advance of tomorrow's gridlock. He ran his tongue over his front teeth and tasted the food he'd eaten hours earlier. He could still see Morley's body as it lay in front of him. He could smell the blood oozing. He could see Morley's open eyes staring up at him. Spates' breathing grew more labored. He tried to compose his thoughts. He needed to decide whether to cancel today's operation along the rail line or go ahead with it as planned.

Neither of his other two accomplices, the train engineer and the laborer who agreed to plant the explosives on the train, knew Morley. They would not connect the murder to the operation. Sure, Morley was important, but he wasn't critical, Spates told himself. Wallace was good enough. The engineer had already pulled out of Atlanta and was headed to D.C.

Spates lifted his hand and looked at it. It was shaking. *Okay,* he said to himself, *you can do this.* He had to do it. He went to the garage, got in his car, and drove to the same place he'd been the night before when he'd dropped off the backpacks filled with cash. When he arrived, he removed another backpack from the trunk and placed it along the fence where the cash had been deposited. Inside the backpack were explosives that Spates had purchased on the dark web. He was guaranteed the explosives were potent enough to ignite one of those white cylindrical fuel cars with large red letters reading FLAMMABLE MATERIAL.

He hurried back to the car. He knew he was out of his league. He didn't know what he was doing. He was acting out of total desperation.

Chapter Seven: Morning

"I'M HEADED to Crystal City to wait on a train," Stone said when Katz answered his phone.

"Want to come along?"

Katz was making coffee, his usual eight ounces of water and five scoops of Misha's

Arabian Mocha Java beans, coarsely ground. Snowe had already left to check on Katie. She had hardly slept and he was worried about her. She was consumed with Moriarty and her daughter.

One of the cardinal "rules of the game" Katz had learned was not to care about the client. It didn't matter whether you were an attorney, a cop, a judge, or a social worker. Caring clouded your judgment and it could hurt you in the end. He learned that from Sean Matthews, an attorney with whom he'd set up shop after leaving the Commonwealth Attorney's office a decade ago. The partnership lasted six months. Matthews, it turned out, didn't care about anyone or anything but himself, which was more than Katz could tolerate.

Katz didn't answer right away.

"Hellooo? Anybody home?" Stone asked.

"Sorry. I'm just a little spaced out. We were out late last night. We actually went to a cemetery looking for Maggie Moriarty."

"That's wild. By the way, what's the latest on the little girl?"

"Someone found Katie in an alley behind Meggrolls. She's in child protective custody. Abby went to check on her this morning." He paused. "I think she's way too invested in the case."

"Know why?" Stone didn't wait for Katz to answer. "She wants to have a family." Katz said nothing. "If you're not going to accommodate her, you're going to lose her, partner, just like you lost her back in the day."

"We can talk about this later."

"That's called avoidance."

"I'm not avoiding anything, Stoner. I'm acutely aware of the fact that there's a problem with our relationship. And I know it centers on the fact that she wants a family and I don't." *This is weird*, he thought. He was talking to Stone like she was his big sister. "Sometimes I'm very assertive, particularly with work," he continued. "But when it comes to my personal life, I'm almost passive. I just let things take their course. If Abby and I are going to spend our lives together, it's either going to happen or it's not."

Stone sucked in her breath. "I don't really buy that, Mo. You're a nice guy and all, but I've always thought of you as very self-centered. Too much so. Not in a Machiavellian way. Just ambitious. Sometimes to a fault. I don't think you're laid-back at all. I think you're just focused on you."

Although Katz didn't seem to be in the mood to have this conversation, Stone persisted. "At some point, you've got to quit putting yourself at the front of the line. If you do, you're going to end up at the tail end. And, in terms of your relationship with Abby, I'd say you're pretty close to being there now."

He said nothing.

She sensed he was tuning her out but added, "I'm not saying this to hurt you, but as a friend who cares about you. About both of you."

He was trying his best to tune her out, even though a part of him wished more people were as forceful as Stone. Last year, when he reestablished relations after many years with his parents, his mom — who had been hospitalized with COVID-19 — asked whether he and Snowe were still together. He figured she wanted the comfort of knowing her son was in a solid domestic relationship before she died. He said, "Yes, of course, why do you ask?" But the truth was more complicated. Snowe *spoke* to him, but he didn't always *listen*, even if he heard what she was saying. His failure to listen was driving them further apart every day.

"Yesterday, when I was leaving the briefing, I ran into Phil Landry," Katz said.

"What's Landry got to do with this, Mo?"

"He said something about my being a lot of parts that don't add up to anything. It kind of hit home."

"Landry said that to you?" she asked, seeking context.

"We ran into one another in the parking lot. I always seem to set him off. I think he has a lot of pent-up resentment."

"And hatred."

"That, too."

"Well, I wouldn't normally give him any credit in the insight department, but he's right in this instance. You're sorta all over the place, everywhere and nowhere at the same time."

"I think it all must stem from my childhood," he laughed.

"Yeah, well, I think everything stems from childhood. I mean, look at me if you want to talk about issues."

Katz was finished with the psychobabble. "So, in response to your question, yes, I'd love to join you," he said.

Stone sighed, resigned to the fact that Katz had once again blown off the topic.

"Good," she said, and gave him the details.

**

ABBY SNOWE faced a Hobson's choice. She could use inside information to get temporary custody of Katie or she could disregard it entirely and stand no chance of success. As a probation officer, she had access to Katie's file as well as her mother's. She knew the good, the bad, and the ugly. She could use it to her advantage in developing a case to gain custody if Moriarty needed to go into treatment and be separated from her daughter for a while.

She tried to reconcile the potential conflict of interest by telling herself that she was uniquely qualified to care for Katie. But she wondered if she was being disingenuous and magnifying her own importance without bothering to look at other alternatives.

She stopped at a red light. She had just left the foster care family that had taken in Katie last night on an emergency basis. She turned and glanced at the little girl lying asleep in the back seat. She looked at herself in the rearview mirror. Her eyes told her she was doing the right thing. If she could wrestle custody from Moriarty for just a short period of time, she could make sure both mother and daughter got on the right path to navigate through life.

But what if she was put under a microscope? How would she look? In addition to raising eyebrows that she had used her position to gain an inside track on gaining short-term custody, what about her own personal lifestyle? She lived with a man to whom she was not married. She had no other children. She was a workaholic. She didn't really have a *home*, not in the Norman Rockwell sense of the word.

She and Mo passed like two ships in the night, speaking in code about their work to preserve confidences and only occasionally intimate to satisfy their needs, before going their separate ways again.

God, she thought. *What have I gotten myself into?*

She picked up the phone and called Stone, who would provide honest feedback, she knew.

Stone, on her way to Crystal City, looked at the name that came up on her phone and disregarded the call. She could guess what it would be about. The last thing she wanted to do was become an unlicensed, unpaid shrink for Snowe and Katz.

"Sherry, this is Abby," Snowe said after the call went to voicemail. "I wonder if you could call me. I've got little Katie in the car with me, Tony Fortune's daughter. She's going to be with me for the holiday weekend, maybe longer. Her mother's still missing. I want your opinion about how you think Mo will react to this. You know, bringing a child into our home?

"Maybe it's an odd question, but I value your opinion. Anyway, give me a call back. Thanks."

Snowe was angry with herself after she ended the call. That wasn't the real question. She knew how Katz would react, which was negatively. At his core, he was selfish and self-centered. It would be inconvenient for him to include a child in his life, particularly a child who was not his own. She didn't need confirmation from Stone about that. The *real* question was whether she was crossing a line if she sought temporary custody.

**

MID-MORNING, the train slowed along the tracks that ran through Crystal City. That was the deal. Slow to a crawl for 60 seconds. Then pick up steam and continue across the Potomac River into the District of Columbia.

Money had already been wired to the train conductor's bank account. He hadn't asked any questions and Spates hadn't provided any details. The inference was that Spates was unloading something, maybe drugs or illegals, or even guns, but there had been no suggestion that Spates was onboarding explosives to detonate in Southwest D.C.

The train idled for more than a minute. The conductor smiled to himself. "Take all the time you need, brother," he said softly in the rumbling engine room. If Spates believed money would buy the conductor's silence, he was sadly mistaken. The first thing the conductor did after receiving a communication from Spates was contact his local police department in Hanover County, outside of Richmond. He wasn't going to risk his livelihood for a measly 10 grand. *Screw that*, he concluded.

While the train idled, Levin Wallace ran between two cars and with difficulty hoisted himself up on the metal joints between them. He wished he had practiced beforehand. Everything seemed much larger and higher than he had imagined it. This was scary.

A bright orange backpack hung from his back. His instructions were simple: secure the backpack to the rail car and get off the train before it started moving. And make sure the backpack is secured to a car adjoining one of the white cylindrical containers with large red letters reading HAZMAT and FLAMMABLE MATERIAL.

Stone, Katz, and two members of the counterterrorism team watched with binoculars from a nearby high-rise building. "It's unfolding just as planned," she said.

"Don't worry," said one of the team members. "Something will go wrong. It always does. It's Murphy's Law."

Wallace began ascending the ladder along the side of a boxcar. Because he was nervous and scared, it took him longer than expected. Just at the moment when he reached the top, the train lurched forward. Wallace struggled to slip off the backpack and complete his task. The train picked up speed. In his haste, Wallace pivoted wildly. His trouser leg was caught. "Shit!" he hollered. Now the train moved faster. Wallace bent down to free his trouser. Instead, he lost his balance and rocked backward, hit his head on the car, and fell. Wallace was perilously perched between two cars. The train whistle blew. Now it was moving at full steam.

"Spates' guy didn't clear the train," said one of Stone's officers. They watched as the train proceeded. Wallace was clinging helplessly to the car and attempting to get back on his feet.

"They'll stop the train on the trestle to blow the explosives," Stone said. She turned away from the window. "Let's go."

A short distance away, Spates watched in dismay. Wallace was proving to be as useless as Morley. With Wallace stuck on the train, bad things were bound to happen. Spates didn't want to be around to see it happen. If only he'd gotten a better return on his initial investment, he thought as he raced to his car.

One Year Ago

THE REAL ESTATE MARKET had risen dramatically over the past decade. Ironically, the pandemic was beginning to look as though it was a blessing for real estate as well. But Spates was disappointed with his profit margin. He had put everything he had in real estate along the railroad lines near the U.S. Capitol. He had suffered through one real estate bubble and, while he had a tidy profit in store if he sold now, he wanted more. A lot more.

He had waited for a terrorist attack in the city. He was patient. But it never materialized. He was briefly hopeful after the siege on the U.S. Capitol. But that was quickly contained and security in the area had even increased. Perhaps he had to fabricate an attack himself to realize the return he would reap under the Terrorism Risk Insurance Act.

In fact, the only thing that had materialized was the novel coronavirus. He had been to a wedding in Columbia, South Carolina, in mid-March. He came down with COVID-19 probably because someone at the reception was asymptomatic. Fortunately, he recovered without getting critically ill. For a while, though, he thought he might be a goner. And during that time he thought about his lost opportunity.

He remembered the comment by one of his colleagues when they were writing the bill.

He sat on his bed overlooking the railroad tracks paralleling 14th Street. He got up and walked down to the circle at Maryland Avenue SW. The Wharf was shut down and the city was eerily quiet. As he walked, he had a crazy thought.

What if I actually do it? What if I stage a terrorist act? Nothing to injure anyone, just something strong enough to cause some property damage. Like arson, except with a twist. Right here, on this track, near the Capitol.

Maybe it wasn't so crazy, he thought. After all, he had crossed the line before and never suffered any adverse consequences. Sure, he thought, this was a lot bolder than anything he had ever done, but, in the end, if you got away with the small stuff you could get away with anything.

Too many close encounters without consequences emboldened him. He stuffed prohibited earmarks into bills; nobody noticed. He paid kickbacks for favors; no one alerted the authorities. He blackmailed regulators into doing his bidding at the expense of exposing their peccadillos on social media. He crossed the line repeatedly. In fact, he did it with such abandon that by now he probably lived permanently on the other side of the line.

Lines were territorial, Spates thought as he walked along the waterfront. They existed so they wouldn't be crossed. Some were about sex and others dealt with drugs or alcohol. Some were transactional, while others concerned societal boundaries.

Get close to the line — well, that was expected. Call it curiosity. Cross the line once or twice, that was sort of expected too. Call it experimentation. But cross the line repeatedly, you're looking for trouble. Cross it repeatedly and get away with it, and you're writing a death sentence for yourself.

He knew he should have stopped taking risks long ago, but he couldn't, not now, not after he'd succeeded so many times. Deep inside he knew his number would be up one day. It felt that way to him now.

As he recovered from the infection and got back to work, he vowed never to remain idle again. Cardiac and neurological damage and symptoms lingered, however. He had to take action. Who knew? The next pandemic might take him down for good.

**

THE TRAIN chugged along the tracks. Within a few minutes, it approached the trestle across the Potomac River. Once it was on the trestle, it stopped.

Instead of the explosion Spates expected, all was quiet. The materials that Spates arranged to purchase over the dark web were bogus. In fact, they had been provided by the feds. The stuff looked authentic — particularly to an amateur like Spates — but they were duds. At no time had anyone been at risk in connection with Spates' ill-fated plot.

Within a few moments, three helicopters appeared upriver, heading toward the trestle that ran parallel to the 14th Street Bridge.

The tip of each blade of each chopper formed a vortex, and those blades struck the vortices created by the previous blades, echoing over the river.

A passenger in a car on the 14th Street Bridge heard a boom. It might have come from the helicopters, or maybe there was a fender bender in another lane of traffic or a firecracker lit and thrown along the riverbank. The passenger posted on social media that he might have heard a bomb. That post was translated to read that a bomb might have exploded on the 14th Street Bridge. Within a few minutes, a message went viral that a bomb was heard exploding over the river.

People were understandably nervous. The January insurrection had shocked the nation. Domestic terrorism was foremost on everyone's mind. The breach of the Capitol building, a symbol of the United States and democracy, had created an indelible image in everyone's mind, similar to the collapse of the World Trade Center towers nearly 20 years before.

BREAKING NEWS

There are unconfirmed reports that a bomb has exploded on or near the 14th Street Bridge.

A freight train is stopped along the trestle paralleling the bridge. Commuter traffic across the bridge has been reduced to a crawl in either direction. Metro rail service from the Pentagon to L'Enfant Plaza has been temporarily halted while officials determine if there is any risk to passengers.

Automobile passengers heading across the bridge reported hearing the explosion at approximately 9:45 a.m. A stream of steady traffic had been pouring into the city for Memorial Day weekend. Northbound traffic is now backed up to the Pentagon.

**

A MAN stood between two train cars. He had an orange

backpack strapped on his back. His hands were flailing. His pant trousers were torn.

Helicopters hovered over the train. Their blades slapped the sky and created ripples on the water below. Automobile passengers in the parallel lanes of the 14th Street Bridge snapped photos. The pictures went viral, along with the warnings of a possible bombing.

The man on the train continued to teeter. People on the bridge placed bets on whether he would regain his balance or fall. After a few minutes of hilarious or horrifying drama — depending on whether those watching thought his predicament funny or frightful — he lost his balance and plunged into the water.

One of the helicopters swept over the spot where he disappeared into the river. Two divers jumped from the chopper. A flotation device sprung open as soon as they hit the water. The divers went under in an effort to retrieve the man.

Cars had come to a dead stop on the bridge. Drivers and passengers got out of their vehicles and hung over the bridge's railings, watching and filming the attempted rescue. Some people took selfies of themselves with the helicopter, train, bridge, and water in the background.

BREAKING NEWS

The body of a man who fell into the Potomac River from a train stopped on a trestle parallel to the 14th Street Bridge was recovered this morning by the U.S. Park Police.

The man, who has not yet been identified, is alleged to have been part of a plot to detonate a bomb in Southwest D.C.

Police and antiterrorism personnel have confirmed that they have been monitoring the man's movements since earlier this morning.

The plot to set off a bomb along the railroad tracks running near the U.S. Capitol was discovered several weeks ago, and those involved have been under surveillance, according to police sources.

No bomb has exploded, as was alleged earlier this morning. Police report that the bomb planted on the train was inert.

With the exception of the victim who fell from the trestle, there have been no injuries or casualties reported in connection with the incident.

**

MARIA PENA arrived early and sat in Farragut Square. There were dozens of people on the sidewalks, although not in the numbers traditionally welcomed to Washington for the Memorial Day weekend. People in masks alighted from the Farragut West Metro station and streamed to and from local hotels and restaurants. A food truck was setting up shop.

She heard that something had just happened along the Potomac River. She wondered if there was a connection to the operation in which she was involved. Although she was a considerable distance from the river, she thought she heard the faint sound of helicopters.

In her haste, Pena had forgotten her medication. She hadn't eaten a complete breakfast either, settling for orange juice and a slice of toast instead of cereal and yogurt, her normal routine. Her mother always used to say that breakfast was the most important meal of the day.

Pena missed her mother terribly.

Twelve Years Ago

"WHAT'S WRONG?" Pena asked hesitantly. A day ago her mother had been ebullient. But today she looked drawn and haggard, her dark hair falling limply over her shoulders and her mouth turned down, as though fishhooks were pulling on either side of her pale lips.

"Your father's been placed on leave," her mother said. The words came out of her mouth, but there was no life to them. She was in a state of shock.

"Why?"

"Leave without pay," her mother said, either avoiding the question or not hearing it.

In the days ahead, Maria Pena would learn her father had been reprimanded for pursuing a misconduct case too vigorously. The media used to call him a hero, a crime fighter, the Serpico of the South. But those lofty accolades turned to harsh criticisms. He was vilified for trying to destroy the reputation of a good cop. He was portrayed as the very person against whom he once raged.

It started with an article in *The Chronicle*. The article turned into a series. The reporter gained instant notoriety. He unearthed information about her father that bore no relation to the man who had raised her.

Pena didn't believe it. Her father was her hero. But no one cared what she believed.

Overnight, her father was removed from his job. The energetic man who went to work each day with enthusiasm and dedicated his life to helping others now moped around the house. He became a pariah in his close-knit neighborhood. Friends shunned him. As a result, he rarely went outside.

Then her mother fell into a state of depression. But that was only the beginning of it. A month after her husband was placed on administrative leave without pay, she committed suicide.

**

PENA SAT on the bench trying to regain her composure. She reached for her flip phone to check the time. The phone was missing. She must have left it at home. She jumped up and asked a passer-by for the time. She learned she was five minutes late. Panicked, she quickly turned and started running. Startled, nearby pigeons took flight. One of them flew to the statue of Admiral Farragut in the center of the square and landed on his head, eyeing her suspiciously.

As she rushed to the hotel, Pena turned to see whether anyone was watching her. Everyone looked suspicious. They all appeared to be staring at her, like in those dreams where she ran down the hall without wearing any clothes. She hurried down the sidewalk and across the street. She entered the hotel gasping through her mask.

She turned to the left, facing the concierge's desk. No, that was wrong! She was instructed to go directly to room 909. She turned to the right and stopped in front of the shiny gold elevator doors. The bell announcing the arrival of the elevator sounded and the doors opened. She dashed inside and punched 9. As the door was closing, a hand reached inside. The doors opened. A man entered. She glared at him. "Sorry," he said. "I hope I didn't alarm you." He hit 8. Pena moved quickly to the back of the elevator, like a boxer retreating to the corner at the end of a particularly grueling round. The elevator stopped at 8. The man alighted from the elevator. As he left, he turned and stared at her, pressed against the mirrored paneling. *What the hell is wrong with her*, he thought.

The door closed and Pena issued a loud sigh.

**

SULEIMAN WAS not feeling the rapture. Colors were not vivid. Sounds were not crisp. His handler said it would happen and that he had to be strong in the moment. Mohammed Atta had not hesitated steering that commercial jet liner into the World Trade Center on 9/11, his handler said.

Yet there was something about his handler that he did not trust. It was nothing he could identify but it was there, like a foul odor or bitter taste. Deep inside it made him question the logic of what he was doing.

Now he felt only a nauseating fear. He tried to block it out. But it would not go away. It was like a stomachache after eating bad food.

He made his way to Room 909. When he entered, there was a woman seated on the edge of the bed. There were two backpacks on the floor. He looked at the woman and then at the backpacks.

Without saying anything, he crouched down and unzipped one of them.

The backpack was filled with books. Books! He checked the other pack and it also held books. There were cookbooks, self-help books, novels, and textbooks, all on random topics.

"What's going on?" he asked the woman. "And who are you?"

Pena told Suleiman her name. She told him about the man she had befriended. She did not share certain details, like the fact she had slept with him.

Suleiman eyed her suspiciously as she spoke. She seemed a little off to him. But, he concluded, they were in this together so it was best for them to work together.

"I thought this was some kind of suicide mission," he said. He was relieved to see the backpacks filled with books. But that didn't really make a lot of sense to him.

"I honestly don't know what this was supposed to be," said Pena. "I always felt I was being duped. I didn't feel as though he was being completely honest with me."

Suleiman said he felt the same way.

"I sure didn't want to harm anyone," she continued. "For over a year, the protests have been peaceful. I view Lafayette Square and Black Lives Matter Plaza as sacred spaces. The last thing I wanted to do was defame them, you know?"

Suleiman knew. He agreed completely. This whole thing was a setup. Their emotions had been preyed upon. Yet, all that was inside of the backpacks were harmless books.

"So what do we do?" she asked.

"Well, since these backpacks contain only books, I don't think there's anything wrong if we carry out the operation as requested. What do you think?"

Both had questions and neither had answers. As a result, they decided to go through with the plan.

Suleiman strapped a backpack over his shoulders. Pena did

the same. They both went downstairs and outside. Together they proceeded to their destinations.

"Where are you supposed to go?" Suleiman asked.

Pena said the southwest corner. He said he was instructed to go to the northeast corner.

"We should keep in touch with one another," Suleiman said. "If something happens, we can alert one another. And, once we figure out what this is all about, we can meet and compare notes."

Pena said that was a good idea but she had been unable to find her mobile phone before heading out this morning.

"You don't have a phone?" Suleiman asked, incredulous.

"It wasn't where I always put it and I didn't have time to continue searching," she explained. He gave her his phone number. They agreed to meet back in the park at 6 in the evening.

"Hey," Suleiman said suddenly. "Maybe it's not a good idea for us to walk together. We should probably split up and go in different directions." Pena was hesitant. She would have been more comfortable walking to the park with him. But he was already pulling away from her, giving a little wave goodbye.

The sidewalk was wide and filled with people. Throngs moved in every direction. At intersections, masses filled the curb waiting for the lights to turn. There were singles and couples, groups of students, parents pushing baby carriages and holding the hands of small children, and multigenerational families with grandparents proudly carrying their young grandchildren. Everyone was going somewhere to celebrate the holiday.

Suleiman was glad he was just a decoy and not a person carrying explosives. He imagined the carnage that would have occurred. Limbs would have been torn from bodies; shrapnel would have pierced arms, legs, and faces; and the joy and carelessness of the day would have been shattered forever. Carrying books was innocuous, but odd.

Pena felt the same way. She was spared the recrimination she would have felt if she had actually harmed people or property. Yet she could not understand why in the world she had been groomed to carry books to Lafayette Square on Memorial Day weekend. It really didn't make any sense.

**

THE NINTH FLOOR of the GreyStone Hotel consisted of two wings separated by heavy sheets of plastic. One wing, containing Rooms 901 to 909, was in use, although only two rooms were currently occupied. The other wing was under construction, and because of that guests avoided staying on the ninth floor. Rooms 910 to 919 were gutted. Every piece of flooring, wall, and ceiling had been tossed down the wide mouth of the plastic construction chute that descended through a window to a huge dumpster in the alley below.

Following the purchase of the GreyStone last year by a hotelier with deep pockets, the grand old edifice was in the middle of a construction project to restore it to its nineteenth century grandeur. First, the lobby was renovated, with massive chandeliers, ornate ceiling tiles, lush carpets, and walls composed of glass, wood, and polished brass. Then the guest rooms underwent construction floor by floor. Everything was torn out and replaced with expensive antiques, state-of-the-art electronics, plush bedding, and luxurious baths. If COVID-19 had not set back the renovation, the work would have been completed last year.

Only one wing of the ninth floor remained to be finished.

The glitz of the GreyStone rivaled Washington's best hotels and went toe-to-toe with such popular destinations as the Madison, the Mayflower, and the Willard. The GreyStone was built during the Gilded Age, when Carnegie and Rockefeller were the titans of industry, McKinley and Teddy Roosevelt made up the winning presidential ticket, and Manifest Destiny was the guiding principle of the republic.

When the Depression descended and Hoovervilles dotted the nation's landscape, the hotel lost its luster. By the dawn of World War II, it was a fleabag destination for hobos and tramps. In the early 1960s, it was a shooting gallery for drug addicts and a hook-up joint for prostitutes.

In the 1980s, the hotel was bought by a national chain and was slated for a major renovation. But the chain went bankrupt and the renovation never happened. Since then, it changed hands twice, including last year's sale.

Over time, much of the original façade had been plastered over. It bore scant resemblance to its original self, like facial reconstruction gone awry. Architects and historians studied every nook and cranny as part of the current renovation. No expense was spared to replicate the graceful and elegant sandstone structure that was once the gem of Farragut Square.

Three H-Pack backpacks sat on the dusty floor of the wing under construction. To a casual observer, they might have been construction workers' day packs, loaded with lunch and thermoses of water or coffee. But no one was working in the hall or in the rooms. The construction crew was off for the weekend. Tools lay on the floor. Cups, water bottles, soda cans, and sandwich wrappers were swept into a corner. A thermos stood against a wall. Exposed light bulbs lit the deserted rooms. There was not a sound in the corridor. It almost seemed serene.

Suddenly, the entire hotel rocked as though an earthquake had shifted the ground under the building. Windows shattered in offices across the alley. Bricks and plaster jettisoned through the air and dispersed on the ground nine stories below. Pieces of the façade splattered on the cement alleyway. A gargoyle toppled from the rooftop. A plume of smoke filled the air. When the debris finally settled, a hole the size of an interstate billboard could be seen on the side of the building.

Without understanding what had happened, hotel guests ran

out of the lobby. Pedestrians on the sidewalk spilled into the streets. Drivers reacted in a variety of ways; some pulled to the curb while others gunned their vehicles and ran red lights. Cars smashed into one another at intersections filled with people fleeing in all directions.

BREAKING NEWS
This is a developing story

A bomb has exploded on one of the upper floors of the historic GreyStone Hotel at Farragut Square, sending pedestrians rushing for shelter.

The explosion came on the heels of an incident on the train trestle over the Potomac River parallel to the 14th Street Bridge. That incident was reported to have involved an explosion as well, although that fact is now disputed.

These explosions occur less than five months after a vicious attack on the U.S. Capitol when a mob of thousands, protesting the outcome of the November 2020 election, breached the Capitol, invaded the Senate chamber, and ransacked House and Senate offices.

Federal and District law enforcement have arrived at the scene of the hotel bombing. The entrance to the hotel has been cordoned off. The hotel was recently renovated and the top floor is still under construction. The few guests who have ventured back to hotels since last year's pandemic were rewarded by being forced to evacuate the building.

Evacuations are underway at a number of retail and commercial buildings in the surrounding area, where windows were shattered from the force of the bombing. Due to the holiday, most offices in the buildings are unoccupied.

Passers-by were stunned by the explosion.

"It was like a mini-9/11," said one man. "I didn't know whether a drone or small aircraft might have struck the building. In fact, I'm still not sure what happened."

Another passer-by equated it to the Capitol attack. "I felt as though the domestic terrorists had returned," she said. "Our democracy is under siege."

According to authorities on the scene, the entire hotel will be swept for explosives.

No one has claimed responsibility for the blast. At this time, authorities do not know whether it is an act of terrorism or related to the construction itself.

"Right now, it could be a disgruntled employee for all we know," said one official.

**

THE WHITE HOUSE and Eisenhower Executive Office Building were evacuated. Metro lines serving the area were shut down for fear of a bomb at either the Farragut North or Farragut West stations. The likelihood of a bombing squared with the information that Stone had provided last night to law enforcement officials. She based her information on the files found on Landry's computer. An APB had been put out for Landry, but he had not yet been located.

The streets around the hotel were caged in total gridlock. The whereabouts of top government officials were confirmed. Security details were doubled. All of the D.C. monuments were closed. A hockey game scheduled for that evening was postponed. The Mall became a gathering place for thousands of people who had nowhere else to go.

Television stations raced reporters to the area. Counterterrorism experts assembled in cable network studios expressed concern that a massive soft target was forming in the heart of the city.

In response to Stone's alert, a robust police force had already been assembled for today's expected festivities. Now, that force was augmented with security personnel, canine units, and police. Security was tight everywhere, including Lafayette Square and Black Lives Matter Plaza.

BREAKING NEWS
This is a developing story

Law enforcement officers are fanning out across the city in response to a bombing at the GreyStone Hotel and reports of potential attacks at Metro stations.

"We are on guard against a possible terrorist plot," said one law enforcement officer who spoke on the condition of anonymity. "There's been no corroboration of the report, but we aren't taking any chances."

The explosion on the top floor of the GreyStone Hotel occurred in an unoccupied part of the hotel undergoing renovation. There were no fatalities, and all guests have been accounted for, according to a spokesperson for the hotel.

The explosion reverberated through Farragut Square, creating chaos and confusion among the throngs of people gathering in the area for the holiday. Minutes earlier, a train was stopped on the trestle bridge across the Potomac River running parallel to the 14th Street Bridge.

Reports of a bomb exploding on the train have proven to be false. However, a man fell from the train and drowned in the Potomac River. His body has been recovered by a rescue team launched minutes after he plunged into the water.

No other fatalities or injuries have been reported from the train incident.

NATIONAL TERRORISM ADVISORY SYSTEM (NTAS) ALERT

The regional threat level for the Washington, D.C., metropolitan area has been raised to "elevated" effective 11:15 a.m. Eastern Standard Time.

Metro riders and residents living in proximity to Metro stations are requested to be on alert for pedestrians carrying orange H-Pack backpacks at Metro substations.

This "elevated" alert is provisional. It does not constitute a verified terrorist threat. This warning is NOT imminent. It does not mean there is a verified, specific, and impending terrorist threat against the United States.

NTAS alerts provide timely, detailed information to the public, government agencies, first responders, public sector organizations, and others.

All changes, including the announcement that cancels an NTAS Alert, will be distributed the same way as the original alert.

**

THE NTAS alert was emailed through DC Alerts, Facebook, and Twitter. The information was immediately relayed via online news feeds, radio, and television. The news popped up on phones, laptops, and tablets. Commuters were asked to avoid the Metro stations until further notice.

"Have you already put out your analysis?" the Chronicle's editor-in-chief, Alice Caraway, barked over the phone to Mann.

"Just now," Mann said.

Mann's agreement was to hold the inside story until something developed. He kept his promise. Up until now, he played it straight, including a piece publicizing Stone's role in the events. The NTAS alert issuance was the development that justified releasing the story. With the click of a finger, the article posted to the Chronicle's website and was pushed to media outlets around the country.

BREAKING NEWS
11:30 a.m.
The Washington Chronicle
Analysis by Tom Mann, city editor

An elevated alert warning was issued moments ago by the National Terrorism Advisory System to guard against a possible terrorist incident engineered by Philip Landry, director of security operations for the Department of Homeland Security. Associates described him as a discredited and disgruntled employee.

Although the likelihood is remote that an actual terrorist-related incident is underway, there is a hint of danger in the air. It is the sort of danger that arises when a child brings a loaded gun to the playground for a game of cops-and-robbers.

According to this reporter's examination of files obtained by the Chronicle, Landry enlisted three individuals to carry backpacks to Metro stops.

Those backpacks are possibly filled with incendiary devices.

Law enforcement officials place a low probability on the likelihood that any explosives will be detonated in the D.C. area. The purpose of the operation is not to actually detonate explosives, according to law enforcement, who say that the operation is intended to create the appearance of a crisis so that Landry can defuse it.

The identities of the three individuals enlisted to carry out the operation are unknown.

"This sort of Machiavellian enterprise is standard operating procedure for Landry," said an official on the condition of anonymity who was not authorized to comment on the ongoing investigation.

Two years ago, Landry orchestrated an apparent terrorist-related incident on the Woodrow Wilson Bridge, the source said.

The official version of that operation was that Landry was part of an elite cadre of antiterrorism experts who foiled a plot to bring surface-to-air missiles into the District.

The reality, based upon interviews conducted by this reporter with sources who prefer to remain anonymous, was that Landry had manufactured the whole thing in a vainglorious effort to advance his career.

It is also believed that Landry was sympathetic toward the mob that attacked the U.S. Capitol in January. According to informed sources, he opposed efforts to arrest and prosecute the people who participated in the mayhem.

The Wilson Bridge plot culminated in the downing of a helicopter and a firefight with would-be terrorists. Several individuals died in the mayhem.

Following that incident, Landry was rumored to be a strong contender for secretary of Homeland Security.

But as the truth about his operation leaked, his candidacy for the position lost its luster. He was sidelined to his current position.

Today's events bear an uncanny resemblance to that earlier plot.

While it is believed to be unlikely that the backpacks will be detonated, no one is taking any chances.

Security has been increased around all Metro stations and an all-points bulletin has been issued for Landry.

Security officials have expressed concern about innocent people who are walking around this morning with H-Pack backpacks, the type carried by the people Landry is believed to have enlisted.

"I hope no one takes the law into their own hands and confronts anyone wearing a backpack under the mistaken belief that they're stopping a terrorist from carrying out an attack," said one official.

"If any one of them gets shot, it's going to be a tragedy," the official added.

**

STONE'S EYES crawled across the iPhone's screen studying the article that the Chronicle had just published. She stopped at the line that read: *The operation is intended to create the appearance of a crisis so that Landry can defuse it.* Stone muttered out loud, "Wrong, Tom. That's what he wants you to believe. The operation is actually intended to kill the messengers. It's all about inflicting pain. The son of a bitch is turning the tables on us."

117

**

THE CHRONICLE EDITOR called Mann back. "Great stuff," she said. A half-hour later, she was in the office, having hurried in from her home off Rock Creek Parkway. Caraway was tiny physically, but steely, with wire-rim glasses and short blonde hair. She was dressed in a T-shirt and yoga pants. Her face glowed with satisfaction and approval.

"You're back, Tom. Full throttle. This is going to be a huge story for us. I couldn't stay away. I had to come down to the newsroom. This'll get people to take us seriously and give us a fighting chance of competing against *WaPo*. Stay with it."

He nodded. "I will."

"By the way," she said. "When did you first learn about this? I mean, there was a lot in that story. It didn't all materialize this morning."

"I got a tip the other day," he said. "I promised not to run with it too soon."

"No doubt from that policewoman you wrote about in that puff piece earlier this morning," she said.

He smiled. "Plus, I wanted to be sure of the facts, for the paper's sake if not for mine."

"Are you're sure you're sure?"

"Yeah," he answered. "It comports to all the facts I've uncovered." He studied the look of concern clouding her face. "Don't worry. I haven't allowed personal feelings to seep into my reporting. I'm playing it straight."

She gave him a hard look.

Eight Years Ago

MANN WAS RADIOACTIVE. He was no longer a Woodward or Bernstein of *The Washington Chronicle*. Questions had arisen about his exposé on the Pena Inquiry. There were rumors Phil Landry had manipulated him. The stories destroyed Pena. At the same time, they took the heat off Landry.

If the rumors were true, Mann had unfairly destroyed a good man's reputation and enabled a bad guy to escape justice. As time passed, the truth became evident. Landry had indeed duped him. The allegations bore no resemblance to the truth. At one time the Chronicle's golden boy who won a Pulitzer for the Pena articles a year ago, he now faced the possibility that it would be taken from him. It was akin to relinquishing a World Series ring or having your name removed from a university building.

Where would he go? What would he do? As unsettled and angry as he was at himself, he felt nothing but disdain toward Landry. He had been tricked, plain and simple. He had discarded one of his prize attributes — skepticism — and promoted a storyline that not only failed to tell the truth but that inadvertently told a lie.

**

MANN KNEW what he had to do to persuade the boss. "My source is a woman named Wilson," he explained. "She works for Landry. She showed me documents about him soliciting people to do some shady shit. I reviewed the information with Sherry Stone. She believes the documents are legit. The NTAS also took the story seriously enough to issue an elevated warning. So I'm confident that I'm on solid ground."

She still looked unconvinced. He realized now why she rushed to the office. It wasn't to be where the action was, but to see whether he had his head on straight.

"It's solid," he reiterated.

"Okay. Just please be careful," she said. "If you have any second thoughts, hold the story. We can't afford any mistakes." She tapped her fingers on his desk. It reminded him of the scene in *All the President's Men* when Jason Robards portrayed *The Post's* legendary editor Ben Bradlee. "Don't go off the rails again," she cautioned.

Mann smiled. "I'll stick to the facts, wherever they lead," he promised.

**

THE SCENE could only be described as surreal. An acrid odor of explosives filled the air around Farragut Square. Emergency vehicles rushed between stopped traffic to the scene of the bombing. People alighted from Metro stations throughout the city and ran onto the sidewalk.

Pedestrians massed on the sidewalks and pushed into the streets, sealing the spaces between cars like grout between tiles. People inside buildings ran outside to escape a potential explosion. People outside rushed indoors to avoid being a sitting target.

All the while, everyone made an effort to avoid congregating too closely with one another, a reflexive action that had become ingrained because of the coronavirus.

No one knew what was next. Some believed the worst was over. Others suspected the worst was still to come. That sentiment extended throughout the city, including in the area around Lafayette Square and Black Lives Matter Plaza.

**

MARIA PENA WAS LOST. The park was supposed to be at this intersection. She looked for a statue. There should be one at each corner of the park. In the center there should be a statue of Andrew Jackson on a horse. But from where she was standing, she could see no statues. She felt disoriented.

She surveyed the pedestrians and tried to divine who was headed to the park, but it was impossible because people were running in all directions. She followed a woman with a large picnic basket, then changed course when she saw a man with a bundle of flowers under his arm. He ended up going into a residential building. She felt like she was walking in circles.

Suddenly a man yelled, "There's an H-Pack backpack!" He

120

extended his arm and index finger at her as though he was holding a rifle. "She's got one of the bombs!" People scurried in every direction. They tripped over one another in the stampede. Couples separated. Parents hollered the names of their children. For an instant, pandemonium prevailed.

Pena began running. Her mask slipped off her face and fell to the ground.

"Stop!" A uniformed officer stood in a firing stance, her service revolver held at shoulder height. Pena pivoted. Everything was spinning. The street seemed splintered like a kaleidoscope. She dropped the backpack. People gasped. Some averted their eyes and covered their faces, fearing the worst. Pena thrust out her arms and walked into the intersection.

"Stop!" The policewoman now had one eye on the discarded backpack and the other on the crazy woman walking down the middle of the street doing her best Frankenstein imitation. "Stop, or I'll shoot!"

**

BONITA WALLACE was scared. Early this morning, her husband said something about going to Crystal City and catching a train. She did not pay much attention to him at the time. Now he was on the news, identified as the victim of a fall from a bridge into the Potomac River. Even though he had told her to leave the backpack alone, Bonita grabbed it and fled the house. The money was safer with her than in the apartment. Someone would break in and steal it. She'd already been robbed once this year.

Clutching the backpack, she took a bus to the Green Line. She missed her stop at L'Enfant Plaza, thinking the transfer must be at Metro Center. Having little familiarity with the Metro system, Bonita wandered about aimlessly. She tried to orient herself. Maybe she could walk to Crystal City, she thought. She sought directions from passers-by. But her English was poor and everyone was rushing.

She headed in the direction of Lafayette Square.

Seeing the backpack, people avoided her. Then they started pointing at her and running.

A security officer appeared. He was one of Landry's goons. *Shoot first, ask questions later.* Wallace did not match the description of the woman he'd been told would come to the park but she was wearing the ubiquitous orange H-Pack backpack.

"Hold it right there!"

She removed the backpack and held it in front of her like a child grasping a teddy bear. Her eyes opened wide. "No!" she cried.

"Put the backpack on the ground! Do it now!"

She panicked and ran toward him. He fired five shots in rapid succession, hitting her face and upper torso. Her body jerked backwards and the backpack flew out of her arms.

**

"STOP!" the policewoman hollered again at Maria Pena. "Stop, or I'll shoot!"

A hand suddenly reached out and grabbed Pena, blocking the line of fire for the officer, who stood with her firearm pointed at the couple. Pena felt comforted and secure. She looked at the hand and then the face in front of her. "Papa," she cried. "What are you doing here?" Fernando Pena embraced his daughter, tears streaming down his face. The policewoman darted toward the backpack and motioned for people to move away from it. A siren blared. The street cleared. People huddled on the sidewalks.

More police arrived. The crosswalk was cordoned off with plastic cones and yellow police tape. Sirens grew louder and louder. A large police van appeared. The bomb squad alighted, dressed in armor. An explosives detection canine trotted out, also wearing a vest.

Pena and her father were hustled to the sidewalk. The members of the bomb squad approached cautiously, unsure of what they had been summoned to investigate. The canine sniffed the backpack but gave no signal. Eventually, the backpack was opened, revealing its threat: books.

More sirens echoed through the canyon of downtown office and apartment buildings. Wooden barricades were assembled along the curb to establish a perimeter. Crowd control directed people to move briskly. Everyone complied. The policewoman walked over to Pena to question her.

"What are you doing?" asked her father. "She's done nothing wrong. All she was doing was walking down the street with a backpack full of books."

Police walkie-talkies crackled.

"Man at Union Station with H-Pack backpack."

"Three suspects with H-Pack backpacks detained at Smithsonian."

"Unattended H-Pack backpack found at Dupont Circle."

"Woman stopped at Gallery Place with H-Pack backpack."

Suddenly, there were dozens of Maria Penas all over town.

**

AHMED SULEIMAN approached Lafayette Square.

"Don't move!" hollered a policeman. "Do not take one more step or I'll fire and ask questions later," the officer warned.

Suleiman stopped. He dropped the backpack. He held up his hands. With the mask around the lower half of his face, he looked like a bank robber. Out of the corner of his eye, Suleiman spied Uncle Trey. *What the hell is he doing here?* Suleiman asked himself. Carr made no effort to interfere with the officer, standing passively on the side and hoping for the best.

The officer radioed for assistance. "I have a suspect in Lafayette Square," he said. The radio crackled as the dispatcher responded.

"They're books," Suleiman spoke to the officer. "All I got is books."

"Under control," the officer said, his firearm trained on Suleiman.

"Backup unit and a bomb squad requested."

"Did you hear me? I said, all I got are books. I don't even know why you're stopping me. I didn't do anything wrong." Carr took a step forward. It appeared as though everything was going to be cool. If only Ahmed would stop mouthing off at the cop.

BREAKING NEWS
This is a developing story
Tom Mann, City Editor © The Chronicle

Thirty minutes have passed since an explosion inside a landmark hotel rocked the nation's capital.

The threat level remains elevated but it has not been raised to imminent.

The absence of any additional bombings, along with the threat level remaining at an elevated level and a strong police presence throughout the city, has led to speculation that the crisis may have abated.

"Nobody's expecting another bomb to explode," said one law enforcement officer, who requested anonymity as this is a developing terrorist-related incident. "Right now everyone's efforts are focused on hunting down Phil Landry."

Police believe that Landry, director of security operations for homeland security, is behind the mayhem that has engulfed the city.

Landry reportedly left at least one incendiary device at the GreyStone Hotel late last night, according to sources. The sources also said that Landry had recruited three people to carry backpacks filled with bombs to Lafayette Square. One bomb detonated before it was picked up by anyone.

No one was injured in the hotel explosion.

Police and antiterrorism experts believe that the individuals enlisted by Landry rejected his plan at the last minute. The names of those individuals are unknown, as are their current whereabouts.

"Those people probably ran away as fast as they could once they realized what was happening," one law enforcement official speculated on the condition of anonymity.

Dozens of people carrying H-Pack backpacks, the type believed to have been used by Landry's recruits, were stopped and searched. They carried just about everything but bombs: lunches, cosmetics, and electronics. At least two individuals had backpacks loaded with books. "Bookworms," one official said in describing them.

At the same time Landry was orchestrating the Lafayette Square bombings, a plot was underway to explode a bomb on a train traveling across the railroad bridge that parallels the 14th Street Bridge over the Potomac River, according to law enforcement officials.

Police acknowledge they had advance knowledge of the train plot and were monitoring the situation in the days leading up to this morning's explosion.

Police also acknowledge they learned of Landry's plan last night, following up on a tip from an anonymous source.

In addition to searching for Landry, police are seeking Hugh Spates, a Washington-based lobbyist and developer, in connection with the foiled train bombing.

Spates is also being sought in connection with the murder of Danny Morley, whose body was recovered early Saturday morning at an underpass along Route 1 and Four Mile Run at the Arlington-Alexandria line.

Police have said that they believe there is a link between the shooting and the train plot.

While police do not acknowledge that Landry and Spates were working together, there is growing speculation that the two men are co-conspirators in an overlapping criminal enterprise to terrorize the capital during the Memorial Day weekend.

"It makes sense when you think about it," said one veteran officer. "One guy wants to make money and the other wants to advance his career. They're both greedy (expletive) intent on enriching themselves at the public's expense."

**

MANN TOOK a chance with the story. He reverted to his old self. He had promised himself and his editor that he would avoid repeating his previous mistakes. Yet here he was, writing a quasi-fictional account of what was happening in the city. But he believed he was right. And he still sought retribution against Landry. The unnamed sources were fictitious. The idea that the two events were connected was speculation. The same was true about connecting Landry to the explosion at the hotel. It was all conjecture. In fact, the only real quote was that there was no existential threat to the city. Ironically, the veracity of that statement was the only one he questioned.

**

WHILE THE terrorist alert level remained elevated, an unexpected orderliness settled over the streets of Washington. Behavioral experts predict that, in an emergency, people come together and help one another. Whether it's a car running off the road into a stream, a twister touching down in a residential community, or a communicable disease threatening the health and well-being of an entire population, people pull together to get one another out of harm's way.

Online reporters and radio broadcasters reminded listeners that static pools of people constituted soft targets. So people kept moving, navigating streets like water coursing along a riverbed.

"Keep it moving," advised traffic controllers dressed in orange vests. Their composure at intersections reminded people of the orderly mayhem when exiting a stadium after a championship game. *We got this*, people seemed to be saying without actually uttering a word. Order replaced chaos. Pedestrians stopped at intersections when the lights turned red, and then proceeded on green. No one pushed. No one jaywalked. Cars crawled along, bumper to bumper, unimpeded by the pedestrians. Bikes and scooters weaved in and out of traffic but avoided the throngs that controlled the sidewalks.

The orderliness resembled a wave at a stadium event, except people weren't jumping up and waving their hands. They just moved in tandem. A mantra took hold: *Stay cool, calm, and collected. We're going to get through this thing together.*

It helped that everyone was wired and that the crowds were sparse compared to most previous Memorial Day weekends. People with earplugs listened to nonstop updates on local radio stations WTOP and WAMU. Others read newsfeeds from *The Chronicle*, *The Post*, Politico, Bloomberg, and other news sources. Everyone was connected to one another. News alerts continued to spread across airwaves. The basic facts were the same. A train was stopped on a trestle over the river.

The explosion at the hotel was a one-off. Nothing else happened in the past two hours. Each passing moment heightened the sense of safety and security. Breathing returned to normal. The pace of the crowd slowed. Someone stopped and gave a traffic controller a bottle of water.

As an air of confidence ringed the city, the mayor held a press conference. It wasn't just any press conference. It was held in front of the Metro Center subway station, a symbolic ground zero. District and regional law enforcement officers surrounded the podium. They weren't wearing masks or vests. If they weren't afraid, there was no reason for anyone else to be alarmed.

"While we remain vigilant, and while the terrorist alert warning remains elevated, we are confident that the danger has passed and that no one need fear any additional terrorist-related incidents," said the mayor. Minutes before she spoke, the mayor held a conference call with the commanders of antiterrorist groups throughout the metropolitan area, including Stone, who had arrived in D.C. an hour earlier. The mayor received confirmation that the chances of another incident were nil.

Based on the group's consensus, the mayor decided to allow public events to resume. The hockey game was back on. Colorful kites started flying on the Washington Monument grounds. And motorcycles rumbled through the city from Arlington Cemetery to the Vietnam War Memorial.

Two conspicuous loose ends remained for law enforcement. One was finding Hugh Spates. The other was locating and arresting Phil Landry.

Chapter Eight: Afternoon

CALLERS SPOTTED Landry at a bagel shop in Bethesda, a car lot in Fredericksburg, and a bus stop in upper Northwest. Every lead was investigated, however far-fetched it appeared and despite the fact that many sightings were of a person wearing a mask. Sooner or later, one of those leads was going to pay off.

Someone reported seeing Landry enter a white van parked at Roaches Run. An Arlington cruiser with two uniforms pulled into the parking lot at the waterfowl sanctuary. A minute later, a U.S. Park Police cruiser joined them. The officers got out of their vehicles and surveyed the area. Sure enough, there was a van in the far corner of the parking area, and a sedan parked near it. No passengers were visible. A check of the license plates confirmed that both vehicles were registered to Landry.

Neither the Arlington cops nor the Park Police officer approached the van for fear it was booby-trapped. Assuming Landry was inside, and given this morning's bombing, it was logical to assume the van might be wired with explosives. Something about this one felt right to them. The Park Police officer requested backup. Over the next 30 minutes, an armada of law enforcement vehicles arrived. People in vehicles parked in the area were told to leave. Wooden barricades and orange cones sealed the entrance and exit. Reagan National was notified; private charter flights that flew over Roaches Run were diverted from the runway at the north end of the airport and provided with alternative landing schedules.

Then an army of media trucks with communications towers pulled into the parking lot at Gravelly Point. This was getting serious. Everyone could feel it.

**

KATZ AND STONE had started the day together. After leaving Crystal City, they went to Gravelly Point to observe the train on the bridge. Following the explosion at the GreyStone Hotel, a chopper landed at Gravelly Point and took Stone into the District. She was finishing the meeting with the mayor when Landry was reported to have been spotted at Roaches Run.

In the meantime, Katz called Santana, who picked him up at Gravelly Point and took him to the U.S. Attorney's office in the Eisenhower Valley. When Katz heard the news about Landry being spotted at Roaches Run, he recalled Landry's inquiry the previous day about placing a two-person crew at the wildfowl sanctuary to observe the train. Now he understood why.

But if Landry knew the van might be spotted by the police, why didn't he move it last night?

**

A HELICOPTER carrying Stone swooped down over Roaches Run and landed in the southbound lanes of the G.W. Parkway, closed from the 14th Street Bridge to the edge of Old Town. Stone jumped out. She was immediately surrounded by fellow officers. No one had approached the van and no one had exited it.

As the chopper landed, the command center received a text from Phil Landry. It read: "*Tell that policewoman to call off her stormtroopers or I'll blow this van to kingdom come.*"

The communication was relayed to an electronic tablet handed to Stone. She read it and then looked around. "Let's get some drones in the air," she said. "And launch a small vessel over there as well," she commanded, pointing to the water. Then she responded to the text: "*Phil, no one is going to rush the van. We'd like to find a peaceful solution. Let's find a way out of this. S. Stone.*"

She pulled her phone from the pocket of her blue windbreaker and called Katz. "I'm down at Roaches Run now. Landry just texted the command center from his phone. He's inside a van in the parking lot threatening to blow up the vehicle. Where are you?"

"I'm already on King Street. I left my office about ten minutes ago, as soon as I got a call about Landry being located. I should be at Roaches Run in another ten minutes." Katz noticed the traffic lights at each intersection along King Street were all green. "Maybe five," he amended as he cruised across town from Duke Street to Slaters Lane.

"Roger that," she said. "Look me up when you get here. I may need your valuable counsel."

As Katz hung up, a roadblock appeared ahead. He slowed, unbuckled his seat belt and reached in his pocket for his badge. He came to a full stop and flashed the badge at two officers in armor holding long guns.

"Good to go, Mr. Katz," one of them said, waving him forward. "Please be careful. We don't want to lose you." He nodded and proceeded along the parkway past Daingerfield Island and the airport.

The azure sky was gone and clouds the color of creamy wool covered the sky. Gravelly Point was to his right, Roaches Run to the left. The place was a parking lot filled with cruisers, ambulances, fire trucks, bomb squad vehicles, and a couple of SUVs used to transport bomb-sniffing dogs.

There were over 100 law enforcement officers at the scene, Katz calculated. He brought his car to a stop right on the parkway and got out, jumped over the guardrail separating southbound and northbound lanes, and proceeded to the parking area. He could see Stone up ahead. The only non-official vehicles in the parking lot were a sedan and the white van. The cab was empty. There were no windows on the side or back of the vehicle. Yellow police tape created a perimeter around the van. No one was standing closer than 30 yards away.

"Any more communications?" Katz asked as he came alongside Stone.

"He just texted," she said, showing him the screen of the tablet she held in her hands. It read: *"S. Stone: Do you think I'm a fool? The* second I open the door they'll blast the living daylights out of me. I'm not coming out! And if you don't pull back, you leave me no choice."

Katz thought it odd the message was addressed to S. Stone. "I don't get it," he said. "This isn't like Landry. Martyrdom isn't his game."

Stone shrugged. "What's he got to salvage? Blowing himself up might be the easiest way out of this. It'll buy him headlines for a couple of days. He'll like that." She typed: "*It's time to give it up. Come out with your hands over your head.*"

That was followed by a series of exchanges.

"*Get back or I'll blow this tin can.*"

"*Don't be a fool. We can sort this out. I give you my word.*"

"*You have 2 minutes to clear the field. Then I'm gonna blow.*"

"*Don't.*"

"*Have your people move further back. 30 yards isn't far enough.*"

Katz looked over Stone's shoulder, reading the one-liners being lobbed back and forth. "How does he know how close the LEOs are to the van?" he asked.

Stone paid no attention, busily typing a return text. Behind her, a large message board projected the online communications.

"Let's pull back," someone hollered. "If that idiot carries out his threat, we don't want anyone getting hurt."

Stone turned to Katz. "What did you say?" He was no longer there. From the corner of her eye, she watched as he jumped the guardrail and got back in his car. "Where the hell is he going?" she asked out loud. Her question was met with empty stares.

"Clear the area," someone repeated. The LEOs and EMTs on foot moved back, and there was a roar of engines as others began maneuvering their vehicles further away from the van. Stone looked down at the tablet.

Meanwhile, Katz raced down the parkway, took the ramp for southbound I-395 and exited onto Route 110. He drove under the 14th Street Bridge to the aquatic center, parked, and ran up the embankment to Green Point. From that vantage point, he overlooked Roaches Run, Gravelly Point, Reagan National, and the Potomac River.

Stone was carrying on her communications.

"Don't do this, Phil. Don't make it worse."

"Have everyone get back further. 60 seconds and counting."

Stone sensed Landry was not backing down. "Get everyone away from the van," she shouted. "I can't stop him killing himself, but I don't want him taking out any of our people." Everyone started to back further and further away from the van. With thirty seconds left on Landry's time clock, no one was within 1,000 feet.

"That's more like it. T-minus 30 and counting."

"What can I do to talk you off the ledge? This is insane."

Like Katz, Stone found Landry's actions incomprehensible. The media painted Landry as a rogue cop responsible for the mayhem that occurred earlier today. Yet she knew he had nothing to do with the train incident. Linking Landry and Spates was irresponsible on Tom Mann's part. It might attract readers, but it had no basis in fact. Furthermore, none of the H-Pack backpacks confiscated around Lafayette Square contained bombs. While the documents found by Landry's assistant suggested that Landry was concocting some kind of crazy plan, there was no evidence that anything had actually come to fruition.

It was anyone's guess as to the cause of the explosion at the GreyStone Hotel, Stone reasoned. It could have been connected to the construction. Again, she was irked at Mann for drawing conclusions based on pure speculation. She was confident that he had not gotten those quotes from anyone in law enforcement. She was certain that he made them up.

While Landry might be complicit, Stone thought it was improbable he'd ever be indicted of a crime, let alone convicted of one. *So why is he threatening to take his life?*

BREAKING NEWS
This is a developing story
Tom Mann, City Editor © The Chronicle

Nearly 25 years ago, on July 27, 1996, a bomb exploded at the Summer Olympics in Atlanta, Ga.

The 100th anniversary of the modern Olympics was marred by a terrorist attack. However, that bombing was only part of the tragedy. In addition to one dead and over 100 injured, it destroyed the reputation of Richard Jewel, a 33-year-old rent-a-cop who was mistakenly identified as the bomber.

No one is going to make a misidentification like that today.

Phil Landry, a counterterrorism expert with a checkered past, bears complete responsibility for putting the D.C. area on edge at the outset of the Memorial Day holiday weekend.

He coordinated a train explosion earlier this morning over the Potomac River.

He led law enforcement authorities on a wild goose chase for would-be terrorists carrying bombs in H-Pack backpacks to Metro stations.

He planted explosives in the GreyStone Hotel that destroyed the edifice's southwest corner earlier today.

And he is currently threatening the lives of dozens of federal, state, and local officials.

Shortly after noon today, Landry texted a *Chronicle* reporter. In the text, he threatened to harm officers who have surrounded a van where he is hiding out at Roaches Run, the wildfowl sanctuary south of the 14th Bridge and across the G.W. Parkway from Reagan National Airport and Gravelly Point.

"I will kill the LEOs [law enforcement officers] surrounding me if they dare come any closer," he texted to this reporter.

A Questionable Career in Local Law Enforcement

Landry has a history of being at the center of controversy. Twelve years ago, he was investigated for a series of questionable convictions obtained from penny-ante criminals.

According to people familiar with an internal investigation conducted by the U.S. Department of Justice, Landry pressured individuals into confessing to crimes they did not commit to rack up a string of high-visibility "wins" for the department.

According to sources who spoke on the condition of anonymity, Landry threatened to prosecute family members of the individuals unless they confessed to crimes on which he wanted to "close the book."

Due to pressure from Landry, several individuals went to jail for confessing to crimes that they did not commit, the sources said.

One of those individuals was Trey Carr, who was released from the penitentiary last year. "I don't hold no grudge against him, but what he done was wrong," Carr said when contacted by this reporter earlier today.

An Investigation Gone Awry

. The inquiry into Landry's activities was terminated after people questioned the integrity of the person heading up the inquiry. That person — Fernando Pena — was accused of lying, stealing, and cheating, all crimes of moral turpitude that would have made him ineligible to conduct the investigation and would have tainted the inquiry's findings.

Landry was responsible for planting the stories about Pena. Those stories were contrived and false. No one feels more embarrassed to say that than this reporter, who was complicit in allowing Landry to sell a false story to the public.

Mea Culpa

Landry fed this reporter information about Pena that had the effect of discrediting Pena and exonerating Landry. Over time, it became apparent that the information was false and misleading. This reporter has remained silent — until now.

**

MO KATZ stood on the bluff overlooking Roaches Run. He watched as LEOs withdrew further and further from the van. Across the parkway and behind the barricades at Gravelly Point, he observed a crowd of bikers, runners, and onlookers. A helicopter hovered over the railroad trestle adjacent the 14th Street Bridge, which was shut down to traffic. Traffic backups grew on I-395 and around the Tidal Basin. An airborne drone looped around Roaches Run. A small craft sped across the waterfront at the sanctuary.

The wool blanket of clouds now covered the sky. There was a promise of rain in the air. In the distance, thunder rumbled and lightning glimmered. As Katz scanned the area he spotted a man in a hoodie by the soccer field at Gravelly Point. He was looking through binoculars and had a phone in his other hand. A laptop was set up next to him on a small aluminum and canvas chair. The man was facing Roaches Run.

Suddenly, a fireball accompanied by a loud boom flashed across the parking lot. The van split apart like popcorn exploding from a pan. Flames spread out in all directions. Pieces of the van and the car parked next to it shot across the lot and glass shards dropped to the pavement like confetti. The smell of burning rubber and fuel filled the air. The explosion set off antitheft systems in several vehicles.

Beep! Beep! Beep! The devices barked like electronic dogs.

The remnants of the van settled into dozens of mini bonfires across the parking lot.

It happened as fast as the striking of a match.

Everyone who had moved back now raced forward. Fire trucks and ambulances revved up their engines and hastened toward the van. Firefighters in full protective gear jumped out and quickly manned hoses to douse the flames. They warily approached the steaming wreckage in search of Landry.

Distracted by the explosion, Katz had taken his eyes off the man with the binoculars. Now, as he looked back to the spot where the man had been, nothing was to be seen.

The entire parking lot was now a crime scene. Pieces of the van's interior — seats, computers, screens, table, papers — were strewn about everywhere. Every item was burnt or smashed. The sedan was heavily damaged as well, with chunks of it blown away.

Amidst the debris lay pieces of a body. The pieces were more lumps of charred meat than a body. Some bits of skin, clothes, and hair were still smoldering. LEOs and EMTs stood among the remains. There was no life-saving to be done here. The smell of burnt flesh joined the other noxious odors from the explosion, and those who weren't wearing masks covered their mouths and noses with whatever was handy.

As a finale to the mayhem, the clouds burst open and a spring shower began to rain down. Police rushed to their vehicles to grab tarps and plastic canopies to cover the materiel at the scene.

"What a fucking mess," someone uttered.

Ignoring the rain, Stone hollered, "Get the forensic crews and coroner over here right away! I want this stuff photographed and catalogued before anything is removed from the scene. Get me fingerprints!" As she spat out orders, people scurried about.

Meanwhile, Katz had abandoned his lofty perch and driven back to Roaches Run.

"Where the hell have you been?" asked Stone when he returned.

"Testing out a theory," he said. They stepped away from the center of activity. "It seemed to me that the person you were communicating with had x-ray vision. I mean, he knew what was happening outside of the van. I wanted to find out."

"Whether he had x-ray vision?"

"No," he smiled. "I wondered whether the person on the other end of the line was outside of the van."

She looked at him quizzically. "And?"

"And I think he might have been. I saw someone with binoculars over by Gravelly Point looking this way. I honestly thought this was all a bluff. I never expected the van to blow, not really. But now that all hell has broken lose, it's got me wondering."

She nodded. "Interesting theory. Keep me informed the more you test it out."

**

"HEY, ROSCOE, it's Mo Katz."

Roscoe Page was a legend in the D.C. area. A former high-ranking intelligence officer who had served both Democratic and Republican administrations, common among career civil servants, he was now making a fortune running a security and investigative firm at Tysons Corner. Their paths had crossed through the years. "To what do I owe the honor?" asked Page.

"I have a question about tracing text messages."

"I assume this has to do with Landry texting Sherry Stone, Tom Mann, and others in the run-up to his dramatic exit," Page said. It was already all over the news.

"I'm just not convinced it was Landry."

Page was seated in his car parked in his driveway in McLean. He pushed back the seat and leaned his head back against the headrest. "What makes you say that?"

"My gut. I needed to call someone I can trust, someone who understands electronic communications. Think of the terrorist attacks at the Pensacola naval air station in 2019 or in San Bernardino in 2015. There's always a problem trying to access communications."

"You really think Landry's alive?"

"I think Landry was on the other side of the parkway by Gravelly Point. And that's why I'm curious to know whether it's possible to trace the source of those communications."

"So, to be clear, you're not talking about the device? You're talking about its location?"

"That's right. Landry was using his phone. The question is whether the phone was inside of the van."

"You don't need my help, Mo," Page laughed.

"Why not?"

"Just search the scene. If the phone is among the wreckage, you should have your answer. If there's no phone, call me. Otherwise, you don't need my help or anyone else's."

Katz felt foolish for not thinking it through.

Sensing Katz's embarrassment, Page said, "Don't feel bad about it. There's a lot going on." Then he added, "What makes you think Landry would pull a stunt like that?"

"To give himself a clean getaway," Katz speculated. "I was at Roaches Run when Stone received the texts. There were things written that could not have been known by someone sitting inside the van, such as the location of personnel stationed around it. Plus, it doesn't make sense that he would kill himself. There was no need for him to take such drastic action."

Page thought about it for a minute. "He was probably watching the scene on television," he said. "I heard they found television monitors, or pieces of them, from inside the van. He would have known what was going on outside the van simply by watching the tube. Or maybe he had hidden cameras on the van. As to taking his own life, well, there are stories about his involvement in a string of wrongful criminal convictions. Everything was closing in. It doesn't surprise me."

"Yeah, maybe you're right," Katz said.

"If I can be of any further help, give me a call," Page said.

Page backed out of the driveway. An hour ago, he had received a call from Ari Hammond instructing him to release a copy of the Ruth Hammond report to Tom Mann of *The Chronicle*. Now he gets a call from Katz. There was no way these two incidents were unrelated, he thought to himself. He turned up the street.

It was a forty-five-minute drive to Mann's home in Brookland. Page needed to touch base with Abe Lowenstein. Whether or not Landry was alive, the whole thing was going to be an embarrassment to the senator unless he quickly initiated some damage control.

**

FIFTEEN MINUTES LATER, Lowenstein called Katz. "Do you have a few minutes to talk about Phil Landry?" asked the senator.

"Of course," Katz said.

Lowenstein steered Katz's confirmation hearing through the Senate four years ago. Since then, they had remained in close contact, often seeking advice from one another on a variety of issues, some legal, some not. As part of that relationship, Lowenstein entreated Katz to work collaboratively with Landry. Katz always resisted. The current revelations confirmed Katz's suspicions and validated his resistance.

"This is hard for me," Lowenstein said. "I feel betrayed. Phil and I came to this town together. Our careers dovetailed. I'm embarrassed I never saw through him and that I tried to get you to work with him. Your instincts were right on."

"We're all blinded by our loyalty and friendship," Katz said. "It's not unique to your relationship with him. It's just something that happened."

"Still," the senator said.

Katz knew the score. Beneath it all, Lowenstein was just another politician whose number one priority was his own reputation. Two people were dead, an explosion rocked a luxury hotel in the heart of the city, a nefarious plot involving H-Pack backpacks was disrupted, and a van was blown sky-high at Roaches Run. Yet Lowenstein's concern was whether his relationship with Landry might reflect poorly on his public image.

"If it's any consolation," Katz said, "Landry fooled a lot of people for a long time. You're not alone in that category."

"I appreciate your saying that."

Katz didn't respond. He hadn't meant it as a compliment.

"I mean, even thinking of his statement about January 6, I think

140

Landry wanted those bastards to wreck the Capitol." Lowenstein hesitated. "Do you think I should do some press?

"Katz was surprised by the question. "Why? What for?"

"To distance myself. I could talk about what a bastard he was. Emphasize that I helped deep-six his plan for a Cabinet level position a couple of years ago."

"I don't know," Katz replied carefully. As Katz remembered it, the senator had held fire until it was clear Landry was a lost cause.

"Maybe consult your public affairs folks," Katz added.

"They're all out of town for the weekend." Lowenstein paused. "Actually, I don't trust their instincts half the time. I pretty much follow my gut. Make a few calls to friends like you, and then adopt a course of action. Think I'll call a couple of reporters who've given me favorable looks in the past. See if I can get some face time."

"Good luck."

"By the way, what's the latest on the incident out at Roaches Run?" It was the first in a series of rapid-fire questions. "Did Landry play a role in the H-Pack backpack scare this morning? Do you think Landry was working with that ex-congressional aide to detonate a train bomb?"

Katz deflected the inquiries. "You'll need to talk to someone in the know, like Sherry Stone." He gave Lowenstein her number.

"If I can't reach her, I'll wing it," Lowenstein said. "I'm the chairman of the Senate Intelligence Committee. I know everything," he added facetiously.

"More than me, that's for sure," Katz replied.

"I doubt it," Lowenstein said wryly. He added, "By the way, in case you're wondering, I just heard from Roscoe Page. It's why I called you."

"I figured."

"He says you think that Landry might not be dead, that he might have faked the whole thing to create an elaborate escape."

"It's possible. I'm working on a theory, senator. The only two people I've discussed it with are Roscoe and Stone. I'll fill you in as soon as I figure it out."

**

THE LOCKS of Page's white hair curled over his collar. He ran his hand through them. He knocked twice. He was loathe to drop the envelope through the mail slot in the door, so when there was no answer, he turned and walked away as discreetly as he had approached. He was almost to the curb when the door opened.

Page turned around and walked back to the house. "I'm Roscoe Page," he said, stifling the reflex to shake hands.

"I know who you are," replied Mann, wearing a mask. "Your reputation precedes you." Mann looked at the envelope tucked under Page's arm. "Is that a present for me?"

"May I come inside?"

He opened the door wider and Page stepped inside. Classical music was playing in the background. Mann ushered Page from the foyer to the living room.

"I got my vaccination shots for COVID-19," Page said. Mann removed his mask.

Papers were strewn about the floor, coffee table, and sofa. Mann was dressed casually in a T-shirt and khakis. "I've got a show this evening," Mann explained, waving at the mess.

Page handed Mann the envelope.

"Tell me what I'm looking at," Mann said as he sat down and pulled the contents out of the envelope. He flipped through the pages.

"It's a copy of my firm's investigation into the attack on Ruth Hammond several years ago in Crystal City," Page said.

Mann looked up at Page. "Who?" His heart skipped a beat.

"Ruth Hammond. She did the preliminary research into Phil Landry's scam in Alexandria Circuit Court. Her work led to the Pena Inquiry. You remember, don't you?" Page held Mann's stare.

"A couple of years after the inquiry fell apart, Ms. Hammond was brutally attacked in a parking garage. The crime was never solved by the police. But I solved it, and my findings are in the report you're holding."

"Who asked you to give it to me?"

"Ari Hammond, her brother."

"Why now?"

"You'll know the answer to that question after you've reviewed the report."

Page didn't stick around and Mann didn't waste any time reviewing the documents after the entrepreneur left. The report confirmed a suspicion that had resided in the pit of Mann's stomach for years. He felt ill. But only for a moment. There was work to be done and a story to be told.

**

Tweet from #TheChronicle

Sen. Abe Lowenstein, a dear friend and a very smart guy, will offer insights and commentary this evening on *Mann Up/Newsmakers Saturday Night*. We're on-air, online, on point, and right on! Join us!

**

During the afternoon, dozens of people were questioned about bringing H-Pack backpacks into the city. No one coordinated the investigations. As a result, they Balkanized into a dozen disparate inquires.

"We're exacerbating the problem," said one intake officer processing the interviews. "We don't have grounds to detain these people. We're potentially looking at massive civil rights violations and lawsuits up the wazoo."

One by one, the suspects were released. No standard operating procedure was established for detaining, questioning, or releasing them. In some instances, names and addresses were taken. In others, people were simply released without any identification being shown or recorded.

Stone was standing in a police substation in the District that was collecting the names of detainees. Two names on the list caught her eye. She asked if either of the individuals was still at the station. One was, she was told.

Her phone rang. She answered it without checking the source of the incoming call.

"Mo asked me to see how you're doing," Mai Lin said.

Stone had received two calls from Katz earlier. She deliberately did not answer either one. She was beginning to have her own suspicions. If she was right, it might be best to connect the dots later. "Everything is copacetic," she replied.

"Are people being questioned for bringing backpacks into the city?"

"They're being released," Stone answered. "I'm good with that. I don't think there's any need to hold them. I mean, what for? They didn't do anything. Why do you ask?"

"No reason. Just wanted to see how you were doing."

Stone wondered what angle had Katz's attention. "Well, there's nothing suspicious here," she said. "I'm preparing to leave soon." After the call ended, Stone went to the desk sergeant and asked if she could interview the woman with the backpack who was sitting on a bench against a tile wall. The one whose name on the list that caught her attention.

"This way, Maria," Stone said a moment later.

Hesitantly, Pena complied. Stone took her into an interview room and closed the door. The square cinderblock room held a small rectangular table with a chair on either side of it. There was no recording device and no mirror that enabled people on the other side of the wall to observe their conversation.

"How well did you know Phil Landry?" Stone asked as they sat down.

Pena jumped up. "Who?"

"Phil Landry," Stone replied calmly. "And please sit back down." Pena complied.

"I'm not here to hurt you or do anything wrong, okay? I know you were involved in an intimate relationship with him for the past several months."

Pena sat ramrod straight in the chair. "I'd like some water. And how long are you going to question me?"

"Five minutes, max. I just want to gather a little information, that's all."

"Okay," Pena said, relaxing a little. She didn't need that water after all. "I was having an affair with Phil. I just didn't think anyone knew about it."

Stone had not known about the affair. She was working off a hunch. In the papers she reviewed in Wilson's apartment, Landry indicated he was having sexual relations with one of his three targeted individuals. When Stone saw the name Maria Pena on the list at the police station — along with Ahmed Suleiman — she suspected Pena might be that person.

It was the first piece that fit the jigsaw puzzle she was trying to solve in her head.

"Do you know who he is?" Stone asked. "I mean, do you know anything about Phil Landry?"

"No. Why, should I? He seemed like a nice man to me. I can't understand why he would be involved in any of those terrible things they're saying."

Stone lowered her head and ran fingernails across an eyebrow. *Wow. The girl is so far behind the curve she doesn't even know this is the guy who destroyed her father.* "When was the last time you saw him?"

"What do you mean? I saw his picture on television today. Is that what you're asking?"

"When was the last time you were intimate with Phil?"

"You mean, like sex?"

"Yeah, Maria. I mean, like sex."

"A couple of weeks ago."

"How about last night? Did you meet with him at the GreyStone Hotel last night?"

"What are you talking about?" Pena started to cry.

It was the last thing Stone needed. This interview needed to be conducted with a modicum of discretion. *Just nail down this one final fact and get out of here*, Stone told herself.

"Did you drive to the GreyStone Hotel last night to meet with Phil?"

"No. I stayed home. I was by myself." She looked at Stone through her tears. "It's not like I can prove it. But I did not see Phil Landry. I swear."

Stone nodded. "Okay, wipe your eyes. We're done."

As Pena pulled herself together, Stone smiled to herself. Again, she'd gotten information off a bluff. She had not known whether there was a sexual liaison last night at the GreyStone but, given her mounting suspicions, it was logical to believe there could have been one.

After releasing Pena, Stone was confident the narrative created by Tom Mann was inaccurate.

Stone contacted the investigator in charge of the bombing at the GreyStone. She asked if she could come over to the hotel. She anticipated the response to her question so was quick to say, "I realize it's outside my jurisdiction. I'm just interested in seeing whether there are any similarities between the hotel bombing and the explosion at Roaches Run."

Just one officer's request to another to nose around, "Columbo" style, she insinuated. It worked. "Come on down," said the cop in her best Monty Hall imitation. Thirty minutes later, Stone was at the GreyStone.

While there was no evidence of damage to the lobby, an

inspection of the hotel's infrastructure — plumbing, electricity, heating and cooling — was pending.

Stone found the security manager and inquired about security cameras. She was told there was a four-hour blackout the night before. It didn't surprise her. She pressed the security manager, who turned her over to the hotel's IT guy. He finally came clean after Stone said the info would be kept confidential. He explained there was a recurring request from a guest who wanted his sexual liaisons to stay anonymous. One of those liaisons was last night. The security manager knew about it too, the IT guy said. They were both in on the take.

"A lot of politicians and diplomats visit on a regular basis," he said. "Or at least they used to until the pandemic. Nowadays not so much. Still, I sympathized with the guy. Plus, it's a few extra dollars in my pocket."

Stone ran up the stairs to the ninth floor, two at a time. She pushed open the heavy metal door from the staircase to the interior of the hotel and examined the wing undergoing reconstruction where the bomb had exploded. There was a huge hole in the wall, now covered with plastic sheeting.

She studied the contents of the wing, including a heavy-duty plastic and rubber chute that dropped from a window to a huge dumpster in the alley. Then she examined the other wing. The doors to all the rooms were locked.

When she came back down, she told the IT guy she wanted to see the room where the liaison had taken place. He was resistant. "Don't fuck with me," she said. "You've been a good boy so far. Start giving me a hard time and you're only looking for trouble." She saw fear behind his bluster. "If someone pays you to temporarily dismantle the security cameras to facilitate his liaisons," she said, "he probably uses the same routine every time he comes here, which includes using the same room. I want to see it."

The IT guy acknowledged she was right but that there was a

deviation from the norm on Saturday night. For the first time, the guest requested a different room. And the request was made by text from an unfamiliar number.

He took her to the room.

Nothing appeared out of the ordinary when she looked it over: king-size bed, end tables, credenza, plasma television, desk, table and chairs, plush carpeting.

"Who cleaned the room this morning?" she asked. He said he did not know, but he could find out later. "Do it now," she insisted.

He resisted. "The maid, she…"

"Don't worry," Stone said. "I don't care about whether she's legal. Around here, the local police don't volunteer information to the feds as a matter of policy."

Fifteen minutes later, Stone was seated with the maid, Juanita Salazar. The coronavirus had devastated members of her family, many of whom worked in health care and custodial services. Despite the risks posed to her, Salazar felt fortunate to be working and drawing an income.

She explained the room had definitely been occupied. The bedcovers were pulled back and the pillows were on the floor. But, Salazar added when prodded, there was no evidence of sexual activity: no stains on the bedsheets, and no condoms or gels around the bathroom or in the trash. There were no cigarettes in ashtrays or drinks on the tables either.

"Anything else?" Stone asked.

"Nada," Salazar said. Then she paused. There was one thing. A sock was left in the closet. "I throw it out," she said. Stone asked if Salazar could find it. She also asked if anyone had inquired about the liaison. "No," Salazar said. "Everyone just go to the explosion." She pointed in the direction of the wing under construction.

"Okay," Stone said. "And listen, this is just between us. I'm not going to tell anyone."

"Gracias," said Salazar.

148

Stone went back to the IT guy. "How were you paid?"

"It's always an anonymous electronic payment to my PayPal account," he said. "Except this last time was different. An envelope showed up in my mail slot in the back room. I still got it. Do you want to see it?"

Stone demurred. That was a job for the D.C. cops. She was already way outside of her jurisdiction.

As she was leaving the hotel, she called Vanessa Wilson. "Can I drop over and review those files again?"

An hour later, they met at Wilson's house. Neither of them bothered to put on a protective mask.

"What are you looking for?" asked Wilson.

Stone did not share the nature of her inquiry, but a review of the paperwork confirmed her suspicion. Based upon the descriptions of Parties A, B, and C outlined in the documents, she was convinced that Pena and Suleiman were two of the three people Landry had enlisted in his project. Landry — that sick fuck — had intended to take Pena and Suleiman to slaughter, along with Party C, whoever he or she happened to be.

Stone saw it clearly. The plan called for the threesome to carry H-Pack backpacks from the GreyStone to Lafayette Square. H-Packs might be ubiquitous but they were also easy to spot, which was why Landry had selected them. He had carefully chosen trigger-happy personnel to be posted at specific spots where he directed the threesome to go, Stone reasoned. Landry expected them to kill Pena, Suleiman, and Party C when they showed up with backpacks.

Stone thanked Wilson, got back in her car, and called Trey Carr, whom she had tracked down. There was no answer. She left a message: "Call me."

Chapter Nine: Evening

CARR CALLED STONE within an hour. They met in Farragut Square. A few food trucks were parked along the perimeter of the rectangular park. A bronze statue of David Glasgow Farragut stood on a pedestal in the center of the park, a pigeon atop his head.

"You don't look nothing like the way you did then, but I've never forgotten what you tried to do for me," Carr said. "And I'll always be grateful."

Stone was the rookie cop who questioned Landry's tactics when Carr entered a plea in Alexandria Circuit Court.

"Sooner or later, we become who we're meant to be," she said.

"True that," Carr said.

"I wish I could have actually done something for you," Stone said. "I was unsure of myself. Landry intimidated me into remaining silent even though I knew something was wrong."

"It wasn't on you," Carr said. "There was a prosecutor and a judge involved as well. They're the ones who should have stepped up. You did the best you could at the time." Carr smiled broadly. "It's really good to see you."

They both remembered the Pena inquiry ended in an ash heap. After the media shit storm, DOJ pulled the plug and abruptly terminated the inquiry. Instead of prosecuting Landry, DOJ sent him a letter of apology and exonerated him.

"It was a sham," Stone said.

"Landry used that reporter," Carr said bitterly. "None of those stories was true."

Stone got up from the bench where they were seated, walked over to one of the remaining food trucks, and bought two cups of coffee. The crowds passing through the park had been reduced to a trickle. The pigeon atop Farragut's head was joined by several relatives. In the distance, a siren blared as night descended on the city.

She brought the coffee back to the bench and handed Carr one of the cups. She reached in her pocket and removed a plastic bag. In the bag was a sock, which she casually let drop to the ground. She slid the plastic bag back into her pocket. Carr's eyes followed her movements but he said nothing. "You probably aren't too unhappy about the news of Landry's death," Stone said.

"I'm not ashamed to admit it," he laughed. "The man deserves to go down in history as an evil son of a bitch."

Stone nodded in agreement. "Did you know Landry ginned up a plan to create a phony terrorist plot to kill innocent victims?

"Say what?"

"Yeah," she said. "And Ahmed was one of his victims."

"My Ahmed? How do you know something as crazy as that?"

She smiled. "He was a kid when you were sent up. I remember him in court on the day of your sentencing."

"Really?"

"You don't remember?"

"Can't say as I do. And you're saying Landry was going to set him up for a kill?"

"That's right. Ahmed and a woman named Maria Pena."

Carr sipped his coffee. He studied her. "Is this going somewhere, Officer Stone?" he asked.

Stone ran a fingernail through her hair and around her hoop earring. She curled her fingers around the coffee cup. The Olmsted streetlamps in the park were aglow. She bent her head and stared into the coffee cup. "Yeah," she whispered, "It's going somewhere."

They lowered their voices. Buses, scooters, cars and taxis moved down Connecticut Avenue and across K Street. Pedestrians cut diagonally across the park's sidewalks. No one paid any attention to the couple on the bench; they might as well have been two homeless people sharing stories about life on the street.

When they finished, Stone picked up the sock from the ground using the plastic bag like she was scooping up dog shit, wrapped the sock in the bag, and threw it in the trash.

Mann Up/Newsmaker Sunday Night

THOMAS MANN: "Good evening. I'm Thomas Mann and this is *Mann-Up Newsmaker Sunday Night.* I want to thank everyone who's watching us online. Our virtual guest this evening is Senator Abraham Lowenstein, chairman of the Senate Intelligence Committee. Welcome, senator, and thank you for being available on such short notice."

Sen. Abe Lowenstein: "Thanks, Tom. It's good to be with you this evening. And the trip over was no bother at all."

Mann chuckled. One of the benefits of the online programming was the convenience of pressing a button and appearing on the show. There was no commute these days and no studio time prepping for the appearance.

Mann: "It's been quite an eventful day in Washington. A terrorist scare in the midst of the Memorial Day weekend here in the nation's capital. It brought a chill to my spine. For a moment, it seemed like January 6 redux. Fortunately, that's not looking like it's the case. What can you tell us about what transpired earlier today?"

Lowenstein: "First and foremost, we can rest easy knowing that there is no threat of any sort posed to residents of the District of Columbia or people enjoying the Memorial Day weekend. It's worth repeating, given all we've been through these days. I want to repeat that, Tom. No imminent threat exists."

Sadness creeped over Lowenstein's face. The wound to his psyche caused by the January 6 rioters remained open and bleeding. And the security measures implemented afterwards — including construction of a barbed wire fence around the perimeter of the Capitol, referred to as the "Green Zone" as though it was a secure area in Kabul or Baghdad — broke his heart and made him yearn for the good ole days when such barriers did not exist.

Mann: "I can see it in your face, Senator. I'm sure viewers can as well. It's been a tough six months."

Lowenstein just shook his head. Mann thought he saw the elder statesman wipe a tear from an eye beneath his glasses.

Mann: "Do you have any specific intel that you can share with us to put everyone's mind at ease?"

Lowenstein: "I've been briefed throughout the day in my capacity as chairman of the Intelligence Committee. Of course, some of the information shared with me is secret and I can't disclose it. But much of the information about today's events is unclassified and has been disclosed by the media. Based upon the information available to the general public, we know the following.

First, there was a report of some kind of disruptive activity planned to take place at Lafayette Square. That plan never materialized.

"Second, there was an explosion at the GreyStone Hotel. The investigation is ongoing. There is no link to terrorism. In fact, preliminary findings point to construction materials left behind by a crew refurbishing the ninth floor.

"Third, a train was stopped over the Potomac River headed in the vicinity of Capitol Hill. There were no explosives on that train and reports to the contrary have proven to be wrong. In fact, the train incident was being closely monitored by law enforcement and an effort is currently underway to apprehend Hugh Spates, who is also being sought in connection with a fatal shooting that occurred in Northern Virginia at Four Mile Run.

"Fourth, and finally, there was an explosion at Roaches Run. A national security expert named Phil Landry reportedly died, although no positive identification has been made and some of the circumstances surrounding the incident are still being evaluated by investigators."

Mann: "Was there a connection between the train incident and the explosion at Roaches Run?"

Lowenstein: "There very well may be, Tom. As you've reported, both events may have been coordinated by Landry and Hugh Spates.

I'm embarrassed to say I knew both of them, and once considered Landry a personal friend."

Mann: "We all make mistakes from time to time in judging others, senator. I know you've always tried to see the good in others. It's a hallmark of your personality as one of our nation's leaders. No one should think the less of you because you once trusted Phil Landry."

Lowenstein: "That's kind of you to say, Tom, and it means a great deal to me hearing that from someone of your caliber. You're a Pulitzer Prize-winning journalist with impeccable credentials. A lot of people in this town and around the country trust your judgment. As for Landry, I would only add that, in addition to being deceptive and conniving, he was one of the most, if not *the* most, manipulative people with whom I've ever been associated. He betrayed my trust and the trust of our entire national security community."

Mann: "I'm hearing rumors about some of Landry's other criminal dealings."

Lowenstein: "Phil Landry was a monster."

Mann: "Did you say mobster?"

Lowenstein: "No, I said monster, but I might just as well have said mobster. He was a thug who preyed on the innocent and caused nothing but pain and misery to many, many people."

Mann: "If you've just joined us, I'm Thomas Mann and this is *Mann-Up Newsmaker Sunday Night*. Our guest this evening is Abraham Lowenstein, chair of the powerful Senate Intelligence Committee, who's sharing with us some of the inside information about today's terrorist-related events and the men behind the chaos. We'll be right back. Stay with us."

The screen showed a logo of Mann's show while new age music played in the background.

"We're off-line," Mann said. Although their age differential was stark — Lowenstein was hitting 70 while Mann was in his early 40s — they both understood the ways of Washington. They were unabashed in slinging mud at their enemies and throwing accolades to their friends, as evidenced by the ongoing interview.

"I appreciate your fitting me into the program on short notice," Lowenstein said.

"No problem," Mann replied. Mann's scheduled guest for tonight's program was a retired military leader who had resigned in disgrace from a prior administration and was trying to reestablish his reputation in Washington. He was bumped as a favor to the senator. As between the chair of the Senate Intel Committee and a guy trying to remake his career, the man with the power won every time. "When we come back live, I'd like to delve more into Landry," Mann said.

"Fine with me."

"In fact, have you heard about Landry allegedly assaulting a young woman in a parking garage six years ago?"

"That's news to me."

Mann wasn't surprised by the response. The first he'd heard of it was when he opened the envelope that Page delivered to him. In addition to being shocked by the report's findings, he felt partially responsible for the whole thing.

"Are you aware that Landry was investigated years ago for fabricating convictions in Alexandria Circuit Court?" Mann asked.

"Vaguely," Lowenstein answered. "I asked Landry about it. He assured me it was a false accusation leveled by people who wanted him removed from the department. And his version was confirmed by DOJ, which exonerated him from any culpability."

"What about the woman who initially raised questions about Landry's activities? Are you familiar with her? Do you know what happened to her a couple of years after the Pena Inquiry ended?"

"Don't know anything about any of that."

"A woman by the name of Ruth Hammond was badly assaulted in a parking garage in Crystal City. She never recovered from the attack. Suffered permanent brain injury and is confined to a wheelchair to this day."

"So horrible," Lowenstein said.

The conversation ceased. The producer said the show was about to resume. "And we're live in five. Four. Three. Two. One."

Mann: "We're back with Senator Abraham Lowenstein, chairman of the Senate Intelligence Committee, discussing today's events and the men responsible for the chaos that has engulfed the nation's capital. One of those men was Phil Landry, a disgraced national security official who has been the cause of controversy for years. And now we're learning that Landry may have been responsible for a brutal assault that occurred in Virginia. It's a cold case. No one was ever charged with the crime and it remains unsolved to this day. The details are still being assembled, but let me share with listeners the facts as they've been relayed to me." He opened a folder and removed a document with notes and highlights he had made earlier in the evening.

"The victim's name was Ruth Hammond. She was a whistleblower who exposed Phil Landry for pressuring penny-ante criminals into pleading to felony offenses in Alexandria Circuit Court. In other words, she exposed him for sending innocent people to jail. This was when he worked for the Alexandria Police. The allegations were investigated in an effort known to people who followed the story as the Pena Inquiry, after the man who headed it, Fernando Pena. Landry was exonerated of any wrongdoing. But, as I've already written on my blog, in my tweets, and in the *Chronicle* online, Landry never should have been acquitted of his misdeeds. I bear partial responsibility for that terrible miscarriage of justice because I was fooled by Landry into writing a series of articles that raised questions about Pena. Those articles turned the tide against Pena. I won a Pulitzer for my reporting. But if ever there was an instance where an award was undeserved and should be returned, it was that award.

"According to information that I have in my possession, Landry visited the building where the assault occurred a few hours before it happened. He left after the assault occurred. Based upon surveillance records and deductive reasoning, a forensic analysis concluded that Landry committed the crime. The forensic analysis has never been made public, until tonight. Tomorrow, I'll be writing about this newly uncovered evidence in *The Chronicle*. I hope to redeem myself for my own faulty reporting in the past, and I hope you'll join me in my quest to get to the truth about the role of Phil Landry in manipulating the criminal justice system, assaulting a whistleblower, and, this past weekend, spreading fear and panic through the city before killing himself."

Lowenstein sat silently during Mann's exposé. He had expected the show to serve as his opportunity to disassociate himself from Landry. But that was not Mann's intention. Mann was using Lowenstein as a prop to begin a discussion about Landry's involvement in a brutal assault, employing the studio at times as his own confessional.

**

WITHIN MINUTES, Arlington County officials contacted the police department to dig up the old records about Hammond's assault. Much of it had been converted digitally. A few scraps of paper remained, held together by rubber bands that disintegrated when they were touched and by paper clips that had rusted and left imprints on the faded paper. Everything needed to be reexamined.

Mo Katz listened to the show. He had only a vague recollection of the Hammond case. Yet it resonated in his mind. It was important, he felt.

**

MANN: "Okay. Let's go online for some reactions and comments. Hello, you're on *Mann Up: Newsmaker Sunday Night* with Thomas Mann and Senator Abe Lowenstein. What's your comment?"

A third frame appeared on the screen beside the images of Mann and Lowenstein. There was no face depicted on the screen; the caller had chosen not to turn on the video.

Caller: "My comment is that Phil Landry was the spark behind the plan to blow up a train near the U.S. Capitol yesterday. Hugh Spates is being reported as the one who basically planned the attack. I know Spates and I don't think he had the guts to do it alone. The mastermind behind it had to be Landry."

Mann: "My thinking exactly. What's your name, caller?"

Caller: "My name isn't important and if it's alright with you I'd just as soon not provide it on-air. What is important is I worked with Hugh Spates on Capitol Hill after 9/11 writing the Terrorism Risk Insurance Act. At the time, I joked about someone buying real estate near a potential terrorist target to cash in financially if an attack ever took place. Everyone thought it was funny at the time. Apparently, Spates didn't."

Mann: "Any comment, senator?"

Lowenstein: "From everything we're learning, it's entirely possible that Spates and Landry were acting in unison. Of course, we'll know for certain once Spates is apprehended, which is only a matter of time."

Mann: "Thank you, caller. Let's go to our next call. Hello, you're on the air with Thomas Mann and Abe Lowenstein. This is *Mann Up: Sunday Night Newsmaker*."

The message line was instantly flooded. Phil Landry was suddenly complicit for everything that had gone bad in the past five years. Someone even mentioned he might have had something to do with the novel coronavirus.

**

RUTH HAMMOND turned off the laptop and wheeled herself into the foyer. She saw the luggage on the wooden floor. She spun around. She was sad, but hardly surprised. Although he hadn't said anything, she sensed he would be departing. She reminded herself to be grateful. After all, he'd been with her two weeks. *Two whole weeks.*

Hammond moved her wheelchair into the living room. She pulled the plaid blanket tighter around her knees and thighs. How she missed an active life. All of the things that others took for granted had been robbed from her. The ability to walk, for starters. The ability to speak in coherent sentences. And the basic dignity of being able to care for herself, to take showers, stretch her limbs, perform day-to-day tasks.

She never complained. How could she? After all, she knew she was in danger the moment she became a whistleblower. Yet it did not deter her. She always suspected Phil Landry. Based on the program she just heard, he had been the one who attacked her. She wondered about the origin of the report that Mann mentioned, and whether Ari had anything to do with it.

So it was Landry lurking in the shadows behind a pillar in the parking garage, leaping out, grabbing her, throwing her to the ground, and stomping on her body and head until she was unconscious. He must have assumed she was dead. And she would had died if there had not been another late-night worker who found her. She sometimes wondered whether she would have been better off dead.

Hammond wheeled herself to a window and looked out at the black night. She closed her paper-thin eyelids and felt the void.

"Tomorrow."

She started.

Ari's hand fell on her shoulder. "I'm leaving tomorrow. I'm returning to Paris. When I return, I plan to stay with you indefinitely." His fingers applied pressure to her frail, bony shoulder.

Hammond recalled the news item she'd heard earlier in the day. *Phil Landry's dead. Blown to pieces and burnt like a piece of trash.*

"I know," Ari said softly. "Finally, closure."

Hammond put her hand on top of her brother's, her fingertips resting on his knuckles. It felt as though she had slid her hand inside of a glove. It was a knight's glove, protective and comforting.

"He got what he deserved," Ari said. "What he had coming."

And his reputation is destroyed along with the rest of him. That's the most important part, to me. He destroyed everyone associated with the allegations leveled against him. Allegations which were true! It's only right that his reputation as a "disgraced" and… Oh, what was that other word that I heard or read? No matter. It's enough that his epitaph reminds the public that he was a monster, like they were just saying on that program.

Ari got behind her and took control of the wheelchair, pushing it into the kitchen. "Let's make you some tea," he said. "And I got a couple of pieces of chocolate cake. Let's celebrate."

PART THREE
Monday, May 31

Chapter Ten: The Rhythmic Cycle of Life

Three Turns Around and Taking Notes

Before I go further, it is time for you to complete your cycle. Stop reading and get started! I want you to complete the three-cycle history of your life. If you have not completed three cycles, chart your life to this point in time. If you have lived more than three cycles – four, even five – than do a thorough examination of your entire life's experiences. We cannot proceed further until you have done that.

Use the diagram below.

Year 1, 12, 24 and 36

Years 9, 21, 33   Years 3, 15, 27

Years 6, 18, 30

It should take you several hours or days, perhaps even weeks, to complete the chart. Be painfully honest. Don't neglect memories. Put everything down. If you find something in the second or third cycle that is unique, stop and think how it connects to previous events. Your successes, moods, failures, luck, drive, misfortunes, adventures, conformity, confidence. They are all tied together. They are circular. They have come and gone over a twelve-year period just like the cycles of the moon over a one-month period. Or the sun over a twenty-four hour period. Everything going round and round, following a path charted by some invisible hand, controlling your destiny.

One more thing. While you're doing this, look around. Listen to the news. Read articles and reports. You will begin to discover the twelve-year cycle everywhere. In the lives of public figures. Movie stars. Relationships.

Begin looking, and you will find it everywhere.

Inserting Free Will into the Equation.

One of the great attributes that we humans possess is the ability to evaluate past behavior. I don't know whether we are unique in that regard, or whether it exists elsewhere in the animal kingdom. It does not matter. The important thing is that we possess it.

The other thing we have in spades is free will. The ability to do, or not do, a particular thing. We can choose to accept or reject a job. To pursue or discard a lover. To accept hard times or walk away from them. To build something by ourselves, or with a mate, or within a community, or all three.

That free will also enables us to repeat actions, or to consciously avoid them. Combined with our capacity to evaluate our past behavior, we can chart a course in life that avoids past mistakes or magnifies past successes. We can duplicate or triplicate our past experiences, and we can also avoid repeating them. We can chart a new course. A different course. A better course.

In effect, you can create your own destiny. You can put in motion a sequence of actions that go beyond your own behavior. You can change the course of events. You. And I am going to show you how to do it.

We are now at the point where we know the cycle of our own life. We know our rhythm. We can look behind and we can look ahead. We know where the high notes are going to be, as well as the low notes.

So what are we going to do about it? There are several options. One is to do nothing. Another is to actively work to accentuate the high notes and eliminate the low ones. And the third option is to take a radical approach. Demolish the past! Build the new future!

I have tried all three of these options. And I have concluded the smartest of the three choices is the third option. Let me explain.

There are certainly times when we should avoid action. After all, action and inaction are equally potent forces. Indeed, attaining wisdom is knowing when it is sensible to act, to react, or just stand in place.

When is it appropriate to do nothing? I would answer by saying it is appropriate to do nothing when you know you are in store for better times or when you know that the bad times ahead are not strong enough to topple you, or might even open the door to a favorable outcome. You know this from experience, from the rhythm of your life. If you agree with me that your life is a series of cycles, then you have the foresight to know when it is in your own best interest to just hang in there.

But sometimes you have to act, even if that means breaking rules. Be bold. Right the wrongs of the past.

I believe that cycles define our lives. I believe in free will. But I also believe in fate. If this sounds contradictory, I suppose it is. Life is complex. Life is also simple. So maybe contradiction abounds in our lives. Or maybe it does not. I have no answer to these things. Philosophers have debated these points for centuries. All of this leads me back to my initial point: Take the aggressive, assertive, active route. Radically alter your life. Take a course of action that allows you to heighten benefits and minimize problems without losing your sense of self. Do not be afraid to love. If need be, do not be afraid to kill.

Chapter Eleven: Morning

I pledge allegiance to the Flag of the United States of America, and to the Republic for which it stands, one Nation, under God, indivisible, with liberty and justice for all.

IN 1868, U.S. Gen. John A. Logan designated a day to decorate the graves of Civil War soldiers. It was called Decoration Day. "If other eyes grow dull, other hands slack, and other hearts cold in the solemn trust, ours shall keep it well as long as the light and warmth of life remain in us," Logan wrote in General Order No. 11. Since passage of the National Holiday Act of 1971, Memorial Day has been celebrated on the last Monday in May.

On this Memorial Day, in Washington, sparse crowds gathered on the Mall, at the World War II Memorial, and the Vietnam War Memorial. Others went to Arlington National Cemetery to see field upon field of white gravestones accentuated by lush green grass, each with an American flag planted next to it, the result of loving acts of labor by families and volunteers. And at cemeteries around the country, flags were planted at graves commemorating the veterans of war.

Throughout the holiday weekend, tributes were made to those who died in war. Mixed in with those statements were expressions of thanks to those who died in another kind of combat, namely fighting to care for the victims of COVID-19. Doctors, nurses, and hospital workers all received praise. Also among those recognized were men and women who worked throughout the pandemic to feed the nation, including farmers, truckers, and grocery store workers.

Finally, emphasis was placed upon patriotism. Photos and videos of the U.S. flag used as a battering ram to breach the U.S. Capitol had left a searing image in the minds of Americans. Peaceful dissent was one thing, but January 6 had crossed the line into the unimaginable and the unacceptable. Everywhere, people paid humble allegiance to the fact that liberty was a precious commodity, easily extinguished by a violent mob.

**

KATZ ASKED Santana and Lin to join him in his office. If his request interfered with Lin's schedule for her two-year old, she didn't say anything. She and Santana both knew Katz would not be calling a meeting on a holiday unless it was important. Something was brewing.

"I'm not sure where to begin," Katz said, "but I have very serious reservations about whether Phil Landry was inside that van at Roaches Run."

"I tend to agree," said Santana. "I can't understand why Landry would panic and kill himself. He's talked his way out of worse situations in the past."

Lin was never one to subscribe to herd mentality. Yet, in this instance, she also agreed with Katz's analysis. "I haven't seen any evidence against Landry that suggests he had to kill himself to avoid prosecution," she said. "There was a dust-up about H-Pack backpacks down at Lafayette Square, but that turned out to be a bust. And we all know that there's no truth to the media stories linking Landry and Spates."

"Spates was under intense scrutiny for weeks," Santana reminded the others. "If he had been dealing with Landry, it would have come to our attention." He paused. "Which reminds me," he resumed. "There are some interesting developments in the murder of the other accomplice, Morley. They found gunpowder residue around the wound, leading to speculation that a gun discharged inadvertently during a tussle."

"No surprise there," Katz said. "It's been my surmise all along. Spates flashed a gun and Morley tried to grab it, or vice versa. Either way, they fell to the ground and scuffled. The gun went off and a bullet lodged in Morley's skull."

"Hey," Lin interjected, "maybe it was Spates inside the van." Katz and Santana reacted with cautious surprise. "I mean, he hasn't been found yet, has he?"

"Nah, that's too crazy," Santana said.

"Has the body at Roaches Run been ID'd yet?" Katz asked.

"No, it was blown to shit, so it'll take time," Santana said.

"Just enough time for Landry to slip away across the border," Lin said. "A diversionary tactic. Wouldn't that be a hoot?"

Katz thought for a minute, then said, "That might not be so crazy. I might have seen Landry yesterday at Gravelly Point. I had a sense something wasn't right when I arrived at Roaches Run, so I went to higher ground at the aquatic center," Katz explained. "From there, I had a panoramic view from the river to the waterfowl sanctuary. I saw a guy in a hoodie with binoculars and a laptop. It could have been Landry."

"Have you told Stone?" asked Santana.

"I mentioned it to her that afternoon. We haven't had much of an opportunity to connect since then."

"She's working on her own theory of the case," Lin said. She exchanged a glance with Santana. This had become standard operating procedure between Katz and Stone. Whether it was the case at Jones Point or Slaters Lane, they each pursued their own theory of a case and then joined forces when the moment was right. "It is curious that no one actually saw Landry inside the van," Santana said. "In fact, no one actually spoke to him. All of the communications were done by text."

"There's something else," Katz said. "Landry knew that Stone was positioning a pair of agents at Roaches Run, but he never moved the van. I think it's odd. I can't believe it didn't occur to him."

Santana guffawed, but added: "I'll inquire about the ID of the vic."

Katz turned to Lin. "I read there were books confiscated from some of the H-Pack backpacks. Is that true?"

"Yeah, it's what's been reported."

"Why would someone be carting around books during a holiday weekend in D.C.?" Katz asked. "Could a backpack filled with books be used as a prop to simulate something else, like a bomb? I mean, it's heavy and bulky. Can you see what you can learn about the people who were carrying those particular backpacks?

"It's just a hunch, but maybe the people carrying those books were the ones Landry enlisted. If we look into it a little deeper, we might be able to figure out their identities. Maybe some of the books were taken from a library, or maybe there's an inscription on some of them. And it's not unusual for people to leave photos, letters, or other papers inside of books, sometimes as book markers or keepsakes. Maybe it's a dead end, but I'd like to do it."

"Whatever," Lin shrugged. "I just think it's a waste of time. Sherry told me there wasn't sufficient reason to hold those people."

"When did she say that?"

"When I called her yesterday. After you asked me to reach her."

"This whole thing is more than a little puzzling," Katz said. "I'd like us to poke around a little and see if we can figure things out, that's all. I'm going to drive down to Roaches Run and take another look."

**

KATZ RETRACED his steps.

He drove along the parkway north of Old Town and pulled into the parking area at Gravelly Point. A few television trucks remained, their antennas pointed to the sky as though tracking alien spaceships. As he got out of his car, he glanced across the Potomac at the arrow-shaped Washington Monument, pointing, like the hand of a clock, at twelve o'clock.

The lot was scattered with empty vehicles belonging to the joggers, strollers, and bicyclists who used the path along the river. A small crowd was also there to watch the bellies of the commercial airliners that flew overhead before they touched down on the tarmac, their engines roaring as thick tires hit the runway.

A plane was making its descent. Katz glanced up. He then glanced at the bluff where he'd stood yesterday. Had he seen Landry here or had it been someone else?

He looked around for clues, but found none. In truth, he didn't know what he was seeking. He simply hoped that being here would trigger something in his mind about the case. But that didn't happen.

He returned to his car, took the ramp onto I-395 south, stayed to the right and swooped down the ramp to the southbound lanes of the parkway.

A quarter of a mile later, he turned into Roaches Run. The entrance was cordoned off in yellow tape. Two officers stood in front of the tape. Katz pulled up to the apron and flashed his badge. He lowered his window. "How's it going?"

"All good, sir," replied the officer. "They're still collecting material strewn about the scene. That cloudburst yesterday slowed everything down." The other officer raised the tape and pointed for Katz to park along the perimeter.

Katz parked and headed over to the burned-out hulk of the van. The explosion decimated the inside of the vehicle. The windows and doors were blown out, the metal frame was distorted, and a portion of the roof was gone. He watched a forensic team sift through debris. A large map of Roaches Run posted at the site indicated the location of all of the items recovered from the van. According to the map, a cell phone was recovered about 20 yards from the wreckage.

Katz circled Roaches Run three times. Familiarize yourself with a crime scene and you'll see things that you might otherwise miss. Santana told him that. As he walked around, Katz noticed that security was porous. He also realized that the phone was a significant distance from the van.

He went to his car and retrieved his tablet. He then sat in a chair under a blue tent near the van. Katz tapped on the search engine. He started pulling threads. Mann's interview with Lowenstein was on his mind, particularly the allegations linking Landry to the assault of Ruth Hammond.

Katz found it odd that the story surfaced at this point in time. Was it coincidence? He initiated his search by keying in the name Ruth Hammond. To his surprise, the first article that appeared featured the author Henry David McLuhan.

Author Addresses Convention in Baltimore

https://McLuhan>author>disability>donation

April 1, 2015 — Renowned author Henry David McLuhan announced today that he donated all of the profits from his best-selling self-help book to a Virginia-based charity, "Restore Our Dignity."

The charity was created by the family of Ruth Hammond, the victim of a brutal unsolved assault that occurred in Crystal City in 2013.

Hammond, 30, suffered permanent brain damage after she was repeatedly kicked in the head in a parking garage of an office building in Arlington County.

McLuhan is the author of the wildly successful "The Rhythmic Cycle of Life," which has been on the bestseller list for over three years. It joins "The Road Less Traveled" as one of the most popular self-help books of all time.

The premise of "Rhythmic Cycle" is that life repeats itself and that people can identify and prevent destructive behaviors from reoccurring, sometimes by taking bold action to prevent cycles from repeating themselves.

There was no photo of McLuhan, but there was one of Hammond. Katz studied the image. It looked familiar. He continued his search.

Charity Created to Honor Victims of Abuse

https://disability>donation>Hammond>RestoreOurDignity.org

May 17, 2014 — The family of Ruth Hammond has created a $1 million charitable organization, "Restore Our Dignity," to assist the victims of physical and sexual abuse.

Hammond was the victim of a brutal unsolved assault that occurred last year in Arlington County.

"We honor the valiant efforts of women and men who are victimized by predators," announced the family in a statement.

"These victims are often left with permanent physical and mental health injuries, and we must assist them to live productive lives after their growth and development has been stunted by abuse," according to the family statement.

In Hammond's case, her attacker stomped her face, head, and body with multiple, forceful blows, resulting in permanent injuries to her legs, shoulders, and brain.

Brutal Assault Goes Cold in Arlington County

https://crime>assault>Hammond>CrystalCity

March 4, 2014 — It has been six months since Ruth Hammond was discovered in the garage of her Crystal City office building lying face down in a heap of blood with a fractured skull, broken limbs, and bruised skin.

"We've exhausted all leads," the Arlington County Police Department announced today at a press conference suspending its investigation.

"We continue to ask the public to assist us in solving this hideous crime," said the department's spokesman. "A predator is stalking our streets, and our community will not be safe until that individual is identified and brought to justice."

According to the police, the attack appeared to be random and undertaken without any advance planning.

"She was simply the wrong person in the wrong place at the wrong time," said one investigator.

Crime Report: Woman Attacked in Crystal City Garage

https://crime>assault>Hammond

October 7, 2013 — Ruth Hammond, a graduate school research assistant, was savagely beaten last night in a parking garage of an office building on Crystal Drive in Arlington.

Hammond, 28, was reportedly going to her car around 8 p.m. when she was attacked and robbed.

Her purse and wallet were missing, along with her car keys, according to police.

She sustained multiple injuries, including a fractured skull, broken wrist, knee, and ribs, and facial injuries.

Hammond was transported by helicopter to Johns Hopkins Medical Center in Baltimore because of possible brain injuries sustained in the beating, according to police.

"Something like this just doesn't happen in Crystal City," said a resident of an adjacent building. Crystal City is a composite of retail, commercial, and residential offices sandwiched between Pentagon City and Potomac Yard.

Whistleblower Case Collapses
By Tom Mann, chief investigative reporter © Chronicle

https://Hammond>investigation>whistleblower

May 11, 2011 — A highly-publicized investigation into alleged wrongdoings by Phil Landry, an Alexandria detective, has collapsed, according to informed sources.

A lead Justice Department official has been removed from the case and a letter of apology has been issued by the department to Landry, indicating the case was without merit, according to two individuals who have seen the letter.

"It's rare to see a case take a 180-degree corrective action," said one DOJ official, who spoke on the condition of anonymity given the sensitive nature of the investigation.

The person who filed the whistleblower complaint against Landry that started the investigation has been identified as Ruth Hammond.

Whistleblower Alleges Fraudulent Plea Bargains
By Tom Mann, metropolitan desk © Chronicle

https://investigation>whistleblower>Alexandria>Landry

January 14, 2011 — Phil Landry, a decorated Alexandria police detective, is under investigation for falsifying information provided to the Alexandria Circuit Court in order to close felony cases.

The U.S. Department of Justice has launched an inquiry into several of Landry's cases following allegations by a whistleblower that Landry perpetrated a fraud upon the court in obtaining several criminal convictions.

Fernando Pena is reportedly heading the DOJ inquiry.

To ensure the safety of the whistleblower, that individual's name has not been made public.

Katz grabbed his phone and called Santana. "That investigation ten years ago into Landry fixing cases," he said. "It got started because of an article by a researcher. Do you know what I'm talking about?"

"Of course," Santana replied. "I'll never forget it," Santana replied. "Her name was Ruth Hammond."

"Did you listen to Tom Mann's radio show last night?"

"No. I heard about it though. He linked her attack to Landry, from what I heard. I've got to listen to the podcast later today."

"Do you remember how her name was made public?" Katz asked. "According to some stories I just looked at, her name was not disclosed when the investigation started. By the time it fell apart, however, her name was all over the place. How did that happen?"

Santana fell silent. "Where are you?" he asked.

"Roaches Run."

"I'll meet you in your office in thirty minutes."

**

SANTANA AND KATZ sat opposite one another at the conference table in the U.S. Attorney's office. The door was closed. A milky sun shone through the windows, bathing the office in a warm glow. Santana looked out the window as he spoke. "Landry was racking up big wins in Circuit Court based upon flimsy evidence. At the time, people said the convictions looked sketchy."

"I remember that," Katz frowned. "I'd just left the Commonwealth Attorney's Office and gone into private practice. In fact, I represented Stone after Landry filed a complaint against her."

"Landry filed it in retaliation for Stone looking under rocks to dig up stuff about his conviction rate," Santana said.

"So I'm learning."

"She didn't tell you at the time?"

"Stone was a mess back then, Curtis. She held most things private. She wanted to beat the rap and stay on the force. I didn't spend much time thinking about Landry's motivation. My job was finding a technicality to beat the rap."

"Makes sense," Santana said.

"So tell me about Ruth Hammond. Who was she?"

"Hammond was a graduate student at one of the local colleges," Santana said. "She interviewed a guy named Trey Carr as part of some criminal justice reform project. He told her that he was pressured into pleading guilty because Landry had the goods on his nephew, a kid named Suleiman.

"Her research came to the attention of Freddy Pena, a veteran auditor at DOJ. He launched an inquiry. For a while, it looked like Pena had uncovered a major case of malfeasance.

"As the investigation heated up, things fell apart. I don't know how Landry did it, but he poked holes into Pena's work and discredited him. *The Chronicle* ran a devastating series on Pena, basically calling him a fraud."

"I remember that," Katz said. "The spotlight turned on Pena. He wilted."

"I always thought it was a tragedy. I knew Pena. He was a good man, did good work. People respected him. I always suspected Landry was somehow pulling strings behind the curtain, considering how the whole thing went down."

"But what about Hammond?" asked Katz. "How did her name get in the public domain?"

"*The Chronicle* exposed her," Santana said, running a thumb and index finger over the corners of his open mouth.

Santana, who had been looking out the window all this time, turned and looked at Katz. It was evident that the case still bothered him. "The way I see it, Mo, Landry fed false information to *The Chronicle* about both Pena and Hammond and the newspaper never fact-checked its own story." Santana stopped abruptly.

"And?"

"I always harbored a suspicion that the attack on Hammond was connected to the investigation. Not that I was pointing the finger at Landry. But I always thought there was more to it."

"I appreciate your candor, Curtis," Katz said. "Ever since the explosion at Roaches Run, I can't put aside the feeling that something isn't matching up. I was there, on the ground. It just didn't feel like all the pieces fit together."

"Yeah, sorry about not closing that loop, I'm still waiting to hear back from the coroner," Santana said, recalling he'd promised Katz that he would confirm the identity of the victim.

The sun slid behind clouds and the milky glow that permeated the office disappeared. A dull, dark tone replaced it. The room grew cool.

Katz glanced at his phone. There was a news update.

BREAKING NEWS
This is a developing story
Tom Mann, City Editor © The Chronicle

Arlington police have reopened an investigation into the facts and circumstances surrounding a near-fatal assault that occurred in Crystal City ten years ago.

As information about the case came to light last night, Arlington police immediately launched an inquiry into the cold case.

On the evening of October 6, 2013, Ruth Hammond was brutally attacked in a parking garage in Crystal City. She was rushed to Johns Hopkins Medical Center, where she staged a miraculous recovery.

Today, Hammond is confined to a wheelchair. She is the chairwoman of "Restore Our Dignity," a nonprofit organization that helps victims of brutal assault.

In 2011, Hammond did research for a graduate school project about possible irregularities in criminal plea agreements in Alexandria Circuit Court. As a result of her work, an official investigation was launched by the Department of Justice under the leadership of Fernando Pena. The investigation was discredited and discontinued, in part because of stories that appeared in *The Chronicle*.

Those stories were based upon false and misleading information supplied to the paper by Phil Landry, the subject of the investigation.

According to newly discovered evidence, Landry is the prime suspect in the assault on Hammond.

The evidence is included in a privately commissioned report conducted by Page Investigative Services for Hammond's family. *The Chronicle* obtained a copy of the report yesterday.

Landry died yesterday, the victim of his own suicide bombing at Roaches Run. At the time of the explosion, Landry was under investigation for conspiring to conduct a train bombing in Washington, D.C.

"No one is going to be surprised if it's determined that Landry assaulted Hammond," said one veteran law enforcement officer, who asked to remain anonymous because the investigation is ongoing. "He was rotten to the core and had been for years," the source said.

Katz immediately called Stone, but she didn't answer.

Four Years Ago

MANN SCORED a television interview with Abe Lowenstein about the discovery of a body in the water off Daingerfield Island. His coverage of that story restored his reputation and credibility with the public and within the Washington press corps. He earned an Emmy for outstanding local reporting.

The Chronicle, now an online paper, hired him back. He promised he'd play it straight from this point forward. He would study every story idea that crossed his desk with a healthy degree of skepticism. *With one exception.* The exception was if an opportunity arose for him to avenge himself for the lies and deceit perpetrated by Landry.

Chapter Twelve: Afternoon

KATZ BELIEVED that the custodian of records was an important position. That person catalogued evidence and stored case files and, in so doing, learned things about a case. For that reason, he developed a relationship with Joey Cook dating back to his days as a city prosecutor and as a criminal defense attorney. Cook, the custodian of the Alexandria Police Department's property room, never disappointed.

"I hear the evidence collected at Roaches Run is being stored in Alexandria," Katz said.

"I can confirm that to be the case," Cook replied in an official-sounding tone. Roaches Run was on federal land in Arlington County. Other things being equal, the evidence should have been transported to Arlington. "Requested by her high excellency, the Honorable Sherry Stone."

"She carries a lot of weight," Katz said.

"She's in charge of the task force, and it encompasses both jurisdictions," Cook replied. "I suppose that's the explanation. I don't think people like her, but they follow her instructions. Everyone can see the writing on the wall. She's a poster child for the police department and she's going to go places in law enforcement."

Cook spoke contemptuously of Stone, whom he'd known since her rookie days. He didn't hold it against Katz for salvaging her career, but that was because he admired Katz's courtroom machinations and not because he believed Stone's misconduct deserved leniency. Despite the fact that she was an exemplary officer today, Cook resented that she stayed on the force.

"That may be," Katz said mildly. "Well, I thought you might know if a cell phone was turned in as evidence."

"Sure was," Cook replied. "Except there was something strange about it." He waited until Katz inquired further — a rough equivalent of *pretty please* — before providing more information.

"Landry's phone was not turned in when most of the other evidence was, including the computer stuff. It turned up today. When I asked about it, I was told it must have been overlooked." Cook cleared his throat. "Your inquiry about it only confirms my suspicion. I think someone hacked into it before turning it in. Makes sense, you know. It's a pain to get the phone manufacturers to help you crack a phone. I figure someone tried to get into it right away, see what was inside."

"Maybe," Katz said. "Who turned it in?"

"Uniform," Cook replied. "It's banged up pretty bad, looks like it was retrieved from a war zone, which, when you stop to think about it, it was."

"When's it going to the lab?"

"First thing Tuesday morning. Why? You interested in looking at it?"

"Nope."

"Well, I'll let you know if I learn anything that raises suspicion about the whereabouts of that phone," Cook said.

"Thanks, Joey," Katz hung up. Katz believed the phone had been placed at the scene during the night. Given the lax nature of security at Roaches Run, it was easy to do, and that supported his view that the party communicating with Stone was outside of the van.

Until now, Katz believed that Landry faked his own death. A new theory was rattling around inside his head. To test it, he needed to know the identities of the people who carried those backpacks filled with books. He wondered if Lin was having any success.

**

"WHAT DO you mean, you don't have them?" Mai Lin asked, incredulous. "Didn't you put anything into evidence?" It took her over a dozen phone calls and emails to track down the official in charge of collecting evidence from yesterday's incident at Metro stations. As it turned out, everybody and nobody was in charge. There was no coordination and, a day later, no one took responsibility for anything.

Twenty people carrying H-Pack backpacks had been stopped around Lafayette Square and Black Lives Matter Plaza. Based on the information assembled by Lin, no single policy was applied. Some people were stopped at the stations and then released, while others were taken to district stations and then released. No one was booked, so there were no photos or fingerprints of anyone, and there were no signed statements. Some of the individuals provided names and addresses, but no one verified their identity and there was no guarantee the names that they gave were their real names.

There was a partial list of the individuals stopped by police floating around somewhere.

Furthermore, none of the items in the H-Pack backpacks were retained by the police for further examination. Everything had been returned or thrown away.

"There's no evidence because there's no crime," an irate investigator replied to Lin. "There is nothing to show you. Zilch. Nada. Nothing." He stretched out his hands and opened his palms. "These people are *very* unlike the mob that desecrated the Capitol. This crew was just walking around with backpacks. They didn't desecrate anything."

"But what if we want to examine the items in the bags?"

"You're — out of luck." He paused between *you're* and *out*. Lin was pretty sure she knew the word he intended to insert. "Anything left behind was either thrown out or donated, you know, like a jacket being sent to a homeless shelter. That sort of thing."

"You should have held onto their belongings," she said.

"What for? They didn't do anything. Those people shouldn't have even been stopped, according to some of our attorneys. We'll be lucky if they don't sue us for wrongful arrest or malicious prosecution."

Lin showed her exasperation. "It can't be wrongful arrest if there wasn't any," she said pointedly. "And it can't be prosecuted if no crime was charged."

"Don't get technical with me, lady. You know what I mean."

Lin shook her head. "I don't believe it. You receive a warning that people may be carrying bombs in H-Pack backpacks to Lafayette Square and you just let everyone go. How can we follow up leads if we're unsure of names and don't have the evidence?"

"Follow up what leads? What evidence? What are you talking about?"

Lin should have stopped quarreling, but she went over the official's head to his supervisor, and over the supervisor's head to a deputy police chief. That's when Katz got a call.

"You better come over and collect your research assistant," he was advised. "She's driving us crazy. She's going to be in the lockup before the day is over if she's not careful. She doesn't seem to know the meaning of the phrase 'outside of your jurisdiction'."

Katz made a few quick calls to defuse the situation.

"This is B.S.," Lin said angrily when she spoke to Katz a few minutes later. "I mean, these people actually threw away or donated evidence." A thought popped into her head. "Got to go," she said and hung up.

**

RATHER THAN throw away the books confiscated at one of the police substations, someone contacted a bookstore to see if they were interested in them. An employee came over and picked them up. The books were now at a used bookstore near Dupont Circle.

The books were in a box in the back of the store. Lin sat on the floor going through them. She looked for inscriptions from owners or authors, or labels from libraries or bookstores. She shook the pages of each book to free any photos or notes stuck between pages.

She had no luck at all until she opened the last book. It was a copy of the new edition of *The Rhythmic Cycle of Life*. Inside the front cover was an inscription that read:

F — We have come full circle. May this merit the redemption you long desired — Ari

Not knowing whether to attach any significance to the note, Lin called Katz, who didn't answer.

Then she called Stone.

"I'm not sure how that's going to help us," Stone said. "There's no correlation between Landry's plan and some person walking around the city with a bunch of books. You shouldn't have even bothered with the follow-up. It's a waste of time."

"If you say so," Lin said, feeling dejected. "I'm going to let Mo know anyway. He might feel otherwise."

"Don't waste his time," Stone instructed. "Mo's got more important things on his mind. I'd just forget about this one."

"Hmmm, well, ok," Lin replied. After she hung up, she sat and thought a minute. Then she took a couple of photos. She attached the photos to a text to Katz.

**

STONE WALKED along the brick sidewalk leading to her townhouse. God had thrown her a curveball. Here she was, a law enforcement officer sworn to uphold the law. She thought back to when Katz defended her in that cocaine case. She was a rookie cop who didn't fit in and was beset with a host of personal and professional issues. Life was complicated.

When Katz took her case, his sole concern was finding a credible defense to beat the rap. He didn't care whether she was guilty of a crime. In truth, she was guilty as sin. Not only was she using coke, but she was using it on the job. Her judgment was marred. And though no one ever found out, she had been compromised in another way: Her drug supplier blackmailed her into overlooking criminal activity that came to her attention.

Many thought she deserved to be fired, convicted, and run out of town. She knew some people on the police force despised her to this day, and she honestly couldn't blame them. She knew she'd made some grievous errors in judgment. But Mo Katz, defense attorney extraordinaire, did not judge her. He discovered procedural errors in the case that saved her. The case was dismissed. The file was expunged. It was a complete vindication, on paper.

She remembered something Katz said to her during the case: "In this business, the guilty occasionally go free and the innocent sometimes end up in jail. But the scales of justice balance out in the end. If you're truly a bad person undeserving of a break, you will eventually go down. It's just how it works. So it's on you, Stoner. If you do okay from this point forward, all is forgiven if not forgotten. If you don't fly straight, you'll go down and no one is going to be able to save you."

Her phone rang. She knew who was calling. She slipped a large leather purse off her shoulder and dug for the phone. Sure enough. She let it ring and go to voicemail. "Hi, this is Sherry. I'm busy, so leave a message. I'll catch you later."

No message was left.

A follow-up call ensued.

Stone dropped the phone into her purse and slung the bag over her shoulder. The phone jangled; the caller had left a message this time. She stopped, pulled out the phone, and went to messages. "Stoner, it's Mo. Give me a call. Thanks."

She clutched the phone in her hand. A breeze swept around the corner and wrapped around her. She stood straight and squared her shoulders against the wind. They had to talk, except she didn't want to do it on the phone. A phone call left a record and she wanted nothing that could suggest they had colluded with one another. If her hunch was right, they had to cover their tracks.

**

KATZ HELD his phone, trying to will Stone into answering his call. Another call came in. "Katz," he said angrily.

"Was it something I said?" asked a rough voice on the other end.

Katz recognized the raspy voice as that of the medical examiner,

Rodney Brown. Irascible and blunt, Brown looked pretty much the way he sounded — old, wrinkled, and stooped. He was also a chain smoker, the only person Katz knew who still smoked a pack a day. To call Brown a dying breed was no exaggeration.

"Sorry if I sounded a little frustrated, Rod," Katz apologized. "Nothing to do with you."

He'd known Brown as long as he had been an attorney, first as a prosecutor and later as a defense attorney. The time of death, the angle of a bullet, and the existence of gunpowder burns on a victim's skin were all factors that contributed to understanding what actually happened in a case and proved critical in informing juries whether a charge was valid or bogus. Brown was good at his job and his expertise was essential in building a case.

"Curtis called about Landry," Brown said. The coroner pronounced *Landry* in a derisive tone. "I never trusted or cared for the man," he added without a prompt.

"You don't have to explain yourself to me."

"I know I don't, Mo, and I know I'm not supposed to speak ill of the dead, but Landry was an evil son of a bitch. He put a lot of innocent people through hell. I'm glad he got what was coming to him." He coughed. It sounded to Katz as though he was sucking on a cigarette. "I only wish it had come sooner.

"Anyway, that's neither here nor there," Brown continued. "I'm calling because Santana wanted to know whether we had a positive ID on the victim of the explosion at Roaches Run." He lowered his voice. "I was a little surprised at the request, to tell you the truth."

"I asked him to check it out," Katz explained.

"That's what he told me. Why? I mean, was there ever any doubt?"

"You tell me."

"It's Landry all right," Brown replied gruffly. "Fingerprints and dental records are a match. Positive ID by his sister earlier today, so far as you can identify a charcoal briquette. She drove down from

Philly. If he treated his family the way he treated others, she was probably relieved."

"Thanks," Katz said. "I appreciate it." He scratched his chin.

"There was one thing, though," Brown said, coughing again. "At first blush, I actually didn't see it myself."

"What is it?" Katz asked.

"Marks, Mo," Brown said in a conspiratorial voice. "Marks on his neck."

"So?"

"So, nothing. The cause of death was the explosion. His body was torn apart and burnt to a crisp, for the most part."

"But you said there were marks."

Katz could hear Brown suck on the cancer stick again before he continued. "I know what I said."

Katz sustained convictions as a prosecutor and won acquittals as a defense attorney on the strength of Brown's testimony. One word from Rodney Brown could change the entire complexion of a case, from the time of the murder to the circumstances surrounding it. Trying to hide his impatience, he asked carefully, "So, what were the marks like?

"Like strangulation."

Katz could hear a match strike on the other end of the phone. "Can you confirm time of death?" he asked.

"Death occurring instantaneously at the time of the explosion, according to my report."

Katz remained silent, thinking.

"Listen, Mo," Brown said. "I didn't mention the marks in my report." He took a deep drag. "What's the point, you know?"

Katz understood the logic of not wanting to look under any rocks. Landry was dead and his reputation was in tatters. Perhaps it was best to just leave well enough alone.

"Are you still there?" Brown asked after a long silence.

"Yeah, I'm still here," Katz said. "Have you shared this

information with anyone else?"

"Only Stoner. I know she'll hold it confidential."

"OK. I'll do the same. Good to talk to you, Rod. I'll tell Curtis you called."

"I'll call him myself, if you don't mind," Brown said crustily. "I want to confirm for him that it was Landry and that there's nothing more to it."

"Okay."

"And I'm not going to recollect part of this conversation after I hang up the phone."

"Understood."

Brown hung up.

But Katz was definitely not going to forget the conversation. Everything was spinning around him. A veteran coroner was breaking the rules. A trusted friend in the police department was not returning his calls. His research assistant had even hung up on him. Katz thought it odd that, even in death, Landry seemed to influence the way people played the game. He had done so much harm to so many people over such a long time that everyone was willing to break the rules if it meant he burned in hell or at least in the memory of everyone who knew him.

Then he realized it was May 31 and remembered the significance of the day. He left the office, got in his car, and drove to D.C.

**

"SHERRY STONE!"

Snowe opened the front door. Stone stepped inside. The foyer spilled into the living room, where Katie was seated on a couch reading a book. The girl glanced up at the tall policewoman. "This is Katie Fortune, the daughter of Tony Fortune, Mo's old client, and..." For an instant, Snowe could not remember the mother's last name. "...Moriarty."

Am I subconsciously trying to erase the woman's memory already?

"How are you, sweetie?" Stone asked.

"Fine," Katie smiled and returned to the book spread open on the couch.

The two women moved to the kitchen. Snowe popped coffee capsules into the machine on the counter and made a couple of espressos.

"I called the other day," Snowe said. They sat at the island in the center of the kitchen.

"I know. Sorry I didn't get back in touch with you earlier. It's been crazy busy. I've had a hard time keeping up with everything."

"How's it going?"

"Not much to do, from my end. Roaches Run is being inspected with a fine-tooth comb now that I've taken control of the situation and placed the investigation under the task force. We'll collect and catalogue everything, but it's not a crime scene, so there isn't very much I have to do. As for what happened in the District, I don't really have anything to do with that. I'm not sure how the hotel bombing is going to turn out, but at least there wasn't any terrorist-related street incident."

Stone seemed uncharacteristically calm and low-key to Snowe, who expected the policewoman to be more animated in describing events. Snowe took note of the fact that Stone had wrestled control of the case from Arlington County, where Roaches Run was located. The fact that the sanctuary was on federal property made the power grab seem less obvious, Snowe thought.

"Sounds like everything's turning out okay."

"Yeah. No innocent people got hurt and Landry went up in a ball of hellfire."

They laughed. "I didn't mean it that way," Snowe said.

"It's okay. I did."

"Listen, the reason I called you," Snowe lowered her voice, "I'm trying to get my bearings on this whole thing with Katie."

"What whole thing?"

"I'm interested in seeking some kind of guardianship, depending on how everything turns out. I want to be sure I'm not using my professional position to get an inside track."

"And you're asking my advice?"

"Mo trusts you. He says you're pretty well grounded when it comes to doing the right thing. A lot better grounded than some of the others on the force."

"Mo said that about me?"

"You look surprised."

"Well, yes and no. We go back a ways, as you probably know. He was my defense attorney once upon a time. He got me out of a jam when I deserved to be severely punished."

"That's old history, Sherry. Mo always talks about the scales of justice balancing out in the end. If people get a break, it's on them as to whether it keeps."

"Believe me, I've heard the gospel according to Mo."

"Well, if you deserved worse than you got, it would have found a way of catching up with you. But it hasn't. You've been a stellar member of the force. Which takes me back to my point. Mo trusts you. So do I. I'm seeking your opinion on whether I'm crossing a line."

Stone searched for words. "I can't really answer that question for you," she said. "You need to consult your ethics office. But, for what it's worth, I don't see a conflict. You're not abusing your position. You're simply trying to help a child. *No harm, no foul*, in my book."

They finished their espressos in silence.

"By the way," Stone said, "I was hoping Mo would be home. I haven't been able to return his calls. Will you tell him I dropped by?"

**

THE PRIEST expressed surprise at seeing the U.S. Attorney kneeling in a pew. The interior of the church was dark. The only light came through the stained glass windows that adorned each side of the chapel and from the candles lit in front of the altar. "I haven't seen you since the funeral for Tony Fortune four years ago, come November."

"I don't go to church," Katz replied. "Or temple."

The priest stroked his full gray beard. His protuberant eyes were watery and bloodshot. He plopped his rotund body in the pew beside Katz. The wooden bench sagged with his weight. "You don't have to come here to find God." He tilted his head. "So long as you pay homage to Him, it doesn't much matter where you do it."

"I suppose that's true," Katz nodded.

"What brings you here?"

"Today's Tony Fortune's birthday," Katz said

"Is that so?" The priest smiled. He remembered Fortune and the many close brushes with the law that he shared in the confessional.

"Yeah, May 31. The first time I represented him it was in connection with an incident that occurred on his birthday." Katz didn't elaborate but he remembered the facts. Fortune blew a tire on the 14th Street Bridge returning to Virginia from D.C. A cop stopped to help and found a brick of coke in the trunk, a birthday present from a good friend. Katz got the case dismissed because it wasn't Fortune's car. "His funeral was here, so I thought I'd drop by and say a prayer."

"Good of you to do that," the priest said. "It's funny that you stopped by this afternoon. I had a dream the other night and you were in it."

"No kidding. About what?"

"I wish I could remember. Dreams are weird. You sort of remember them, but not really."

"You know, I had a dream about Tony the day he was murdered in Georgetown back in '17. I was in a hospital bed recovering from getting wounded. It was so real I thought he was actually there."

"It was tragic, Tony getting shot and all. You worked out a nice settlement for Maggie. Look what she did with all that money. It can't make you feel good."

"It makes me feel terrible." Never in Katz's wildest dreams did he think the money would be used to facilitate a drug habit. Now Moriarty's life was in tatters, and her daughter essentially had no family. "My girlfriend's trying to help Maggie and Katie now. It makes me feel like we're trying to make amends."

"You're not to blame," said the priest.

"I appreciate your words, but it doesn't really change the way I feel," Katz confided. "I got her the money and, instead of being a springboard to a better life, it started her on a downward spiral.

"I should have anticipated she might be overwhelmed with the settlement. I should have come up with some kind of game plan to teach her how to make the best use of it. I feel as though I failed all of them, Tony, Maggie, and Katie. I wish we had a chance to try to get everything back on an even keel."

"Maybe you'll have that opportunity. As I'm wont to say, it's in God's hands."

The priest left. Katz stayed in the pew silently eulogizing Fortune. He lit a candle before he left.

**

OUTSIDE THE CHURCH, Katz walked down a cobblestone path to the gated entrance as he scrolled through emails and text messages on his phone. Birds were rustling in the bushes along a chain-link fence. He opened an email from Lin. Then he clicked on the attachment. It was a photo of the inscription on the inside cover of *The Rhythmic Cycle of Life*. It read:

F — We have come full circle. May this merit the redemption you long desired — Ari

He reread the inscription. For an instant, he stopped breathing. When he finally inhaled, he did so slowly, filling his lungs with cool evening air and exhaling through his nostrils. His mind focused on the salutation and the signature: "F" and "Ari." He recalled his earlier conversation with Santana. There were still some pieces that didn't fit into the puzzle, but he possessed two key ingredients: identity and motive. Thanks to Lin's legwork, he now knew the identity of Landry's killer.

Chapter Thirteen: Evening

HUGH SPATES emerged with a backpack and took the elevator to the basement of his apartment building. A minute later, his car ascended from the underground parking garage and bounced onto the street. The headlights pierced the night as he swung to the left.

He heard on television that he'd been the target of a federal investigation for several weeks. People he had enlisted — Morley and the train conductor — were working against him all the time. He was angry, humiliated, and scared. His phone was probably tapped, and both Morley and the train conductor were probably wired for some of their conversations, he concluded. He hoped there was no wire on Morley at the time of the shooting.

He picked up the interstate at New York Avenue, drove across the river into Virginia, and exited on southbound Route 1. He had left his phone at the apartment for fear he would be traced. He turned on the radio. There was wall-to-wall coverage about the explosions at the GreyStone Hotel, about a man who plunged to his death on the trestle bridge, and about the van exploding at Roaches Run.

"What a fucking disaster," he sighed.

As he crossed the intersection of Route 1 and Gunston Cove Road, he saw lights in the rearview mirror. A cruiser had activated its emergency equipment. He pulled to the shoulder, which was adjacent an industrial area populated by a junk yard and huge outdoor parking area for RVs and boats. Spates bit his lip. He put on his mask. He had considered renting a car, but decided against it. He was a fool to think he could avoid law enforcement simply by driving in the dead of night. After all, there was probably an APB out for his arrest.

"What's the problem, officer?" he asked, lowering the window on the driver's side as the officer approached. The officer had not sat in his cruiser to check the license and registration, which told Spates he was dealing with a rookie who had noticed something about the car and was likely to cut him a break. Thank goodness for the new world of community policing, he thought.

"Did you know you've got a rear light out?" the officer asked.

"You're kidding," Spates laughed. "I just got the car inspected in April."

"I'm going to issue you a citation, but if you get it fixed before the court date the case will be dismissed. You can send the information to the clerk's office and you won't have to appear in court."

"Listen," Spates said. "I don't want to get on the interstate and drive if a light's burned out. The safest thing for me to do is get it fixed right now. I noticed a service station at the intersection back there. If it's okay with you, I'll turn around and get it fixed now."

"I doubt there's a repairman working tonight," said the officer.

"I'll check," Spates said. "If they can't take care of it, I'll postpone my trip until the morning. I want to be safe, both for myself and others."

The officer considered what to do. Part of him wanted to just let the guy go based on the promise to fix the light and stay off the road until it was repaired. But there was something that bothered him about this guy, who seemed to be too accommodating. The officer reached for his flashlight and shined it inside the car. The light illuminated an orange H-Pack backpack in the back seat.

Is this the guy they're looking for in connection with the incident on the rail line? Is he armed? Did he play any role in that murder the other night?

"License and registration, sir," said the officer, trying to sound nonchalant.

"What's going on?" Spates acted surprised.

"I just want to make sure there aren't any outstanding warrants before I let you go," the officer explained.

Spates fidgeted for his wallet. He pulled out his license and handed it to the officer. Then he reached over to open the glove compartment for his registration.

The officer recoiled. *If he's armed, he could be reaching for his gun.* "Sir, please put down your hands and exit the vehicle," the officer said.

At that, Spates quickly shifted the car into drive and floored the accelerator pedal, pulling the car off the apron and back onto Route 1. He tore off his mask, filled with saliva and sweat.

The officer drew his service revolver. Even though there was no traffic, he did not shoot. Instead, he called for backup. "A suspect is driving south on Route 1 at a high speed," he reported. "The suspect had an H-Pack backpack in his vehicle and may be connected to this weekend's activities. The suspect may be armed and dangerous. Repeat, the suspect may be armed and dangerous."

The car sped down Route 1 toward the ramp onto I-95 at the Occoquan River, the dividing line between Fairfax and Prince William counties. The officer's report was broadcast to both police departments, as well as the Virginia State Police.

How did things get so messed up? I wasn't involved in anything with Phil Landry. I don't even know Landry. And the incident with Morley? That was a mistake. Morley was more responsible for his death than I was. I only wanted to collect on an insurance policy for damage to property.

This stretch of Route 1 was unfamiliar to him. According to the signs, he should stay in the right lane to continue on Route 1 and in the left lane for I-95. He hesitated. Then he floored it, racing across a flyover. Below and to his right, Spates saw traffic backed up as the car careened forward, banked left, and began its descent.

Spates expected a police blockade. To his amazement, there was none. The backup was caused by a tractor trailer blocking the right lane up ahead. He hugged the jersey wall as he crossed the Occoquan River and veered to the far left lane. Ahead was nothing but open road. He adjusted the rearview mirror. Only light traffic behind him.

Spates checked the gas tank, which was full, and then shifted back into the right lane to exit onto the Prince William Parkway.

Dusk fell, providing cover as Spates made his getaway. If he stayed on side roads all night, who knew where he would end up? If he cut back across the interstate below Norfolk and followed the coast, he might be able to disappear along the Carolina shore.

For an instant, everything seemed manageable. Was it too much to hope for things to return to normal? Perhaps. But now, as night folded around him, Spates believed there might be a path out of the madness.

**

KATZ SAT in his office reviewing the articles he had Googled earlier in the day. He tried to make sense of everything based upon the new information he had learned from Lin's email attachment.

Reese appeared at the door. "Got a minute?"

Katz nodded for him to enter.

"So, I had my first jury trial, aggravated assault, with a woman who struck her ex-boyfriend's car and claimed sexual assault as her defense. Well, it turns out there was another part to the story. I heard it earlier today from a nurse at the Alexandria Hospital."

Katz's eyes opened wider.

"According to the nurse, that woman previously sought medical attention on several occasions. Her ex-boyfriend beat her up pretty bad on a regular basis. Last fall, for example, she was three months pregnant and suffered a miscarriage after a particularly violent beating."

"The nurse told you all that?"

"Yeah. I'm not sure whether she was breaking a privilege of confidentiality, but I guess she felt it was important for me to know about it. I did the math. The woman rammed her car into her ex-boyfriend's on what probably would have been her due date." Reese paused. "None of that came out during the trial, but she somehow managed to channel that grief to the jury. I missed it. I was so fixated on winning a conviction that I never even thought there might be some underlying motivation for her action."

"That's a compelling story. There are some lessons in it."

Reese sat down.

"One is to trust a jury," Katz said. "They don't always get it right, and sometimes they infuriate you by the things they take into consideration, or discount, in reaching a verdict. But their instincts and collective wisdom are powerful and you have to trust them to do the right thing the vast majority of the time.

"Another is that justice has a funny way of revealing itself. We don't always see it clearly. Sometimes it hides. But justice always settles scores. Sometimes it plays a role in a criminal case and other times it just weaves its way through our lives without leaving any trace. But justice won't be denied."

"*Justice delayed is justice denied,*" Reese said. "That's what's written outside the federal courthouse next door."

"I don't know if the meaning of the words over the courthouse door are apropos to what I'm trying to communicate."

"Maybe not," Reese said. "I guess those words stand for the proposition that justice should be swiftly meted out to the guilty. What you're saying is that, sooner or later, justice prevails."

"Exactly, David."

"You did that as a prosecutor, didn't you? Made sure that people paid the price for stepping outside the lines, I mean."

Katz leaned back in his chair. "It's what I did as a prosecutor and it's why I left the prosecutor's office." He hesitated before he continued. "Putting people in jail is easy. All you have to do is show the elements of a crime. The harder part is excusing someone's behavior because they're avenging themselves for a past injustice. Look at that woman in your case. As a prosecutor, you sought a prison term because the action she took constituted a crime. But a jury chose to forgive her. You yourself said they saw things you didn't."

"Yeah."

"So that's the hard part. Seeing the whole picture."

"When you were in defense practice, that's what you did, wasn't it? Tried to make people see the whole picture? Maybe try to get them to overlook something or see extenuating circumstances?"

"That's right."

"Do you miss that?"

Katz sat up in his chair. "Do I miss what?"

"Do you miss making that judgment? Trying to show the underlying motivation and making exception for it?"

"I'm still doing it, David. It's called prosecutorial discretion. It has to do with deciding what's worth prosecuting and what's not. Some things deserve to be overlooked." Looking at Reese, Katz saw himself about twenty years earlier stepping onto the legal stage as a hotshot Alexandria prosecutor. He thought then that he knew it all. If he'd learned anything during the years, it was that he still had more to learn today. "Time for you to go home," he said. "Give my regards to Mai and give your son an extra hug. And tell her thanks for emailing me that inscription earlier today. It was very helpful."

"Sure thing, Mo," Reese replied, standing up.

"Knowing what you know now, would you have acquitted her if you'd been on the jury?" Katz asked.

"Maybe," Reese said. "Probably. Yes, I would have."

After Reese left, Katz made a couple of quick calls and then headed to Dulles International Airport.

**

SNOWE TUCKED a blanket around Katie. "I like it here, Miss Abby," the little girl said, looking at her with trusting eyes.

"Don't you miss your mommy?" Snowe asked.

Katie shook her head. "She left me. I was scared a lot of times. Sometimes they were mean to me. They yelled a lot."

Snowe hugged her and said, "No one is going to hurt you or leave you alone tonight."

"I want to stay here," Katie said. "Can you take care of me?" Again, she gave Abby that trusting look.

Snowe's eyes welled with tears. The thought of becoming a mother to Katie overwhelmed her. "I don't know, Katie," she said. "I don't think so, not permanently. We'll see."

After she put Katie to bed, Snowe went downstairs. The house was quiet. The only sounds were those that houses make when they think they're unoccupied, when the soul of the structure sends out the music of the spirits that inhabit it.

Snowe sat in the living room, engulfed in darkness. If some voyeur saw her, he would have been reminded of the mysterious woman in the burgundy dress in Edward Hopper's "Western Motel" painting.

Her mind wandered. Two days ago, she contemplated breaking up with Katz. Now everything was transformed. She walked to the kitchen, found her phone, and called Katz. No answer. She called a second time. This time he picked up. "What's going on?" she inquired. "I thought you'd be home."

"I'm heading to Dulles," he said.

"We have an angel in our home," she said. "Child Protective Services asked if we could keep Katie until they locate her mom."

"Wow." Katz was driving the inner loop of the beltway. He turned down the music on the radio. He signaled left to exit to the Dulles Access Road. White lines and guardrail markers reflected as his headlights swept across the highway. Miles Davis played softly in the background.

"Wow is right," she laughed. "A big wow! What do you think?"

"I think, yes, it's wonderful. Maybe Maggie is going to need some help with her daughter, and maybe we can help her on an ongoing basis."

"I know this is going to sound crazy, but I feel our lives have been touched by grace," Snowe said. "I mean, this isn't permanent, and I'm not trying to get ahead of myself, but maybe we'll be able to play a role, you know, like you said."

"Yeah."

"You sound preoccupied. What else are you thinking?"

"I'm thinking about Tony, for one thing. Today would have been his birthday. I stopped at the church where they held his funeral. It brought back a lot of memories."

Katz maintained a steady speed as he drove along the access road with the hypnotic lights of the highway and vehicles — the white headlights of oncoming traffic and the red taillights of cars ahead of him.

"When will you be back home?" she asked.

He glanced at the dashboard clock. "A couple of hours. I have to close out something."

"I'll be up when you get back." Then she remembered. "By the way, Sherry Stone dropped by earlier. She said to tell you she's trying to get in touch with you."

Katz smiled. "Okay," he said. "Thanks. Love you."

Recent Tweet from #TheChronicle

Join Tom Mann Tuesday night for an online chat with the author of *The Rhythmic Cycle of Life*, Henry David McLuhan. It's *Mann Up/ Newsmakers Tuesday Night*. On-air, online, on point, and right on!

**

SPATES FELT GOOD. He had stopped along the road, opened the trunk, thrown the backpack in, and banged the tail light with his fist. The light came on. Assuming the APB mentioned a burned-out rear light, he would escape detection. And if the officer failed to write down his license plate number or the make and model of his car — and he was pretty sure that was the case — there was no way to identify him.

He had crossed I-95 about fifteen minutes ago. He failed to continue in a southerly direction, however, and ended up on the

Northern Neck between the Potomac and Rappahannock Rivers, hardly surprising given the fact that he had no GPS and was unfamiliar with the roads. He approached a smattering of houses and commercial establishments. The speed limit dropped from 45 to 25. Before he had time to react, red and blue lights appeared in his rearview mirror.

He took a deep breath. The rear light was operating. The H-Pack backpack was in the trunk. All he had to do was talk his way out of a ticket. He hit the brakes, signaled right, and pulled over to the curb. The cruiser sped past him. Spates issued a sigh of relief. *That was close.*

A half mile later, he understood why. As he made a turn, he saw a roadblock up ahead. There were over a dozen cruisers. Their emergency equipment was in full display, with lights streaking across the sky. State troopers and local police lined the curbs and stood behind their vehicles, several holding rifles and sidearm revolvers.

He knew he didn't stand a chance. As his foot applied pressure to the accelerator, the first bullets broke through the windshield. Spates felt a series of stings to his face and torso. He pulled a hand from the steering wheel and swatted the air, as though he could redirect bullets like flies. Glass flew in all directions and blood splattered against the windshield and front dashboard.

BREAKING NEWS
This is a developing story
9 PM
By Tom Mann © Chronicle News

Hugh Spates, a D.C. lobbyist believed to have collaborated with disgraced antiterrorist officer Phil Landry in a terror campaign unleashed on the nation's capital this weekend, was shot and killed tonight attempting to elude police at a roadblock in Virginia's Northern Neck.

Preliminary reports indicate that Spates was stopped in southeastern

Fairfax County early this evening. He drove away at a high rate of speed, but not before the arresting officer noted his license plate number and the make and model of his vehicle.

An all-points bulletin was issued after Spates fled the scene.

At approximately 8:30 p.m., Spates was spotted near Coles Point about two hours from Washington at the tip of the Northern Neck as he approached a police roadblock.

According to two eyewitnesses, he disregarded the barricades and drove his vehicle toward police cruisers and the officers positioned at the barricade.

"It's always unfortunate when a fugitive forces law enforcement to react this way, but we had no choice," said a state police spokeswoman. "We had to protect the lives and safety of our fellow officers."

Spates had been under police surveillance for several weeks in connection with a scheme to set up bombs along the rail line near the U.S. Capitol to collect insurance money. He is believed to have been assisted in that plan by Phil Landry, a disgraced federal security official who blew himself up on Sunday at Roaches Run after unsuccessfully trying to carry out a scare campaign in D.C. Landry may have also been responsible for an explosion at the GreyStone Hotel on Sunday morning.

Landry has been identified by Arlington police as the perpetrator of a heinous assault against a woman named Ruth Hammond nearly twelve years ago. Hammond accused Landry of pressuring criminal defendants into pleading guilty to offenses that they did not commit. The charges were dismissed after Landry mounted an intense public relations campaign to discredit Fernando Pena, who headed the inquiry into his misdeeds. Now it appears that Landry did in fact pressure criminal defendants in order to earn himself a higher solved-case rate.

After Mann completed the story, he called Wilson and asked if he could possibly see those files again. He was not surprised to hear that Stone had lodged a similar request yesterday. Wilson told Mann he was welcome to drop over to her place and look at them.

**

CARS ROLLED along the parallel lanes of the toll road. Ahead, cars cruised to the airport to pick up or drop off passengers. Overhead, a plane roared its ascent, aerial lights flashing. K a t z passed a Metro station. *'Round About Midnight* was playing in the car. The airport terminal came into view. It resembled either a huge fireplace grate or the ribcage of a prehistoric animal, Katz thought. He knew he didn't like it nearly as much as Eero Saarinen's original design, which was like a jewel box before it doubled in size and lost its elegance.

He could have phoned airport security and reserved a space in front of the terminal. Instead, he decided to be inconspicuous and parked at a satellite lot. He walked to the airport. The jazz rhythm stayed with him as he approached the sliding glass doors and stepped inside the terminal. He put on his facial mask. The ticket counter in front of him was deserted. Nobody was lined up to check in. The kiosks stood on the floor like an artistic display in a museum that no one was visiting. No suitcases or luggage cluttered the baggage drop area.

A television screen in the concourse caught Katz's eye. A reporter was standing in front of a number of police cruisers, their emergency equipment pulsating in red and blue in the black night. The banner at the bottom of the screen announced that Spates had been killed.

Katz listened, and then walked over to the departure board and scanned the schedule of late night flights. He found the one he sought and headed for the gate. At the entrance to the sterile area, he flashed his badge and the security officer waved him through. He rode elevators and trains through the labyrinth of the airport to his destination.

Henry David McLuhan was seated in a faux leather chair near

the gate scheduled for the overseas flight. He was reading something on his phone. Everyone in the terminal wore masks, but with his distinctive silver locks McLuhan was easy to spot. At first, McLuhan took no notice of Katz standing next to him. Finally, he raised his head. His eyes met Katz's. "Are you also flying to Paris?" he asked.

Katz smiled. The seating area was half filled with people whose eyes were glued to electronic devices. A few watched the television monitors. Some stood anxiously near the gate with their carry-on luggage, impatient to board. "Can we talk somewhere a little less public?" Katz asked.

McLuhan shrugged. "Why? This is fine." He gestured to Katz to sit in the empty seat beside him.

"Let's take a walk," Katz insisted.

McLuhan noticed Katz was holding a copy of *The Rhythmic Cycle of Life* tilted toward him so that he could see it. Grudgingly, McLuhan got up, tucked his phone into a pocket, and grabbed the handle of his carry-on. Katz led the way to a high-top table in front of a deserted eatery closed for the night.

"Can you explain this to me?" Katz asked. He opened the book to the inside page and placed it on the table in front of McLuhan.

F — We have come full circle. May this merit the redemption you long desired — Ari

McLuhan looked at it and said nothing.

"You wrote that," Katz said. "You're Ari Hammond."

McLuhan bent forward ever so slightly. "That's right. You must have gotten an advance copy of my taping of Tom Mann's show tomorrow night. I come out, so to speak."

Katz flipped to the dedication page, which read: To RH. "You dedicated your book to your sister, Ruth Hammond," Katz said.

"Yes, of course. She's my twin sister. I'm devoted to her. Most of the earnings of my book go to her foundation. I've never made a secret of that."

"That's not true," Katz said. "You've never really acknowledged it, at least not until now. Why are you going public now, Ari? What's changed? Why is it okay to show the world that Ari Hammond and Henry David McLuhan are the same person?"

Nine Years Ago

Ruth Hammond always parked in the same place even though there were no assigned spaces. It was force of habit, like sitting in the same seat in a conference room. The parking space was on the lower level of the underground garage, in the corner furthest from the staircase and the elevator. She parked there in case work got so crazy that she had no time to get outside to walk to lunch or to go to the gym. She used every opportunity to maximize her steps, taking the staircase and walking the furthest possible distance in the garage.

She went down two flights of stairs, opened a heavy steel door, passed by the bank of elevators, opened another steel door, and walked down a handicapped ramp. The garage was deserted. Her car waited a football field away in the far corner.

The place was dark. Her heels clicked on the cement floor. Ceiling lights flashed on overhead as she approached, lighting the area immediately around her. Cement columns stood like trees in a petrified forest.

She preferred working late at night. There were fewer distractions: no phone calls, fewer emails, and fewer interruptions from other staff members usually asking stupid questions and wasting valuable time. Ruth knew that women were assaulted in garages. She was on guard. She remembered a story about a guy who stood beside the open hood of a car as a woman walked by. He asked for help. An instant later, she was being pulled behind the car. Ruth couldn't remember if the woman was raped before she was murdered.

She held tight to her purse strap, ready to fling the hefty bag at anyone who might approach her. In her other hand, she held her car key like a knife, ready to rip it across the face of any would-be assailant. In the distance, tires screeched as a car turned toward the ramp leading up to the street.

Ruth got to her car. She opened the passenger side door. She placed the purse on the seat.

She heard nothing. No footsteps or screeching tires. She saw nothing. No overhead lights turned on. No shadows were discernible. As a result, she had no time to react when her assailant charged, throwing one arm around her head and covering her mouth tightly with a gloved hand while the other arm slammed her against the car.

The next thing she knew she was spun around and struck twice in the mouth. Then several sharp blows landed on her stomach. She fell forward, gasping. A knee struck her forehead. She fell backwards, seeing stars. Her nose was bleeding. She was shoved roughly into the passenger seat on top of her purse.

Duct tape was wrapped around her face, forcing her mouth shut and nearly preventing her from breathing. Her eyes bulged and watered. Her nostrils shot out streams of blood. She was slapped across the face. Once, twice, three times. Her lip was bleeding. Her right eye closed. She tried desperately to fend off the assailant, but he grabbed both of her arms. Now a rope was bound around her.

She expected to be thrown to the floorboard and trapped inside the car, or placed inside the trunk. Instead, she was yanked out of the car and thrown to the ground. Then she was kicked, repeatedly. First in the face. Then the pelvis and legs. Finally a boot stomped on her head, crushing her face and fracturing her cheek bones.

"Bitch!"

That was the only word she heard uttered by her assailant. She never saw a face, or a piece of clothing. Then everything went black.

**

"NO ONE really understands what happens when you are victimized," McLuhan said. "No one recovers, not the victim and not her loved ones. It's just hell, forever." He choked up. "She's confined to a wheelchair. She can't speak in coherent sentences. I know she's aware of things, but it's like someone on life support who's hoping you don't pull the plug because they're more aware of their surroundings than you think."

Katz listened intently as he sat on the edge of one of the bar stools.

"It's so pathetic and unforgivable," McLuhan said.

"When did you learn that Landry was responsible for what happened to your sister?" Katz asked.

McLuhan grimaced. "I'm not obligated to talk to you, Mr. Katz. I may appear to be an extrovert, what with my speeches and everything. But I'm a very private person, and I have no desire or interest in sharing my feelings with you."

Katz was undeterred. "I'm actually not interested in your feelings, Ari. I'm just interested in the facts, like when you first learned what Landry intended to do and how you outsmarted him every step of the way."

"It may sound trite, but I really don't know what you're talking about."

"What about the inscription to Federico Pena. Can you explain that?"

McLuhan looked over at the boarding gate. People were forming a line. "It looks like they're getting ready. I must have missed the announcement. I mean, it was easy to be distracted listening to you. Mind if I excuse myself?"

"I do," Katz said. "I'd like an explanation."

A second announcement was made for priority seating to board. They both heard it.

"I have to go."

"That inscription was written the night of your appearance in the tent beside Constitution Hall," Katz said. "Landry didn't die until the following afternoon. What did you mean by coming full circle and about redemption?"

McLuhan turned. "Phil Landry died in an explosion in a van

parked at Roaches Run. I don't think you or anyone else is going to be able to pin that on me. So, unless you have arranged for someone to issue me a warrant tonight, I'm going to head over there and board my flight."

"I don't have enough evidence to arrest you, but I know you're complicit."

McLuhan looked at the gate. Passengers were scanning their boarding passes and going down the jet bridge to the plane. "I really have to excuse myself," he insisted.

Katz raised the book. "Somehow or other, you found out about what Landry was up to, and you subverted his plan. He staged an act, but you managed a play within a play."

McLuhan looked amused. "Goodbye, Mr. Katz." As he walked away, he said, without turning his head, "Don't try to figure it out. You never will."

Six Years Ago

It took three years to assemble the report. The cost was astronomical. But in the spring of 2015, Ari Hammond finally received the results of the private investigation he commissioned about the attack on his sister. The report traced the movements of every person who was in the building on that day. People who worked there, and people who visited. It included thousands of people. People who worked in the building were examined first, and they were all eliminated as suspects. Roscoe Page, who oversaw the report, was not surprised, reasoning that no one would carry out a brutal act in their own backyard for fear they would be considered the most likely suspect.

Next were the people who visited the building for the first time that day. Each of them was also ruled out. Again, no surprise to Page, who felt the perpetrator had to be someone who was familiar with the layout and habits of the victim.

The third and final group were people who visited the building on multiple occasions in the weeks and months preceding the attack. These were patients of doctors and dentists and clients of law firms, consulting companies, and financial planners. The list consisted of ninety people.

Page's forensic team analyzed the activities of each of them. When did they enter? From where? Was it from the front doors or from the staircase or elevators that went to the underground parking garage? How long were they in the building? When did they leave? Did they depart the same way they entered? Using this methodology, eighty-nine people were eliminated. The remaining suspect was Phil Landry.

Landry had visited an estate attorney's office five times over a two-month period preceding the attack. He was in the building during times that would have allowed him to discover Hammond's work habits and parking routine. He always arrived by car late in the day. After he parked in the two-story garage, he always took the staircase to the lobby. When his meeting ended, he always returned to the lobby by elevator and took the staircase down two floors to the garage.

With one exception. On the day of the attack, he walked into the lobby from the street. He signed in at the concierge desk, received a visitor pass, and rode an elevator to the floor where the estate attorney's office was located. At the conclusion of the visit, he rode an elevator down to the lobby and left the visitor pass at the concierge desk. But he didn't leave. Instead, he walked across the lobby and went to the restroom. Then, according to the surveillance camera, he took the staircase to the garage. While there were cameras in the lobby, staircases, and hallways, there were no surveillance cameras in the garage.

Landry was seen on camera going up the staircase shortly after the time of the attack on Hammond. He walked through the lobby and left by the street entrance. It might not have been enough to hold up in court, but Ari Hammond had no intention of sharing the report with the police. This was good enough.

"Someday," Hammond told Page, "I'm going to need you to deliver a sanitized version of this report to the media. It's a ways off, but we will eventually reveal what happened. Just not yet. I have to settle the score. I'll be in touch if I need anything further."

About six years later, Hammond contacted Page in need of another favor. He wanted to hack into Landry's private email account. Another request followed, an even more delicate one. Hammond needed cameras set up in a room at the GreyStone Hotel visited by Landry about once a month. It wasn't for prurient interests, Hammond assured Page. It was strictly business.

Under normal circumstances, Page would have turned down the requests. But he didn't, and Hammond knew why. Page also wanted to see justice done.

**

AS McLUHAN stood in the queue with his boarding pass, Katz walked up behind him. "I'm not sure how you did it," he said in a low voice. "I don't know if you acted alone or if you had accomplices. I think Pena helped, though I don't know how. But I'll tell you one thing: Landry had neck bruises. So I'm guessing he didn't die in the explosion. He was strangled. In fact, I don't think he was alive in the van when Sherry Stone was texting at Roaches Run.

"I think it was you I saw at Gravelly Point the afternoon of the explosion. You were the one emailing Stone. You masterminded the operation."

McLuhan turned to Katz. "All his life, Landry got away with ruthless and horrible things," he said. "He finally got what was coming to him. It took twelve years, but it happened. All that was needed was a few changes in the rhythm of life. Don't spoil it now, Mr. Katz. Justice has been served." McLuhan had reached the front of the line and displayed his boarding pass. Then he was gone through a door and headed down a ramp toward the plane to Paris.

A WOMAN darted across 29th Street between K and M. Cars were parked tightly along the curb, bumper to bumper. Crowds were thin along Georgetown's streets. Lamplights shined down on nearly deserted sidewalks. Trees in open spaces bent their twisted limbs over the urban landscape.

The driver of the car bearing down on her barely had time to react. The driver slammed on the brakes, but that was after impact. The body had already hurtled through the air and landed by the curb, one arm extended onto the brick sidewalk.

The driver stopped, jumped out of her vehicle, and ran to the motionless body. She called 911 and waited for help. Within seconds, the sound of sirens filled the otherwise quiet night.

The accident occurred along a stretch of street that went over the C&O Canal. The spot was about 1,000 feet from where Tony Fortune was gunned down four years earlier.

**

AT BEDTIME, Ruth Hammond told the nurse she wanted to remain in her wheelchair. She was in the living room now, positioned in front of a window. Earlier, she heard a jet fly overhead. She thought of her brother. She knew he had gotten away. Although she was confined in this mobile cage for the rest of her life, they had won. *Well, maybe not won. No one really wins. But the score is at least even.* She closed her eyes.

BREAKING NEWS

The body of the woman hit by a car in Georgetown has been identified as Margaret Moriarty of Alexandria. She was pronounced dead at the scene. The incident has been ruled as accidental. No charges have been filed against the driver, whose name was not released by police. Alcohol is not believed to have been a contributing factor. Moriarty leaves behind one daughter. Her husband, Anthony Fortune, died four years ago a short distance from where the accident occurred.

**

KATZ HEARD the news while driving back from the airport. Tony Fortune had died on the day Katie was born, and Maggie Moriarty died on Fortune's birthday. Moriarty's death touched his life. He wondered if Snowe was awake and heard the news. If so, what was she thinking? He wanted to call and ask but decided to wait and discuss things in person when he got home.

If Snowe wanted to seek custody, he would support her 100 percent. They would do it as a couple, which probably meant getting married. He was prepared to do whatever it took. *For Abby, for Katie, for Tony.* That's the way he looked at it.

His thoughts returned to his encounter with Hammond — or McLuhan, or whoever he was. He felt unsettled and dissatisfied. He was not sure what he hoped to accomplish. But he expected to accomplish *something*.

He was left with the same questions that bothered him when he drove out to Dulles. *What was Hammond's role in Landry's death? Who else was involved? And was there an underlying motivation beyond the attack on Ruth?*

He ran through the weekend's events in chronological order. First, there was the train mishap. It wasn't supposed to go down that way, with some guy falling to his death in the river. One of Stone's people had said if something could go wrong, it would. He was right.

Next was the explosion at the GreyStone. The hole in the wall was analogous to a tear in a pair of jeans. Everyone got up, dusted themselves off, and resumed the game. It was similar to the way people behaved in response to COVID-19 last year. People were resilient. They knew what was needed to get through a crisis and did it. The holiday mood was put on pause. People regrouped, realized there was no imminent crisis, and proceeded as planned.

The third thing that happened was the van blowing up at Roaches Run. It seemed mysterious and odd, and Katz had gone on a wild-goose chase asking if someone other than Landry had been

216

blown to smithereens, which proved to be a colossal waste of time.

Finally, there was the revelation surrounding Ruth Hammond's attack. Landry's legacy was forever tainted for his shenanigans at the Alexandria Courthouse and attacking the woman who exposed his wrongdoing.

It occurred to Katz that, if the threesome enlisted by Landry had succeeded, things would have turned out a whole lot differently. But they didn't and, as a result, they basically disappeared from view and the incident itself was largely forgotten. But suppose those three people — whoever they were — actually took a bomb, or just devices that resembled bombs, to Lafayette Park? Suppose the GreyStone explosion was caused by an incendiary device intended for the park?

Suddenly, Katz remembered something that happened on Saturday night at Constitution Hall. He was sitting in the audience. Hammond had taken a drink of water and said something about shaking things up. *"Redirect your energy and take yourself off the road that previously led to bad destinations. Use today — right now, tonight, in real time — to change the past. You can do it. You can definitely do it."* What had happened in that moment?

As he turned off I-495 for the Old Town exit to his home, Katz detoured to Prince Street. A parking space was open in front of Stone's townhouse. He slid his car into it. Santana, dressed in sweatpants and a T-shirt, opened the door when he knocked.

"Stoner up?"

"She's sleeping, Mo. Do you realize what time it is?"

"No, I don't," Katz said. And he didn't care. Moriarty was dead. As was Spates. Katie was orphaned. Ari Hammond, aka Henry David McLuhan, had departed for Boston. When he added those facts to all the other events of the weekend — Morley's murder, the train caper, H-Pack backpacks carried around in D.C., the GreyStone explosion, and the van's destruction at Roaches Run — he didn't care if he was now disturbing the dead.

Stone appeared at the top of the stairs, wearing a blue robe. "It's okay," she said. "I'm coming down."

"What's this about?" Santana asked.

"Nothing, sweetie," Stone answered, now at the base of the staircase. "Go back to bed." Santana trudged up the stairs, shaking his head.

Once she and Katz were alone, she said, "What's up, Mo?"

"I need to know what happened this weekend. You've been avoiding me all day. Going to my house this afternoon took the cake. You knew I wouldn't be there, or you wouldn't have come over."

"I'm sorry?"

"Oh, c'mon, Stoner. You haven't leveled with me all weekend. You've been hiding information from me. You figured something out and you're keeping it to yourself. I need to know what it is."

"Why don't you come in and sit down."

Katz entered and Stone closed the door. Together they moved to the kitchen, right off the foyer. "I figured out that Ari Hammond and McLuhan are the same person," Katz said. "I drove out to Dulles to confront him, but it really didn't do any good. I don't know any more than I did beforehand."

Stone adjusted her robe more tightly around her. "Do you want some coffee or maybe something stronger? I got decaf and high test, along with about everything you'd find at a liquor store."

"Decaf's fine."

Stone looked disappointed, but began pulling out coffee cups. "When Tommy wrote his first story about Spates and Landry being in cahoots with one another, I knew he had it wrong," she said. "Their operations weren't connected, but I didn't do a thing to correct the story. I wanted Landry to get caught in the middle of a shit storm." She filled the coffee machine reservoir with water, popped in a decaf capsule, and pressed a button. She shuffled barefoot across the tile floor, her toenails polished bright red. She and Katz perched on stools on opposite sides of the kitchen island.

"I hated that man," she said. "It's been ten years, ten years almost to the day, and it still hurts like it was yesterday." She went back to the machine and placed a cup under the dispenser. "Anything bad that anyone could do to him was good in my book. As events began to unfold, it occurred to me that the news story wasn't the only thing that was wrong. A lot more was going on. But I felt the same way about all of it. I just wanted Landry to burn."

May 30, 2011

Sherry Stone and Phil Landry had never met or spoken until that night. It was a Saturday. Stone had driven to the state penitentiary in Mecklenburg County earlier in the day, listening to *Boom Boom Pow* by Black Eyed Peas twenty times on the radio. Her goal was to speak to convicted burglar Trey Carr. Although inconclusive, there was evidence suggesting that Carr was innocent of several residential burglaries for which he had pled guilty. Similar-style break-ins had occurred after Carr's incarceration, leading Stone, who was looking into those B&Es, to question whether the correct suspect had been charged and convicted.

A lone ranger, Stone didn't check with the chain of command before looking into the matter. If she had, Stone might have been told to back off. A federal inquiry was already studying the facts and circumstances surrounding Carr's convictions and the detective who handled the cases, Phil Landry.

Landry had heard that a DOJ policy wonk by the name of Fernando Pena was heading the inquiry. Pena had taken up the investigation based upon a report by a Catholic University graduate school researcher named Ruth Hammond.

Carr played dumb during Stone's interview. The way he looked at it, Stone was either uninformed or gathering information on behalf of Landry. He didn't open up the way he did to Hammond.

Landry assumed Stone was part of the team investigating his police tactics and was acquiring incriminating information about him from Carr. When Stone returned to the station, Landry was waiting.

"Hey, jerk-off," Landry said, getting in Stone's face. "There are two things you remind me of: cocks and coke. From what I hear, you're either sucking or snorting, on and off duty. There's no place in this department for a sissy coke head. Either you leave the force today or I blow the whistle, no pun intended."

Stone recoiled. It was a one-two punch to the gut. Intimidation and threats. "Fuck off," Stone replied, frightened, pushing Landry aside.

"I'm filing a complaint tomorrow if you're not gone," Landry threatened.

"I dare you," Stone said. "There's something wrong with your cases, Landry. You want me out because you're scared I'm going to figure it out."

Landry called Stone's bluff. Forty-eight hours later, he went to internal affairs and reported the rookie cop for drug use. Stone was ordered to take a drug test that night, and the next day she was suspended from the force.

**

THREE SMALL ceiling lights created spotlights over the marble kitchen counters. Stone put a cup of decaf in front of Katz. "Is this really what you want?" she asked.

He looked at the cup. "Maybe something a little stronger," he admitted.

She headed to the liquor cabinet in the dining room. A ceiling fan rotated in the center of the room. The windows stared out at a deep black night.

"You didn't seem surprised when I said Hammond and McLuhan are the same person," Katz said to her from the kitchen. "When did you figure that out?"

"Carr told me." She returned with a bottle of Green Hat gin and a couple of glasses. She filled the glasses with crushed ice and placed them on the kitchen island, pushing the cup of decaf aside. She opened the bottle of gin and splashed a double shot into each glass. "Yesterday, I reviewed a list of some of the individuals who'd been stopped in D.C. for carrying H-Pack backpacks," Stone said as she settled herself on the stool across from Katz. "I recognized two of the names. One was Maria Pena. The other was Ahmed Suleiman. Do either of those names ring a bell?"

"No," Katz said, sipping the gin. "Except Pena is a name I've heard. Federico Pena."

"It's Fernando," she said. "I think Federico Pena is a politician. I'm not sure. Anyways, you made the right connection. Maria is Freddy Pena's daughter. And Suleiman is Trey Carr's nephew." She took a deep gulp of her drink. "Well, actually, his son."

"I'm not following, Stoner. What's that got to do with Hammond?"

"C'mon, Mo. Freddy Pena and Trey Carr were part of the investigation into Landry. Pena headed it and Carr broke the case open with his testimony. Landry despised both of them. At the time, he threatened Carr. And he was a man of his word. We now know he attacked Hammond for finding out about what he was doing. If Landry hadn't been stopped, he would have continued hurting people. I'm sure he would have gone after Vanessa Wilson, the woman who pulled the documents from his computer this weekend."

"I get Freddy Pena and Carr, but those aren't the names of the people you found on the list. You mentioned their children."

"The way I figure it," Stone continued, "Landry decided to extract revenge against Pena and Carr by harming their children." She finished her drink. "That's what this was all about. Landry planned to sacrifice Maria Pena and Ahmed Suleiman. "Imagine, if you can, both of those kids walking down the street with dummy explosives in H-Pack backpacks. Or maybe one of them carrying a real bomb, and it exploding. They would have been killed by Landry's goons waiting at designated Metro stops. Nobody would have been the wiser and nobody would have asked questions."

Katz was beginning to get it. The thought that had occurred to him during the drive from the airport was crystallizing.

"It would have destroyed Freddy, who's never fully recovered from losing his wife, and devastated Trey, who's having his own issues fresh out of the penitentiary," she added.

Katz finished his gin. He refilled his glass. He looked over at Stone. She waved off his offer. "When did you meet with Carr?" he asked.

"After I saw the list, I interviewed Maria Pena. Then I called Trey."

"Why didn't you tell me, Stoner?"

"Mo, you make it sound like I figured everything out in an instant. That's not how it worked."

Katz got up from his stool and placed his hands on the counter, leaning toward Stone. "That's bullshit. You avoided me. You were uncovering clues and putting together the pieces and you didn't even have the courtesy of telling me about it."

"Like I said, I wasn't sure where it was leading."

"That's not true, Stoner. You knew exactly where it was going to lead."

"We go back in time, you and me," Stone said. "You represented me in a drug case. I was guilty. It didn't stop you. You fought to get a drug charge dismissed and give me a chance to move on. I was guilty as shit. And, yet, wasn't it 'justice' the way the thing turned out?"

Katz backed away and folded his arms across his chest, considering her comments.

Stone held out her glass toward him. "I'm ready for that refill," she said.

Saturday Morning

Carr watched as his son rose from the bench to take the call. As Suleiman turned, he jolted a pawn and it dropped to the ground.

It was a sign, Carr thought. *That horrible man Landry is using my son as his pawn. Not a nephew. A son. It was always a game to Landry. The truth was in the blood, which was always thicker than mud.* Carr pulled out his own phone and called Hammond.

"What the fuck are you doing?" Hammond cried. "You know the drill. This isn't good."

"I'm sorry," Carr whispered, his eyes on Suleiman's back. "I just wanted to check to be sure everything is set."

"Yes, Trey, for the fiftieth time, everything is set. This is the last time I'm going to answer your call. From here on out, just act. You know where to go and what to do. Goodbye." And he hung up.

Suleiman turned and noticed his uncle on the phone.

Saturday Afternoon

Hammond called Carr and apologized for snapping at him. Protocols be damned. He suggested they meet at their usual spot, the tip of Hains Point. Hammond was genuinely concerned that Carr was having second thoughts. If Carr backed out now, the entire plan would dissolve. As they sat together, Hammond pulled out a cell phone. It had a bright pink cover.

"Whose is that?" Carr asked.

"Freddy gave it to me earlier today," Hammond said. "It belongs to his daughter. I already used it to book a reservation down the hall." He began typing and leaned into Carr so that his message was visible on the screen. It read:

Need you tonight. Room 901. Down the hall. Have a special treat. Not what you're expecting. Will not disappoint.

Saturday Night

Carr pulled into the parking area at Roaches Run and parked in a space at the opposite end from the white van. A black sedan was parked next to the van. He slid down in his seat and waited. After a while he saw Landry exit the van, then get in the black car and drive off.

Anticipating Landry's route, Carr got out of his car and waited. In a couple of minutes, Landry's car came off the ramp from the airport onto the parkway. Carr watched until it made a right turn onto the 14th Street Bridge. Then he pulled his vehicle beside the van and walked to the back door. Landry had installed a special lock, but nothing that couldn't be opened. Carr needed less than five minutes to crack it. He returned to his car and popped the trunk.

Inside was a pressure cooker filled with nuts, bolts, razors, and other metal objects.

The carnage of the 2013 Boston Marathon explosions — three fatalities and hundreds of injuries, including 16 with lost limbs — was a stark reminder of the destruction that could be wrought by the innocent-looking device. Carr carried the pressure cooker gingerly to the van.

**

KATZ EMPTIED his glass and put it down.

"That's right, Sherlock," Stone said. "Carr said Hammond provided the device and told him where to put it inside the van."

Katz was incredulous. "He told you that?"

"Yeah, he told me. In fact, it gets better." She pulled the gin bottle toward her and refilled both their glasses.

Sunday Night

Pena arrived at Roaches Run. Carr got in the passenger side of his car. "We ride, Poncho," he said. Pena laughed. Pena turned onto the parkway's southbound lanes, stayed in the right lane, swooped around the airport, and took the ramp onto the northbound lanes of the G.W. Parkway. He drove by Gravelly Point and turned right to the ramp to the 14th Street Bridge. He shifted to the second from the left lane and drove into the District. To the left was the Holocaust Museum. To the right, the Mandarin Oriental Hotel. He stopped at the light at Independence Avenue.

"I can smell him," Carr said.

"Me too," Pena replied. "It's real now. No more rehearsing. We're actually doing this thing." The car drove across town to K Street, where it turned left. At 18th Street, Pena pulled to the curb. "I'm going to the lecture," he said. He leaned into the back seat, grabbed a bag and handed it to Carr. "Good luck," he said, patting Carr's shoulder.

Carr exited the vehicle with the bag.

Pena found a parking space and walked to DAR Constitution Hall. He bought a second edition copy of *The Rhythmic Cycle of Life* outside the tent set up next to the hall, then took a seat under the tent.

A few minutes later, Henry David McLuhan appeared to deafening applause. He sat on a bar stool in the center of the stage. "Good evening," he began. "*The Rhythmic Cycle of Life* is a self-help book. It's based on a simple premise, which is that your life, like history, repeats itself. Life is not linear; it occurs in cycles."

Pena looked at his watch.

"Since your life is cyclical," McLuhan continued, "the key to a successful life is to repeat your past successes and avoid your past blunders. There is no easier way to do that than to understand the cycles of your own existence. It's all about you, literally. You've already been around the block a couple of times."

Everyone laughed, except Pena, who sat nervously in his seat.

**

Carr went upstairs, opened the door to Room 901 and removed the contents of the bag, which included a light black sweater, a bottle of perfume, and a thin piece of wire. He hung the sweater in the closet, leaving the mirrored door open. He sprayed the perfume near the foot of the bed and on the pillows. Then he went to the bathroom and closed the door.

"I'M BEGINNING to understand why you didn't return my calls," Katz said.

Stone laughed. She went to the dining room and got two martini glasses and a bottle of dry vermouth. She came back into the kitchen waving the glasses and bottle. "Care for a martini?" she asked.

"Sure."

"Listen," she said, filling the glasses with crushed ice to chill. "I don't know if the story is true or not. We sat on a bench in the park. I'm assuming he was waxing poetic, because I'm not planning to do any further investigation."

Katz raised an eyebrow.

"Listen, dude, defense attorneys will fight to the death to get their clients off," she said. "You did it all the time. Juries acquit defendants if they find extenuating circumstances. People take justice into their own hands all the time, for better or for worse." She emptied the ice from the glasses, then poured gin and a splash of vermouth into each one. She handed one to Katz. They clicked glasses.

"So what happened next?" Katz asked.

"Wait a second," she said, turning to the refrigerator to get olives.

Sunday Night

Landry smelled the perfume, saw the sweater, and glanced at the light emanating from beneath the bathroom door. He chuckled. He undressed, got between the sheets, and waited for Pena's warm, lithe body to slide in beside him. He closed his eyes. He never heard the bathroom door open or someone moving across the carpet. Carr sprang onto the bed, his left knee knifing the mattress as he drove his body against Landry and wrapped the wire around Landry's neck.

"What the fuck!" Landry sputtered, spinning around and trying to wrap his fingers under the wire. "What the fuck are you doing?" Then Landry's eyes met Carr's. At first, he was in disbelief. *Where is*

Maria? Why is Carr here? What is happening? His survival instincts took hold. He tried desperately to dig his fingers under the wire and pry it loose. His feet thrashed wildly under the sheet, trying to push away from Carr.

"You're gonna die, motherfucker," Carr whispered. "This is for all the grief you caused so many people." He tightened the wire around Landry's neck. "The reputations you tarnished." Another tug on the wire. "The careers you destroyed." Landry struggled for air. "The people you hurt and humiliated." The wire was so tightly wrung that blood began to spurt out of Landry's neck. First, the legs stopped thrashing. Then the fingers quit trying to unloosen the wire. Finally, the body went limp. Carr held the grip. One minute. Two minutes. Three minutes. Then he let go and took a series of deep breaths.

**

McLuhan enthralled his audience. "Once you've been through two cycles," he said, "you should have a very good idea of the rhythm of your life. You should see when good things happen and recognize the events that enable those things to occur. By the same token, you should see when bad things happen. And you should be able to study how to avoid those things from repeating themselves."

A moment later, he took another sip of water from the glass on the table. "These are all ways to shake things up. Redirect your energy and take yourself off the road that previously led to bad destinations. Use today — right now, tonight, in real time — to change the past. You can do it." Then he paused. *You may have good instincts, but mine are a little bit better.* "You can definitely do it."

**

Thirty minutes later, McLuhan was signing copies of *The Rhythmic Cycle of Life* as adoring fans placed their copies in front of him. The Sharpie was working at maximum speed as he took the messages handed to him and wrote the words on the inside page, completing the message with a flourish of his initials, *HDMcL*. When he received a note that simply said, "Full Circle, Finally," he looked up. Pena was standing in front of him. McLuhan put the note in his pocket and wrote on the inside cover:

F — We have come full circle. May this merit the redemption you long desired — Ari

**

Pena found a parking space near the alley. He opened the trunk and pulled out a box of books, throwing his copy of *Rhythmic Cycle* on top of the other books. He walked down the alley, up the steps to the loading platform, and entered through the service door, which was left ajar by a wad of paper wedged between the steel door and its metal frame.

When he got upstairs, Pena knocked twice on the door to room 901. Carr opened it. A body bag was at the foot of the bed. Two empty H-Pack backpacks were positioned against the credenza.

Carr closed the door. First the two men clicked elbows. Then they embraced. "Where are the loaded backpacks?" Pena asked.

"I carried them down the corridor," Carr replied. "One of those packs is set to explode mid-morning. It'll do a lot of damage to the building but no one'll get hurt."

"Okay," Pena said. He kicked the body bag. "Did he give you any trouble?" he asked.

"No trouble. Just a whole lot of satisfaction." Carr looked at Pena. "Let's fill the two backpacks with books. Go downstairs and grab the other box. I'll handle this one."

Pena went back to the car and returned with a second box of books. After both backpacks were filled with books, Carr crushed the cardboard boxes with his boot and placed them in the other wing of the hotel.

Next, Carr and Pena took the freight elevator to the ground

floor and walked outside. Carr moved Landry's car from the alley and Pena backed his car up to the dumpster. Then they returned to room 901 and carried the body bag down the hall and positioned it precariously at the mouth of a construction chute that went from a window on the ninth floor to the dumpster in the alley. Carr went downstairs, popped the trunk of Pena's car, and stood next to the dumpster. Pena dropped the body bag down the chute. After it fell into the dumpster, Carr retrieved it and threw it into the trunk.

Pena went back downstairs. He kicked the wad of paper out of the corner of the freight elevator door and got into his car. A few blocks from the hotel, he stopped. Ari Hammond got into the car. They didn't speak to one another. Pena drove to the Whitehurst Parkway and across the Key Bridge.

Carr took Landry's car. He wore his mask, a way to disguise his identity in case anyone saw him. He drove down 17th Street to the Tidal Basin and across the 14th Street Bridge. Both cars arrived at Roaches Run at about the same time. The place was deserted.

After Pena parked, he and Hammond carried the body bag to the van. They unzipped it, removed Landry's naked body, and dressed him in the clothes he'd worn to the hotel.

"It looks like you forgot a sock," Pena said.

Carr looked around. "Looks to be the case."

"Are you going to go back and get it?"

"No way. The surveillance cameras are operating by now. Plus, no one is going to notice a missing sock. He's going to be blown to shit tomorrow afternoon."

Pena looked at Hammond, who nodded in agreement.

"This is all going to be dust and debris," Hammond said. "*I got the power,*" he sang, mimicking the 1990 hit tune by Snap.

They left the body on the floor of the van, minus one sock.

Carr handed Landry's cell phone to Hammond, who slipped it into his pocket.

**

Once Hammond learned her name, he addressed her as *S. Stone.* That was a mistake. It suggested he did not know her name. He wondered if anyone would recognize his error. He stared at the tablet. She wanted him to surrender. No chance of that happening. He punched the keyboard:

Like I said, I have no such intention.

He looked across the parkway to Roaches Run. Where had Katz run off to? He had to laugh. Katz was a pretty good judge of character. At dinner last night, Katz had correctly identified Hammond as a fraud, of sorts. Except Katz hadn't really put two and two together and figured it all out.

If he had, Katz would have realized that Hammond created his alter ego to acquire a degree of anonymity. He needed to distance himself from being Ruth Hammond's twin brother. By doing so, he would be less likely to become a suspect if it ever came to that. Not that he expected it to. It was only a matter of time before Landry engineered a plot against Ruth again, having failed to kill her the first time around.

When Landry contacted Hammond about a foolhardy plot involving H-Pack backpacks, Hammond deduced there was an ulterior motive. Thanks to Roscoe Page's hacking of Landry's account, Hammond discovered efforts were also underway to enlist Ahmed Suleiman and Maria Pena. It took Hammond a while to figure out Landry's sinister plan, but he finally got it, namely to destroy Fernando Pena, Trey Carr, and Ruth Hammond by annihilating the person they loved the most: a daughter, a son, and a brother.

Another text from Stone. Hammond looked at how far away the police and emergency response crews were standing. He didn't want anyone to get hurt. Time for another warning.

Get back or like I said, or I'll blow this tin can.

Another text from Stone. This was dragging on too long. Time to end it.

You have 2 minutes to clear the field. Then I'm gonna blow.

230

**

It was two in the morning. Pena had dropped off Hammond at Ruth's place, then driven to Gravelly Point. Dressed in dark clothes, Pena walked along the bike path and crossed the deserted parkway at the far edge of Roaches Run.

He walked cautiously in the shadows toward the parking area. To his surprise, no one was patrolling the area around the burned-out hulk of the van. He removed the phone that he had thrown on the pavement numerous times and flung it over the yellow tape into the middle of the "crime scene." It crashed on the pavement, but the sound went unnoticed as he slipped away.

Chapter Fourteen: After Midnight

THE BOTTLE was empty.

"I actually saw Hammond," Katz said. "I was up at Green Point by the aquatic center."

"When you left Roaches Run?"

"Yup. The text you received mentioned a crowd gathering at the side of the van. I thought it was odd because Landry wouldn't have been able to see that from the inside."

"So what did you see?"

"Someone at Gravelly Point with binoculars. He wore a hoodie. I couldn't see his face. At the time, I assumed it was Landry."

"Landry?"

"I thought he had placed someone else's body in the van to stage his own death. I spoke with Rodney Brown to be sure it was Landry."

Stone laughed. "You're kidding."

"No." Katz laughed as well.

"So, it was Hammond?"

"Had to be. He was there texting you. After the area was cleared, he detonated the bomb. Then, sometime later, he returned to Roaches Run and dropped the phone, making it appear as though it had been there all the time. It pisses me off that I didn't recognize it was him. I mean, I'd met him just the other night."

Stone got up. "Let me see if there's more booze," she said.

"I think we should call it a night," Katz said.

Stone did an about-face and returned to the counter. She held out her hand. "What's said here stays here," she said. "Deal?"

"Deal." They shook.

**

THE online producer finished editing the tape for Tuesday night's show. He sat down and ran the tape to make sure there were no glitches.

Thomas Mann: "Good evening. I'm Thomas Mann and this is *Mann-Up Newsmaker Tuesday Night*. Our guest this evening is Henry David McLuhan, author of the wildly popular book, *The Rhythmic Cycle of Life*. Welcome, Henry David, and thank you for being available on such short notice."

McLuhan: "Thanks, Tom. Good to be with you."

Mann: "I should point out to our listeners that tonight's show was pre-recorded. Therefore we won't be soliciting any calls or messages during the program. It's not as interactive as I like the show to be, but it is what it is.

"First question: Is it okay to call you Henry David? I was an English major, you know, and Ralph Waldo Emerson and Henry David Thoreau were two of my favorites. So I'm putting you in revered company."

McLuhan: [Laughing.] "You can call me Henry David, at least for now."

Mann: "Spoiler alert."

McLuhan: "And I'm flattered to be in such august company."

Mann: "At least for now." [Laughter.] "But, you know, I don't think either one of them sold nearly as many books as you." [Laughter.] "On a serious note, you did a show this past weekend at Constitution Hall. It sold out. The first volume of your book appeared twelve years ago, yet today you're more popular than ever. What's the secret to your lasting success?"

McLuhan: "You have to remember, Tom, that the premise of my book is that you can change the rhythm of your life, but it takes twelve years to see the results. So, if I'm more successful, it means that people are following the roadmap I laid out and they're seeing positive results."

Mann: "That must be very heartening to you."

McLuhan: "Yes, of course. It means everything to me."

Mann: "Something else that means everything to you is a

charity with which you're involved. Tell us about it."

McLuhan: "Yes, thanks. It's called Restore Our Dignity. It was created by my sister, Ruth Hammond, following a tragic beating in 2013 in a parking garage in Crystal City."

Mann: "And that leads to our spoiler alert. Did you just say Ruth Hammond is your sister?"

McLuhan: "Yes. And Henry David McLuhan is my *nom de plume*. My real name is Ari Hammond."

Mann: "So much for holding you in revered company."

McLuhan: "Alas."

Mann: "Now, getting back to Ruth."

McLuhan: "Ruth is my twin sister. The beating she endured in that parking garage resulted in permanent disability. It's been a challenge for her, one that she successfully meets each day."

Mann: "You're aware of the fact that Phil Landry — who died in that explosion the other day at Roaches Run — has now been identified as the perpetrator of that horrific incident. How are you coping with that revelation?"

McLuhan: "It's been a relief, frankly. It's brought closure to my sister and to me."

**

KATZ WAS too drunk to drive. He left his car in front of Stone's townhome and walked home. The air was chilly. Streetlights stood sentry over the stillness of the night, spewing light over deserted sidewalks. He walked further up Prince Street than he needed, all the way to Daingerfield Road, where he made a right onto Diagonal and then another onto King before turning left on his street, Harvard.

He found Snowe asleep in bed with Katie nestled beside her. He grabbed a blanket, went downstairs, and settled on the living room sofa.

"Hey," Snowe said a moment later. She sat on the side of the sofa.

"Hey."

"Welcome home."

They kissed.

"I didn't want to disturb you," he said.

"I wasn't really sleeping. Did you hear?" Her eyes were filled with tears.

"Yeah, it was on the news."

"I'd like to seek custody," she said. She clutched his hand.

"It's what Maggie wanted," Katz replied. "It's in her note."

"What do you want?"

"I want it too."

Snowe looked at him carefully. "Have you been drinking?" She furrowed her brow. "Where exactly have you been, Mo?"

"I've been with Stoner and, yes, we have been drinking. A lot. But I've been thinking about Katie in the back of my mind, and I'm ready to commit. Let's do it."

**

STARS TWINKLED in a black sky. Somewhere a card game was still being played. Aces ran wild.

Sherry Stone nuzzled in Curtis Santana's warm embrace, her head resting contentedly on a pillow. Katz and Snowe discussed the future over a freshly brewed a pot of coffee. Freddy Pena walked up and down a creaky hallway all night checking on his daughter, asleep in her room. Trey Carr dressed for a new job as a short-order cook at a greasy spoon on U Street. He glanced out the window and smiled as Sully slammed the door of an Uber and walked up the driveway, returning from a night out with friends. Tom Mann finished looking at the files and accepted Wilson's invitation to spend the night. Ruth Hammond rested in her wheelchair; for the first time, it felt like a comfortable easy chair. And the plane carrying Ari Hammond touched down at Charles de Gaulle Airport as the morning sun broke across the City of Lights.

Epilogue

In 2009, I made a commitment to revisit the premise of my book after completing the next rhythmic cycle of my life. At the time, I felt confident that I had identified a way to review past experiences, identify problem areas, and chart a future course that converted problem areas into successes. The only ingredient I needed to prove that the theory worked was time.

Now, twelve years later, I am confident that it works! At least it did for me. And I hope the same is true for you.

By the time I turned 36 in 2009, I had experienced a series of high moments punctuated by some very low ones. I can modestly say that I had attained a modicum of professional success that exceeded all expectations. I was an accomplished writer and lecturer. Fame and fortune were mine. But there was a space in my personal life that needed improvement. It was a black and painful space. In the second cycle, it was my father's suicide. In the third cycle, my sister's injury.

I did not want to revisit it.

As I began the fourth cycle, I resolved to preserve and increase the professional achievement I had attained while avoiding the black space, in effect channeling from the disastrous consequences of the previous cycle and steering toward something that brought greater satisfaction and personal reward.

I identified shortcomings in the eleventh and twelfth years of my life cycle. Specifically, I saw that I withdrew support for others during those years and let members of my family fend for themselves. Bad things happened and I suffered because of it.

I also realized that good things happened during the fifth and sixth years of my life cycle, and those things happened when I was active and involved in family affairs.

As a result, I decided to become proactive, to duplicate the good things that I experienced early in my cycle and to avoid the bad things that came at the tail end.

Based upon my own experiences, *The Rhythmic Cycle of Life* is a useful tool to making a better life for yourself. Simply examine your past behavior. Construct different approaches to present and future tasks.

You don't need a life coach, a spiritual guru, or a new-age psychologist, and you don't need any professional counseling. All you need is to look at yourself.

You can do this thing. Get started today. And the next time someone tells you, "Never look back," look them squarely in the eye and say that the only way to change the future is to study the past. *The Rhythmic Cycle of Life* beckons.

See you in the next go-round!

Ari Hammond, Ile St. Louis, Paris

June 2021

Acknowledgments

My thanks go to a dedicated cadre of readers from book clubs in the Alexandria area who read the manuscript: Emily Wilkinson, Charles Monfort, and Nicole Spero. Ralph Tedeschi, who runs a bookstore in Williamsburg, Virginia, also read the first draft. They tightened the prose, exposed inconsistencies in the story, and improved the tale by recommending changes that I adopted without reservation. Each of them came at the book from a different angle. Individually and collectively they made *Roaches Run* a better story than the one I gave them to read.

My wife, Robin Herron, meticulously edited the manuscript before it went to my editor, Charles Rammelkamp, and publisher, Clarinda Harriss. Alex White, who proofread *Slaters Lane*, rejoined the editorial team to assist with the newest addition to the series.

I'm honored by the encouragement and support that I receive from Charles, and appreciative for his insights and comments. His suggestions transform the final product. And I am extremely grateful to Clarinda for including Mo Katz mysteries among the books published by BrickHouse Books, her Baltimore-based print house.

Ety Bush manages the website for BrickHouse and I'm thankful for her updating my profile and events. Ace Kieffer has done the layout of all four books and does a masterful job of it. My son, Alex Wasowicz, designed the book covers and developed a theme for the series, beginning with the first Mo Katz mystery in 2017. Bookmobile prints and Itasca Books/BookHouse Fulfillment distributes Mo Katz mysteries, and Mark Jung, Devin Koch and everyone there provides great support.

My local community in Northern Virginia has welcomed the series, and my continued thanks go to *Alexandria Living Magazine*, *Arlington Magazine*, *The Zebra*, the Principle Gallery, the Old Town Shop, and Made in ALX, an online service that promotes and sells the work of local "talented makers."

My thanks to everyone who's reviewed the books on Good Reads and Amazon.com and to everyone who has emailed and texted me about the stories. Keep those cards and letters coming! I can be reached at AlendronLLC@aol.com.

Many cups of Misha's coffee were consumed in this book. Green Hat Gin has been poured into glasses in three of my four books, including this one. My gratitude to the folks at Misha's Coffee House in Old Town and New Columbia Distillers in D.C. for letting me use their labels. Cheers! And "Good Coffee!"

My thanks to Meggrolls and Principle Gallery for allowing me to refer to their Old Town establishments.

Finally, my gratitude to Robin and our sons, Alex, Andrew and Aron. I'm only as strong as the core that surrounds me, and I've been blessed my entire life with a loving family. I treasure and value their love and affection and trust I give back as much as I've received.

Mo Katz will return in *Mount Vernon Circle.*